Praise for the

series

"An interesting and accessible heroine, a super plot,
and many unexpected twists and turns . . ."
—*LJ Smith, author of the Vampire Diaries series*

"A great teen read:
suspenseful, fast-paced, and loads of fun!"
—*K.A. Applegate, author of the Animorphs series*

"A compelling, entertaining,
and at times, seriously spooky read!"
—*Cynthia Leitich Smith, author of* Tantalize

"Suspenseful and original. A good read!"
—*Peg Kehret, award-winning author of* Stolen Children

"Courage, adventure, and remarkable insight . . . Amber is
truly a teen heroine whom readers will identify with and
learn from . . . A must-have for fans of the supernatural."
—School Library Journal

"I loved the various literary allusions, the book related
puzzles in Eli's room and the titles of Amber's favorite self-
help books that only exist in Charles de Lint's Newford."
—*Diana Tixier Herald, author of* Teen Genreflecting

Every month I "lunch" with two talented writers
who inspire and help with my writing:

Danna Smith
and
Linda Whalen

Thanks for your friendship and support!

DEAD GIRL
IN LOVE

Linda Joy Singleton

Woodbury, Minnesota

First Edition
First Printing, 2009

Book design by Steffani Sawyer
Cover design by Gavin Dayton Duffy

Flux, an imprint of Llewellyn Publications

Library of Congress Cataloging-in-Publication Data
Singleton, Linda Joy.
  Dead girl in love / Linda Joy Singleton.—1st ed.
    p. cm.—(Dead girl)
    Summary: Temp Lifer Amber's third assignment takes her into the body of her best friend, Alyce, who is involved in some secret project involving cemeteries, and while investigating, Amber encounters Dark Lifer Gabe, who wants to make a deal with her.
    ISBN 978-0-7387-1407-3
    [1. Best friends—Fiction. 2. Friendship—Fiction. 3. Mothers and daughters—Fiction. 4. Grandmothers—Fiction. 5. Identity—Fiction. 6. Future life—Fiction.] I. Title.
  PZ7.S6177Ddq 2009
  [Fic]—dc22
                    2009009049

Flux
Llewellyn Publications
A Division of Llewellyn Worldwide, Ltd.
2143 Wooddale Drive, Dept. 978-0-7387-1407-3
Woodbury, MN 55125-2989, U.S.A.
www.fluxnow.com

Printed in the United States of America

I pounded on the silk-lined lid over my head, pushing and breathing hard, trying not to panic. But, geez! Who wouldn't panic in my situation? I'd fallen asleep in my own house, own bedroom, own body. Then in the flash of a promise, I found myself lying flat on my back in some kind of box, entombed in blinding darkness. Not only was I stuck in my best friend's body, but it seemed I was in her coffin, too.

Did that mean ... that Alyce was dead?

Or was I?

"Ouch!" I cried as I pinched myself. Still very much alive.

But what was I doing inside a coffin? My thoughts

reeled with confusion as I tried to get a grip on this new reality. Taking over someone else's life was hardcore confusing. It always took a while to adjust to a different body— like breaking in new shoes, only worse because I wasn't walking on soles, I was switching souls. And while I now looked like my best friend Alyce, I had no idea what I was doing *here*—except for a shivering sense of fear.

Keep calm, I told myself. Alyce (unlike me) was level-headed and avoided risky behavior. She researched her teachers before each semester to learn lesson plans; if a guy asked her out, she prequalified him by checking blogs (which was why she never dated); and she wouldn't drive anywhere without Googling directions. My practical, sensible, slightly neurotic friend never left anything to chance and would never have climbed inside a coffin without a good reason.

The two most logical "good reasons" were:

1. Someone locked her in this coffin.
2. She was hiding from someone.

Both choices involved a dangerous "Someone" that I had no interest in meeting. Panic rose to crisis level. Move arms, legs, body. Get out! Now!

Reaching up, I pressed my hands firmly against the silky lid and, fueled with a surge of adrenaline, pushed up with all my energy.

To my utter and total shock—the lid lifted!

When light streamed onto my face, I wanted to shout with joy. But that would just be stupid. I mean, who knew who might be listening?

Grabbing the edge of the coffin, I jumped onto a polished hardwood floor—then stared, open-mouthed. I was surrounded by rows and rows and *rows* of gleaming copper, wood, and stainless-steel coffins. Obviously this was a mortuary showroom, where luxurious death beds came with two-for-one bargains, warranties, and price tags. But why was Alyce in this place? It would make sense if this was an old cemetery, since Alyce often snapped pictures of creepy gravestones. But this modern mortuary was too cheerful, with its murals of angels, clouds, and daisies floating across sunny yellow walls.

Most of the coffins (or is the formal term "casket"?) were hinged open for display. A printed tag attached to a shiny silver coffin read:

Custom "Praying Hands"
Blue-stitched embroidery, squared corners, adjustable
bed and mattress, fully insured product warranty.
All for a discounted cost of $3,999.99.

Wow! I'd heard that the cost of living was expensive, but the cost of dying was even worse. Why did a corpse need an adjustable bed anyway?

The plain wooden coffin I'd been hiding in was the drabbest in the room, without plush cushioning or embroidery stitching. I was about to check its price tag when I heard footsteps and murmured voices.

Coming toward this room!

Closer, closer...

Reluctant to climb back into the coffin, I jerked my head from side to side, searching for a better hiding place.

No closets, tables, or drapes. The murmurs increased. At least one man and one woman were heading this way. When the door knob jiggled, I slapped my hand over my mouth to stifle my shriek.

Quick! Hide now! Sprinting over to the largest coffin in the room, I scrambled behind it and squeezed into the narrow space between wall and coffin.

"This way, please," a woman said as the door creaked open.

Huddling flat against the wall, I watched two sets of shoes enter the room: men's black loafers shuffled after a pair of girly, blue-heeled pumps.

"We're very proud of our showroom," the woman said in a professional tone. "We have the largest selection of caskets in the state."

"I-I don't think I can do this," an elderly man's voice quavered. "She was all I had ... it's just too soon."

"That's understandable," the saleswoman replied automatically, as if reciting from a script. "Is there someone else in your family who could make these arrangements?"

"No. Only me," he added with a sniffle.

His sorrow reminded me of how I'd felt a year ago, when I found out Grammy Greta had died. Whenever Mom used to give me grief over stupid stuff, Grammy had always been there to support me. Losing her was like having all the lights turned off in the world. But I'd discovered recently, when Grammy and I were reunited on the other side, that "dead" didn't mean she was gone. Grammy even had an important job overseeing the Temp Life program—

which was how I had now ended up in my best friend's body.

"Final arrangements are never easy," the saleswoman was telling the man. "They're a necessary part of the healing process. Still, we can wait if you'd rather do this later."

Yes! I thought desperately. Wait till later! Turn around and leave now so I can get out of here.

But the man wasn't leaving. He murmured something indiscernible, then I watched his black loafers follow the clicking heels farther into the room—toward my hiding spot. I scrunched into the smallest ball possible, which was seriously uncomfortable because Alyce's legs were long and bony with knobby knees. I held my breath, afraid that even the slightest sound would boom like a fired cannonball.

The woman's heels tapped closer.

Two caskets away from me!

I struggled for invisibility, afraid to move or breathe. Only I couldn't hold my breath forever, and when I finally let it out, I was sure I was going to be caught.

But the saleswoman only heard her own voice as she launched into a sales pitch. "Green Briar caskets are velvet lined and trimmed in lace with matching pillows. The lids are foam-filled with decorative buttons. And our caskets are rot- and insect-resistant," she boasted. "They're guaranteed to last a lifetime."

Whose lifetime? I wondered, smiling at the irony. It wasn't like a corpse could jump out of the grave to complain about bugs and mildew.

But my smile died fast when the saleswoman suddenly gasped.

"Dear God!" she exclaimed. "What is that doing there?"

Electric fear shot through me. I braced myself for discovery, but instead of the footsteps coming closer, they click-clicked away.

"Who left this here?" the saleswoman exclaimed angrily.

"Is that a dead animal?" the man asked.

"Of course not. It's only a tacky kid's backpack and it definitely doesn't belong in our sales room." She seemed to recover and added, "I'll get rid of it."

Curious, I shifted toward a crack between caskets, pushing Alyce's dark hair out of my eyes to get a better view. A large-boned woman with upswept burgundy hair and a gaudy abundance of necklaces and bracelets was looking down at the floor. Her jewelry jangled as she swooped down to pick up a leather backpack with a ratty rope dangling from its bottom.

Not a rope, I realized with horror, but a curly, furry tail.

This wasn't a random backpack—it was Monkey Bag!

Alyce had nicknamed her beloved backpack "Monkey Bag" and carried it with her everywhere. She must have dropped it when she climbed into the coffin. The backpack was Alyce's most prized possession (a gift from the father who took off when she was four) and contained her digital camera, art supplies, cell phone, wallet, and notebooks. Since I was supposed to be Alyce (at least temporarily) I needed to retrieve Monkey Bag. Yet if I stayed here, I would for sure get caught.

I considered my odds of crawling around the caskets and sneaking out the door. With the saleswoman distracted, I might make it—except I couldn't abandon Monkey Bag. How could I escape *and* get the backpack?

Think of something, Amber! I told myself. Coming up with creative solutions was one of my strongest skills, and would someday help me achieve my dream job as an entertainment agent. A self-help book I'd read called *There's Always a Plan B* advised thinking out of the box to create inventive ideas. But crouched in the shadow of a casket, I had zero ideas.

Plan C: Wing it.

When the saleswoman (tightly grasping Monkey Bag) led the man out of the room, I jumped up and took off after them.

Luckily, Alyce wore soft-soled sneakers. My quick footsteps were so silent even I couldn't hear them. Staying far behind, I pressed against walls and peered around corners before moving forward. I tiptoed down a long corridor lined with pictures of boring-looking people in suits, then past a door marked *Restrooms*, which gave me an uncomfortable urge to use that room.

But there was no time for comfort. Monkey Bag was on the move.

The man said something softly to the saleswoman, his voice choking with a sob. The saleswoman murmured sympathetically, guiding him left at a hall intersection. As they turned, I glimpsed the man's wrinkled, tear-stained face and my heart ached for him. The poor guy must have lost his wife. I wished I could tell him she would be all right. If she'd gone to the other side where Grammy Greta hung out, his wife was safe and happy.

They stopped at a door marked *Office: Green Briar Mortuary Director.* The saleswoman led the man inside, swinging Monkey Bag by its leather straps. The door shut with a sharp bang.

Now what could I do? I couldn't exactly knock on the door and ask for my backpack. The fact that Alyce had been hiding inside a coffin was a big clue she wasn't supposed to be here.

I need help, I thought, mentally broadcasting an SOS into the universe. When I'd accepted this Temp Lifer mission, I thought it would be easy. Not crazy confusing like the first two times I'd swapped bodies. I hadn't known zip about those new identities, but I knew practically everything about Alyce. I expected to breeze through this assignment in a few days. After Alyce's soul had a chance to rest (I visualized an out-of-body beach resort), she'd return to being my wonderful best friend again. We'd have a sleepover and once I explained everything, we'd laugh about my adventures in body-swapping.

But so far, all I'd had was trouble. And when the saleswoman opened Monkey Bag, she'd find Alyce's wallet with her driver's license and Halsey High School ID card. Then the monkey crap would really hit the fan.

I needed a diversion that would (a) lure the saleswoman and her customer out of the office, and (b) give me enough time to sneak inside to rescue Monkey Bag.

While I was thinking hard, my gaze drifted up to a plastic sphere fixed to the ceiling. The smoke detector's tiny light shone green, as if encouraging me to go wild with my ideas. But while I was creating a rather brilliant plan that involved a ladder and a lit match, the office door swung open.

"Someone's been in my office!" the saleswoman exclaimed, looking up and down the halls suspiciously. "I have to report this to security. It won't take long; please come with me."

The grieving man nodded, following obediently.

A break-in? Hmmm... what was that about? Well, not my problem. In fact, this could work out well for me. When the saleswoman left the office, her hands were empty, which meant she'd left Monkey Bag inside. This was my chance! So I went for it—running like I was on fire, ducking behind a wall, my heart pounding and my palms sweating.

The door was unlocked, and there were papers strewn on the floor and two large drawers of a file cabinet hanging open. And there on the floor was Alyce's bedraggled, ratty Monkey Bag. I slipped it over my shoulders, a position so familiar that the straps fit as naturally as skin. Then I hurried out of the room, the door banging behind me.

"Hey, you!" a voice bellowed. "What were you doing in my office?"

I froze in the hallway, caught in the saleswoman's suspicious gaze. For a moment, I couldn't remember how to make this body work. My legs, arms, and racing heart felt foreign. Not my own. But the fear was one hundred percent mine. With a spur of energized panic, I took off running.

"Drop that backpack!" the saleswoman commanded. "What else did you take from my office?"

Ignoring her, I ran faster.

"Stop, thief! Someone catch her!"

Skidding around a corner, Alyce's sneakers squeaked like they were screaming in protest. Up ahead was an exit. I sprinted for the double glass doors, slamming them open, blinking at natural brightness. I was outside!

The sun was disappearing behind the western hills— which surprised me, since I'd assumed it was morning. How long had I been in that coffin anyway? Fortunately, Green Briar Mortuary had more artificial lighting than a shopping mall at Christmas, so I could see just fine. With a quick glance, I took in the lush mowed lawn stretching out to a gated cemetery, the near-empty parking lot, and the startled look of a tattooed gardener as I jumped over the corner of the rose bed he was pruning. He swore, yelling for me to stop.

But I kept running.

Behind me, voices rose in anger. I caught the word "police," which spurred me to run like escaping arrest was an Olympic event and I was sprinting for a medal. I hadn't done anything wrong ... but what about Alyce? If she'd broken laws, she must have had a good reason. Without knowing that reason, all I could do was make sure my best friend didn't get caught.

Racing around a corner of the building, I headed for the parking lot. I hoped to find Alyce's car—but I didn't see it. How had she gotten here? No time to wonder, I realized, glancing over my shoulder. The saleswoman had given up the pursuit, but the tattooed gardener—who was younger and faster—was gaining on me.

Up ahead, a fence spread around the cemetery. I'd once

tried to climb a cemetery fence with disastrous results. Not going through that again. I veered away, down the sidewalk of a street so desolate I didn't see a single car driving by. My breath rasped and my legs ached like they were about to fall off, but I kept running, too scared to give up.

Hearing a shout behind me, I realized the gardener was getting even closer. I pushed myself faster but knew I couldn't keep it up much longer, especially with the pounding in my chest and the heavy backpack slamming against my shoulders.

Attacking footsteps thudded louder, terrifyingly close now. I looked around frantically, searching for a building or yard to hide in. But the paved road, bordered by chain-link fencing and rural fields, stretched on endlessly.

Then I heard a honk and roaring engine.

Startled, I glanced back at a familiar blue Toyota zooming toward me. The passenger window was down. A girl with curly brown hair waved at me from behind the wheel.

"Amber!" she called in a voice I knew as well as my own.

When the car slowed beside me, I stared in shock.

At my own face.

2

"Hurry! Get in!"

I hesitated, but only for the micro-second it took me to glance back and see the gardener barely a leap away. Grabbing onto the door handle, I swung myself inside the Toyota (my mother's car) and slammed the door. My rescuer punched the accelerator and we were out of there. The side mirror flashed a glimpse of the gardener as he flipped me off.

Turning slowly, I studied my rescuer. Me ... yet not me. I had a good idea who was temporarily residing in my body—but still, it was a shock to come face-to-face with myself and realize that she wasn't me. Like being trapped in a crazy dream where shards of reality swirled into kaleido-scope fragments.

First thought: *No way! I can't be both the passenger and the driver of this car.*

Second thought: *Why is my body wearing a dress and (horrors!) nylons?*

Third thought: *Is that a zit growing on my chin?*

Insanity squared by Impossibility = Belief.

The last time I'd seen my real body had been a lifetime ago. Well ... actually only yesterday, but it felt longer. After living other lives for a few weeks, I'd finally, happily reunited with my own less-than-perfect-but-100-percent-wonderful body. Being myself—Amber Borden—was seriously heaven. I'd hugged my parents, played with my little triplet sisters, and cuddled my cat Snowy. It was like a Hallmark Channel homecoming, complete with tears, kisses, and laughter—except that an important person was missing from the happy reunion equation.

My BFF, Alyce.

She'd refused to even speak to me—which I deserved. While I had been body-switching my way through solving problems for other people, my best friend was going through a crisis. She wouldn't say what was wrong, only that she needed to talk. She'd begged me to come over but I'd let her down. So when Grammy Greta asked me to become my best friend (literally), how could I refuse? It was my chance to fix things with Alyce. Besides, if someone had to temporarily live my best friend's life, who better for the job than me?

So Alyce was off taking a soul vacation, and I was residing in her body.

This left my real body minus one resident.

Guess who'd stepped up for the job?

"Grammy?" I asked uncertainly as I clicked the seat belt into place.

She nodded. "Surprise, sweetie."

My voice. My face. My grandmother.

"Yes," she said cheerfully. "It really is me."

"Oh. My. God."

"My sentiments exactly. We have a lot to be thankful for," Grammy Greta said with a reverent glance upward. "This is an amazing opportunity for both of us."

"Amazing. Definitely," I said, feeling dizzy as I stared at myself. I should have expected this, especially since I'd agreed to the plan, but up close and in person it blew my mind. I could hardly believe it was happening. "You really are in my body."

"I promise to take good care of it until you return. Our assignments shouldn't last for more than a few days, so relax and make the best of this experience."

"I don't even know how to start my assignment."

"You've already started."

"I have? How?" I shook my head, even more confused. "By being chased out of a mortuary? I don't know what's going on with Alyce. Is there any way of contacting her? Where exactly is she?"

"You know better than to ask those sorts of questions." Grammy's clipped tone slammed the door on my curiosity. "There isn't much time. I need to get you home."

"Home would be great! I can't wait to see everybody."
My relief was huge—mostly because I'd been dreading facing Alyce's disagreeable mother. Mrs. Perfetti had this way of looking at me like I was a puddle of pee the cat left on her floor.

"Sorry, sweetie, but you misunderstood."

"Can't I go back home with you?"

Grammy shook her curly head (well, *my* curly head actually, but if I started getting picky about pronouns I'd go crazy). "Don't you remember the Nine Divine Rules for Temp Lifers?" she asked.

I bit my lip, nodding.

"Then you know the first rule: *Follow through on your Host Body's obligations and plans.* You're Alyce now, not Amber. While you're in Alyce's body, her house *is* your home."

"But what if her house sucks? She doesn't stay there much and would rather hang at my place. Bending the rules won't hurt anything. We could tell everyone I'm...I mean, Alyce...is sleeping over with Amber."

"Did she make plans to sleep over tonight?"

"Um...no."

"Well, then. You know what you have to do—the sooner the better." Grammy glanced in the rearview mirror, furrowing her brow. "Delay could be dangerous."

"Dangerous?" I asked uneasily, still a little out of breath from all that running.

"There are always risks."

"You mean...Dark Lifers?" I shivered, remembering my recent encounters with dark souls who refused to stay dead and hijacked living bodies. Except for a glowing grayness around their hands, they appeared like ordinary humans... until they reached out with predatory fingers and stole your energy.

"I have no evidence for concern." Grammy glanced over her shoulder. "Still, we must remain cautious."

"But you're in charge of the Temp Lifer program—you should know everything."

"Not for this assignment. I can't tell you much," she added with a shrug, momentarily lifting her hands from the wheel—which spun wildly and sent the car careening toward a telephone pole.

"Grammy!" I cried, clutching my seat. "Hands on the wheel!"

"Relax. I have it completely under control."

She grabbed the wheel and jerked back into the right lane, giving me a determined smile. I had this flashback of myself showing similar confidence when I'd gotten lost driving, exaggerating how I had everything "under control" when inside my fears flapped like birds spinning blindly in a wind tunnel.

Was Grammy nervous, too, and hiding it?

"As I was saying..." With only one hand on the wheel, she turned back to me. "Someone else is handling my job while I'm Earthbound, so I don't have any upside information."

"Then how did you know I was in trouble?"

"I received a short message with a map and a voice relay."

"What's a voice relay?"

"Unexplainable in Earth terms, but what matters is that I've been warned to hurry because of possible danger."

My heart jumped. "Danger?"

"I'm sure it's nothing more than a routine cautionary message." She glanced in the rearview mirror then back at me. "I haven't seen anything unusual although I've had this prickly feeling, like I'm being watched. But my perceptions are clouded while I'm in a physical form. Until our assignments end, I'm human just like you."

Her words seemed like a bad pun considering that she was speaking through my voice. She wasn't "just like me," she *was* me. And I doubted I'd ever get used to the weirdness of body-swapping.

We'd gone far enough now that Green Briar Mortuary was rapidly fading to a bad memory. We passed under a Spanish stucco archway into a subdivision where all the homes were mission-styled: stucco siding, square and rectangular, a few even rising up to bell towers. My grandmother made a sudden left, turning so sharply I banged my elbow on the door. After "ouch" and "sorry," we didn't say anything for blocks. I was lost in thoughts about my assignment, trying to guess why Alyce had broken into the mortuary. Was she looking for something? Hiding from someone? Checking sale prices on caskets?

"You all right, sweetie?" Grammy patted my arm.

"Define 'all right.'" I stared at her. "I still can't get used to you ... I mean, me."

"Isn't it a kick?" She chuckled. "It's déjà vu, since I used to look a lot like you when I was a teen. Although it's hard adjusting to the restrictions of a physical body—not being able to levitate or pass through solid objects. I got scratched trying to get inside this car without opening the door." She pointed to a reddish scrape on her arm.

"Grammy, be careful with my body. It may not be perfect, but it's all I've got."

"No worries. I'll get accustomed to gravity and solid matter soon. Look how fast I've adapted to driving."

"Speaking of which," I said, frowning, "why are you driving?"

"It's faster than walking."

"I'm serious, Grammy. You don't have a license and never learned to drive."

"What's to learn?" She hit the gas pedal too sharply, jerking me forward. "I put the key in and twist. I figured out that the little *D* means drive. And the *R* means right."

"No! *R* is reverse!"

"That explains a lot." The car jerked back, then forward. "What's this red button?"

"Don't touch! That's for hazard lights!" I pulled at her arm. "Grammy, be careful. Mom will go ballistic if you dent her car."

"Your mother always did overreact. Luckily I'll be around for a while to help her get organized and give her advice on raising the triplets."

"Heaven help her," I murmured, remembering how I used to cover my ears with my hands whenever Mom and Grammy had one of their "rows," as Grammy called it.

"What did you say?" Grammy Greta asked.

"That I think it would help if I drove."

"No time for that. I have to get back before Theresa—I mean, *Mom*—misses the car."

"Please tell me you didn't take Mom's car without asking permission."

"How else was I going to find you quickly?"

I groaned, visualizing being grounded for the rest of the school year and probably all summer, too.

A traffic light blinked from green to yellow and Grammy punched the brakes. This time I was prepared, grabbing tightly to the hand rest. I glanced with relief at the empty crosswalk, glad there weren't any pedestrians for Grammy to run over.

"I'm getting the hang of this driving gig," she said with a smile that radiated her own quirky personality. "I always meant to learn to drive. I may still."

"Why bother? You're already dead."

"Dead is such a misunderstood word."

"I was at your funeral."

"Do I look dead to you?"

"No, you look like me and I look like Alyce, but we both know that's not real."

"Being a Temp Lifer is a real and a solemn responsibility," my grandmother said. "It's not a game."

"I know, I know." I rubbed my forehead. "I'm hearing my voice and watching my lips speak to me. It's all so freaky."

Grammy laughed. "Like that movie *Freaky Friday*."

"Worse. That was a comedy and what we're going through is serious drama."

"You're right—our assignments are serious. We must use paramount caution."

"Paramount caution?" I repeated, rolling my eyes. "Grammy, you can*not* talk like that when you're me."

"Talk like what? I'm not clear on your meaning; could you elaborate?"

"No one elaborates at my age. Grammy, do you even hear yourself? You lecture me on how to behave, yet you're not making any changes yourself. I mean, look at how you dressed. I didn't even know I had a pair of nylons."

"I found these in your mother's room."

"You snooped in Mom's room?" I asked, horrified.

"How else could I find something decent to wear? This dress was in the back of your closet. It's a little tight but I think it looks nice."

"Nice as in boring and hideous," I groaned. "There was a reason it was hidden in the back of my closet—it was a birthday gift from Aunt Suzanne."

"My Suzy always did have excellent fashion sense. But I thought you two didn't get along."

"We don't. I should have burned that dress." I stuck out my tongue. "While you're in my body, no more dresses and never, ever nylons. Wear jeans and T-shirts."

She blinked like this was a startling idea. "Well … I suppose you're right."

"Yes, Gram, I am. Trust me on that."

"But outward appearance is a trivial preoccupation with no redeeming value."

"Grammy, you're doing it again."

"Doing what?"

I sighed. What was I thinking when I agreed to let Grammy take over my life? She hadn't been young since the last millennium. This assignment was going to be a disaster. I never should have accepted it—yet I couldn't abandon Alyce to an unknown Temp Lifer any more than I could leave ratty Monkey Bag in a mortuary.

We had reached a familiar neighborhood with an eclectic blend of old homes. My high school was just two blocks to the left and if we kept going straight we'd run into Molly Brown Lane, where a right turn would take us to my house and a left to Alyce's house.

"Almost there." I pressed my lips tight so I wouldn't beg Grammy to turn around. But Grammy had always been strict when it came to rules—at least for other people. Her double standard made Mom crazy.

She slowed to a jerky yield, then hit the gas (too hard) and turned on Alyce's street. Just a few more blocks and we'd reach the Perfetti house.

"Trust your instincts and you'll sail through this assignment," Grammy said, squeezing my hand. "You might even have fun."

I thought of my "fun" at the mortuary and shook my head firmly. "Doubtful."

"When did you become so negative?"

"It's called being realistic. So far this assignment has gone all wrong."

"Can't you find anything positive to say?"

"Well, I'm glad I didn't lose Monkey Bag," I said, gesturing to the backpack now resting on the seat beside me.

"Ah yes, that old ratty backpack." Grammy smiled fondly. "Little Alyce used to carry it everywhere."

"She still does. If she has any important papers or lists, I'll find them in this bag, which will really help me solve her problems."

"Solving problems isn't your assignment." Grammy wagged a finger at me warningly. "We had this discussion last time. Temp Lifers are merely stand-ins until their Host Body can return, strong enough to face their own problems."

"I did more than stand-in for Leah and Sharayah. I improved their lives."

"Not without complications. You were lucky."

Lucky? Is that what Grammy really thought? Sure, I'd made mistakes (knowingly and unknowingly) during my assignments, but they'd been successful nevertheless. I'd thought Grammy was proud of me...but maybe I was wrong. Was this assignment Grammy's way of giving me another chance to prove myself?

"Tell me more about my assignment," I asked in my most businesslike tone.

"You'll find everything you need in there." She pointed to the glove box.

"Huh?" I raised my brows.

"Look inside."

I popped the glove box open, expecting to find stuff like a car manual, maps, and Mom's cell phone. Those things were there, but so was something small and wonderful that made me give a shout-out for joy.

"The GEM! Thank you, Grammy!"

"Not just any GEM." She smiled. "The same one from your last assignment."

Almost reverently, I picked up the palm-sized book otherwise known as a Guidance Evaluation Manual. The plain gold book appeared boring, but it was a communicator to the other side with audio, video, and text connections. All I had to do was ask a question and the book would create its own answer.

"Go ahead. Ask it anything," Grammy told me.

Eagerly, I opened the GEM to the first page. It was blank, but I expected that and knew what to do next.

"Why was Alyce inside a coffin?" I asked the tiny book.

A spot of black ink spread and stretched into words across the page.

Hiding.

Not very informative since I'd guessed that already. While the GEM was helpful, it also had a habit of giving annoying answers that led to more questions.

"Why was she at the mortuary?" I tried again.

Searching.

"Searching for what?"

The lost.

"That doesn't tell me anything," I griped.

While I was deciding what to ask next, pages flipped wildly as if caught up in a sudden storm. Then the book snapped shut like a slap in my face. When I tried to pry it open, the pages stubbornly stayed closed.

"Open!" I ordered, shaking it.

"It has a mind of its own," Grammy said. "You can't force it."

"Stupid book is giving me attitude."

"Don't take it personally. The GEM is only a tool and not designed to solve your Host Soul's problems. Personally, I find them annoying and won't use one for my assignment."

"But your assignment is easy." I glared at my traitorous GEM, then banished it inside the front pocket on Monkey Bag. "You already know all about me. And Mom is your daughter, so you know everything about her, too."

"Do you know everything about her?"

I shrugged. "Mom is Mom. What else is there to know?"

"I'm not really sure...yet," Grammy said, with an odd expression that made me wonder what she was thinking.

Before I could ask, she slammed the brakes and I was jerked forward, then back, like a crash test dummy until we came to a stop on the curb in front of a brown, L-shaped corner house that I knew too well.

But the view through Alyce's eyes distorted the familiar, so that everything I saw seemed different. It was as if I'd entered a foreign country with no knowledge of customs or language. Shadows were deepening with the setting sun, turning the ordinary into the ominous. The sprawling oak I'd climbed countless times to sneak into Alyce's bedroom window stood there, starkly forbidding, its trunk a twisted grimace of pain, its limp leaves drooping like shadowy tears. A chilly breeze shivered its bony branches, which looked like arms waving me away.

Grammy Greta came around to meet me as I stepped out of the passenger door. "Sorry to leave you like this, but I can't stay."

"I know... although I wish you could." I bit my lip.

"You'll be fine."

"Of course, I'm always fine, but... " I swallowed hard.

"Drive safely... Amber."

"I will... Alyce." When she embraced me, I closed my eyes and, for a wonderful moment, I was hugging my silver-haired, soft, comfortable grandmother.

Then she drove away, and I was alone.

The sun was disappearing fast behind distant hills; it was the time most families prepared dinner. But there was no sound of voices from this house, only the soft jingle of a wind chime hanging over the front porch. The front yard was dark without a porch light, and the darkly draped windows were like eyes closed in sleep.

Resisting the impulse to turn around, I walked up the front porch steps.

Crimson flickered through slits in the drapes.

And I smelled smoke.

When I walked into the house, candles flamed from the coffee table, countertops, and shelves. The scent of hot wax and swirling smoke clouded the room in a surreal fog. There was no sound from the TV—unusual, since Mrs. Perfetti continually watched CNN and other news channels.

Then I saw her on the couch, lying motionless. I coughed, covering my mouth to block the smoke as I rushed over to her.

"Mrs. Perfetti!" I gasped. Kneeling by her side, I checked for a pulse and—thank God!—found one. But she seemed to be in a deep sleep and didn't even stir at my touch.

I started blowing out candles, then heard a cough

and rushed backed to Alyce's mother. "Mrs. Per—I mean, Mom!" I cried, gently putting my hand under her shoulder. "What happened?"

"Alyce?" She stirred, her eyelids fluttering open.

"Do you need a doctor? I'll call 911!"

"No, no, no." By the third "no" her voice was stronger, and she started to push herself up. "I'm fine."

"But you don't look fine. And what's with all these candles?"

"Nothing wrong with enjoying candlelight." She stood, smoothing her tousled hair from her face. She had the same brown eyes as Alyce, a deep dark chocolate that I'd always admired. But Mrs. Perfetti's hooded eyes were shrouded in secrets.

"You should see a doctor," I insisted.

"I've told you how I feel about doctors." She glared at me, defiantly. "I was only sleeping."

"With enough candles burning to start a bonfire?" I retorted.

"Don't use that condescending tone on me—it's your fault." She was shorter than Alyce by a few inches yet had a way of making me feel small. "You took so long to come home, I must have dozed off waiting for you. Where have you been? Why didn't you call?"

Mrs. Perfetti folded her arms across her chest, narrowing her gaze with suspicion that made me squirm. Could she tell something was different about me? How was I going to fool her? I was glad for the dim lighting so she couldn't read the panic on my face. I didn't know why Alyce had gone to the mortuary, but I knew better than to share that visit with her mother.

"So where were you?" she repeated.

"With a friend."

"Which means Amber Borden." She brushed her pleated skirt with her hand as if an annoying best friend could be brushed away as easily as dust. "Whenever you're inconsiderate of me, it's because of that girl."

"It's not her fault. I forgot the time."

"Were you at her house?"

That's where we usually hung out, so I nodded.

"I called there." Her bone-thin fingers tapped against the glass top of the coffee table as she breathed in and out a few beats before finishing, "And her father said he didn't know where either of you were."

"Oh … well. That must have been when we were out walking."

"You didn't answer your cell."

I glanced down at Monkey Bag, sure I'd find a dozen missed messages from Mrs. Perfetti when I checked Alyce's phone. "The battery must be dead."

"Or you purposely didn't answer because you'd rather talk to your friend than your mother."

How was I supposed to reply to that? Of course I'd rather be with my best friend. Who wouldn't? But the truth would only make things worse.

"I'm sorry—I won't do it again. But right now I'm more concerned with you," I said in my best contrite voice. "What's with all the candles?"

"It was so dark…" Her voice trailed off to a whisper.

"But with the candles came flickering flames, and shadows that made me feel less alone."

It was so strange how her voice and expression changed from angry to vulnerable. Unnerving... and confusing. But I didn't know her well. Alyce's mother never pretended to like me, so I avoided being around her.

"You shouldn't leave me," she whined. "You know how I worry."

"There's nothing to worry about—except choking from all this smoke. Let's open some windows."

She nodded, giving me a look like a child seeking approval.

Afterwards, when the air cleared and I could breathe easier, I said I was going to my room and slung Monkey Bag over my shoulder.

"But you only just got home." Mrs. Perfetti's voice softened to a whine. "Please stay, baby. I've really missed you."

Her change of tone surprised me. "You have?"

"I've been looking forward so much to our evening together. It's the only time of the day I truly enjoy, and I'm sure you have lots to tell me. I want to hear everything."

"There really isn't much."

"Whatever you say is more interesting than my boring job. Stuck in a cubical inputting computer data eight hours a day, five days a boring week. I left early, then waited to see my special girl. Come here, baby."

I didn't want to, but she'd stepped toward me with such a tender look on her face that it would be cruel to ignore her. So I stood still, reminding myself that I was Alyce, not Amber, as Mrs. Perfetti opened her arms wide and swallowed me whole in a tight hug that smelled of peach shampoo and coffee.

"Um … Mom. You're holding too tight." I pushed away, trying to come up with an excuse to ditch her. "I should go to my room. I have plans—"

"You certainly do—with me." She flashed a big grin, her shift of attitude even more confusing than a hundred burning candles.

"I do?"

"All the ingredients are ready in the kitchen."

"Um … can't it wait? I have things to do." I almost used the "homework" excuse until I remembered that it was spring break and school was still out till Monday.

"What's more important than dinner with your mother?"

My honest reply would be rude. Besides, I was getting hungry and wouldn't mind being served a home-cooked dinner. I'd had a stressful day and could use some pampering. So I said that eating sounded good.

"Wonderful." Mrs. Perfetti slipped her arm around my shoulder. "The chicken is thawed, the vegetables washed, and I set out your favorite spices."

Then Alyce's mother sent *me* into the kitchen.

To cook dinner.

Now, the first thing everyone knows about me (Amber) is that while I love eating, I'm hopeless in the kitchen. The extent of my culinary talent is using a can opener or following microwave instructions. Alyce, on the other hand, has a creative touch that includes gorgeous gift baskets for our school club, photography, and cooking. Alyce often teases me that I'd starve if I had to feed myself.

So when Mrs. Perfetti left me alone in the smallish kitchen with its yellow-tiled counters and dark-wood cabinets, I stared around in horror.

Me, cook? This was like a waking nightmare.

I couldn't do this on my own and knew only one person who might help. Retrieving Alyce's cell phone from Monkey Bag, I deleted the nine missed texts (from her mother), then made my call.

Dustin Cole, my second-best friend, was part hacker/geek/activist and liked to plot covert online strikes against "corrupiticians" (as Alyce nicknamed dirty politicians). His bedroom, or "Headquarters" as he called it, was crammed with electronic equipment that hummed and flashed with artificial life. There was no bed, only a couch and a sleeping bag that was usually covered with crumpled papers and snack wrappers.

Dustin's tone was wary when he heard my voice. "Alyce?"

"Not exactly. Guess again."

"Don't tell me you ... you're ... "

"You're getting warm."

He groaned. "Amber?"

"And the smart guy wins a prize."

"It had better be a really good prize, like my own personal communication satellite," he grumbled. "I need a scorecard to keep up with your body-switches."

"I've only had three—and the first one was an accident."

"Just stay away from my body—that would not be cool."

"But I've always been curious what it's like to pee standing up."

"Convenient but overrated."

"And it would be interesting to see inside a guys' locker room."

"As if I spend any time there," Dustin said scornfully. "I choose not to break bones over contact sports. I have a file of legal keep-out-of-gym excuses, all signed by a doctor. Not necessarily *my* doctor, but whatever works."

"Everything works for you," I said, chuckling. It felt sooo good to joke around with Dustin like nothing had changed.

"So what's the deal with Alyce?" His serious tone reminded me exactly how much had changed. I imagined him leaning back in his chair, tapping his fingers on his desktop. His eyes would be closed to shut out distractions, so he could listen with total concentration.

"She's taking a time-out." I glanced down at my temporary hands with their frosted black fingernails. Alyce was into black, draped outfits and gruesome jewelry but insisted she wasn't Goth.

"I thought you were done with body-hopping."

"I thought so too." I sighed. Then I explained how Grammy convinced me to take just one more assignment. "I had to do it—for Alyce."

"And what about you?" Dustin asked in his quiet,

perceptive way that never failed to disarm me. "Are you okay?"

I glanced at the counter where Mrs. Perfetti had set out onions, tomatoes, cheese, spices, chicken parts, and pasta noodles. "I'm burning in culinary hell. Alyce's mother expects *me* to cook dinner."

When Dustin stopped laughing, he offered to help. "Cooking is easy."

"Do you realize who you're talking to? When it comes to directions, I always end up choosing the wrong way."

"You're good at math, aren't you?"

"Math doesn't have anything to do with cooking."

"Wrong. Cooking is one big math equation," he said.

Then he explained about washing, slicing, measuring, and baking. It took a while to figure out the chemistry of blending ingredients, but Dustin was a great teacher. If he ever gave up his ambition to overthrow the government, he could be a famous chef.

He was saying how to set the timer on the oven when my phone beeped. I was ready to ignore the incoming text—until I saw the name that flashed on my screen.

Eli Rockingham.

Eli, Eli … My ELI! Calling!

Immediately I developed symptoms of a serious illness: dizziness, chills, sweats, racing pulse, an overall state of confusion. I hadn't known Eli long, but what I did know made me ache, yearn, palpitate to be with him again. Was this love? If I could spend some quality time with him while in my real body, maybe I'd find out. Still, it was great to hear from him and I couldn't say good-bye to Dustin fast enough.

Clicking a button, I read the message.

A,
GG TOLD ME WHO & WHERE U R.
XCITING STUFF DOWN N LA.
GTG. MORE L8R.
ELI

Huh? That's all he wrote? His "exciting stuff" probably had to do with being in Los Angeles as a finalist in the *Voice Choice* competition (think rip-off *American Idol* without the voting). He hadn't planned to enter, but due to some confusion during my last assignment, he'd replaced his sister at the audition and made it to the Top Ten. He was even gaining fans in his new role as "Rocky" Rockingham, math-geek-turned-singer.

I missed Eli but didn't blame him for having fun after a lifetime of being the ignored-little-brother of totally hot Chad. Girls, guys, even teachers were won over by Chad's megawatt smile, athletic body, and charisma. Eli didn't know it, but for a few minutes of bad judgment, I'd even fallen for Chad's charms. But I hadn't been in my own body, so it didn't count. Besides, the kiss wasn't even my idea... not that I'd objected. And I saw no reason to tell Eli, especially since I'd quickly discovered that Chad was an egotistic jerk. Where Chad was fake, Eli was completely real and wonderful, and he deserved his fifteen minutes of fame.

Still, I felt uneasy when Eli didn't answer his cell. I sent a text, asking him to call soon. Then I gritted my teeth and set to work tackling the equation of a recipe. It was obvious from Eli's message that he'd talked to Grammy (a.k.a. GG), so it was natural that he wasn't worried about me. That's what I told myself, anyway.

Dinner looked great—but tasted worse than moldy carpet.

Mrs. Perfetti puckered when she took a bite but smiled without complaint. She was all sweetness now, asking about my day. I gave some vague lies about places I didn't go and conversations I never had.

Afterwards, she offered to do kitchen cleanup, so I escaped to Alyce's room. Once the door shut behind me, I relaxed and felt safe for the first time since body-swapping. I might not be home, but at least this was familiar territory. Yet it was weird being here minus Alyce. I kept expecting to hear her voice or see her walk into the room. When I flipped on the light and caught a glimpse of her face in the mirror, the reality of my situation struck me hard. I really was Alyce. While she was gone, I carried the responsibility of her life with every word and act.

I could ruin her life... or save it.

Opting for the "save it" course, I grabbed Monkey Bag to search for clues.

I flipped the backpack upside down over Alyce's bed. Papers, pens, containers of film, batteries, black-and-white photos, a compact camera case with camera, textbooks, etc. spilled onto the black striped comforter. I sorted everything out into piles, being extra careful with the camera, which Alyce had worked part-time to afford.

But where was her purple notebook?

There were still three zippered pouches I hadn't checked because they were too small for a large notebook. I checked them now, finding loose change, a safety pin, a pack of gum, a gold hoop earring, and a folded paper.

Hmmm, I murmured as I unfolded the paper. It was a list:

1. Red Top
2. Green Briar
3. Liberty
4. Pioneer

Green Briar, the mortuary? What was that about? There was no topic or explanation about this list, only a few notations and dates. Red Top was scratched out with a dark scrawled *NO*. Green Briar's only notation was today's date. Liberty had tomorrow's date with a large, black-inked question mark.

I had plenty of question marks, too.

Was this list for a new photography project? Alyce often took pictures of macabre headstones at creepy cemeteries. But there was nothing creepy about Green Briar, with its gleaming showroom and lush manicured cemetery. So what was the connection between the names (places?) on the list? It looked like Alyce had gone to Red Top at some point, then Green Briar today. I guessed the others were planned for the remaining days of spring break.

Did this have something to do with the GEM's cryptic message about Alyce searching for "the lost"? How could I find something without knowing what I was looking for?

Frustrated, I began returning things to the backpack, searching meticulously for more information. Alyce had been searching, too—for something at the places on her list. But why? And did this quest have anything to do with her crisis? The only thing I knew for sure was that I completely trusted Alyce and would do anything to help her.

So where was that damned purple notebook?

A flash of purple caught my eye, sticking out of Alyce's World History textbook. But it wasn't the notebook—just a folder with a green bush symbol on the label. Looking closer, I recognized the symbol.

Green Briar Mortuary.

A knot formed in my gut, tightening like a noose.

Alyce *had* stolen from the mortuary—and I held the proof in my hands.

Of course, I snooped inside the file.
But scored only disappointment.

Nothing but useless old papers, typed in tiny uneven print that probably came from a manual typewriter, listing names and purchases from customers in 1947. The list wasn't even complete, only showing Green Briar customers with last names beginning with *B* and *C.* Alyce had to have had a good reason for stealing this. I tried to reconstruct the sequence of events that must have occurred before I replaced Alyce. I imagined her sneaking into the Green Briar office, searching through cabinets until the saleswoman showed up. Then Alyce grabbed the file and hid inside the casket—where I took over.

What was so damned important about these papers?

Night folded around me as I studied the papers, losing myself in confusing thoughts as I flipped back and forth, rereading names that meant nothing to me. All I gained was a headache. Not the kind of mild headache that could be banished with a few Tylenol. Alyce often complained about migraines, and although I sympathized, I'd secretly thought she was exaggerating. I mean, how could a headache be that bad?

Now I knew.

Pain intensified, crashing into my brow and spreading out across my head. I rubbed my forehead, moaning. Dizzily, I leaned back on Alyce's pillow, eyes closed as I waited for the misery to ease. Not getting any better, either. My stomach reeled with nausea...so awful...sick...OMG!

With one hand on my head and the other on my stomach, I jumped off the bed and ran for the bathroom.

Afterwards, my stomach was emptier and my pain numbed to a dull ache. I was relieved to find a migraine prescription in the medicine cabinet. I also noticed rows of prescriptions for Mrs. Perfetti—for sleeping, pain, and depression. Not a surprise considering her erratic behavior.

Alyce's migraine pills made me dizzy, exaggerating colors and shapes. As I returned to Alyce's room, I caught my reflection in the mirror over a long, dark-wood dresser. High, hollowed cheekbones; deep, dark slanted eyes with long black lashes; and long, velvety raven hair. Full rosy lips parted into a startled "O" on a flushed face. For a startled moment, I forgot who and where I was, struck by a guilty sense of trespassing.

The night-black ceiling and dark-red walls crowded in on me; familiar sights taking on frightening shapes. But there was nothing to fear, I assured myself, not in this room I knew so well. Although Mrs. Perfetti clearly didn't want me (Amber, that is) around, I always came over whenever Alyce asked. Like the time we'd redecorated her room, painting the walls and the ceiling in what Alyce called a "midnight and blood" theme. Mrs. Perfetti freaked out when she discovered that Alyce had ripped off the frothy pink ballet wallpaper and replaced it with collages of black-and-white macabre photographs: a colorless butterfly perched on a skull, a child digging in a sandbox with a syringe, and a large dog hiking his leg on a headstone engraved with two hands clasping for an eternity.

If kids at school saw Alyce's room, they'd be positive she was on drugs or mental. They already avoided her because of how she dressed and her "don't give a damn" attitude. But I knew the real Alyce. I'd watched her art develop from sidewalk drawings to experimental photography, and understood that her emotions ran so deep that ordinary art couldn't satisfy her. I ached with frustration when others only saw her outer layer and put her down for being different.

But I'm here for you always, I thought to Alyce, hoping she might hear or remember later.

Back to searching for info. I opened drawers, checked shelves and boxes in the closet, crawled under the bed. I found some wrappers from butterscotch candy (her fave) and a crumpled science test (grade: C-).

But no purple notebook.

I understood why Alyce had to hide her important things, although it outraged me that her mother searched her room when she was at school. So Alyce would leave boring stuff out and hide the important stuff. To fool her mother, she'd framed a large photo of her father and hung it on the wall by a large picture window. The word "hate" was not vile enough for Mrs. Perfetti's feelings for her ex-husband, so she would never touch his picture—which made it the perfect cover for hiding a hole in the wall.

As I reached for the framed photo, I caught a flash of movement through the window. Was someone out there?

Startled, I stared at the gap in the burgundy red curtains but saw nothing. Rubbing my forehead, I wondered if the migraine medication was messing with my mind. Then something moved outside again. Pressing my face against the cool glass, I peered out and saw only the gnarled oak branches and darkness mingled with my own (well, Alyce's) reflection.

Nothing was lurking out there; must be the wind or my confused imagination, I told myself. Smiling a little at how easily I'd been scared, I started to turn away ... then stopped.

Yes! Down in the front yard! Something or someone ...

My hands shook as I reached for a wall switch and snapped off the light. With the room dark, I could look outside but no one could see me. Not that I really thought anyone was lurking out there. That would just be paranoid. I'd probably seen a large dog run through the yard.

The damp window pane felt cold against my cheek as I peered down into the dark front yard. There was still no porch light on, and the nearest street light was a house away, giving only enough light to shine a faint golden ray across the yard and driveway. It was hard to see anything except shadowy bushes and trees.

Then a shadow moved.

The silhouette of a man crouched down below my window. As he lifted his head, his face was illuminated. I drew back in shock.

I knew that face—although it wasn't his own.

His real name was Gabe Deverau.

A Dark Lifer.

GEM Rule: *Retreat and Report.*

But as soon as I saw Gabe, he vanished in a blink of my imagination—leaving nothing outside except inky darkness. And I wondered if I was hallucinating. Grammy said being in a different body confused things; maybe I was having some kind of post-traumatic reaction after my experience with Gabe. When I'd first discovered he was a Dark Lifer, I was terrified. But I softened toward him after he confided how he'd been betrayed by his fiancée, his heart broken so deeply it carried through many long decades after his death, his bitterness binding him to Earth. He'd done bad stuff and I should despise him...yet I couldn't. He was tortured, charming, poetic, tragic, and intriguing.

My eyes blurred as I stared, waiting to see him again but seeing nothing.

Finally I turned from the window, conflicted by my

duty to report Gabe and an irrational desire to protect him. As if a Dark Lifer needed my protection! His survival skills had already protected him for over a century.

Unsure what to do, I reached into Monkey Bag for my GEM.

The book flipped to an empty page. Black ink bubbled, swirling into letters and words that invited me to ask a question.

"Will you give me a straight answer this time?"

Answers depend on perception.

"How about a simple yes or no?"

Truth is never simple.

I sighed, then waited till the black ink faded and the page was clear again.

"Was someone outside?" I asked the tiny book.

Yes.

I was almost more shocked to get a straight answer from GEM than by the actual answer. Still, I swallowed hard before asking the next question.

"Was it … was it Gabe?"

Refer to Rule #5.

"What's that supposed to mean?" I demanded.

Report all suspicions.

"But I'm not sure what I saw."

More black ink scrawled across the page, repeating the *Nine Divine Rules:*

#1. Follow through on your Host Body's obligations and plans.

#2. Under no circumstances should you ever reveal your true identity.

#3. Consult this manual with pertinent questions.

#4. Resist temptation; guide your Host to positive choices.

#5. If you become aware of Dark Lifers, retreat and report.

#6. Do not commit acts against your Host's moral code.

#7. Respect your Host Body; no tattoos, hair dye, or piercings.

#8. Your time in a Host Body cannot exceed a full moon cycle.

#9. Guard your Host Body well. If your Body dies, so will you.

The fifth rule was in bold, as if the GEM insisted I make an official report. But I'd feel silly if the DDT (Dark Disposal Team) popped in for a false alarm. The flash of a face wasn't any more substantial than smoke, and without proof, I refused to call an alarm.

As I reached this decision, the words on the GEM vanished and offered a new blank page. I ignored the topic of Dark Lifers and asked about Alyce's purple notebook.

Dark squiggly lines curved and shaded until there was a picture of a school locker, a big dent on the bottom corner and the number *281*.

"That's Alyce's school locker," I said.

Yes.

"She left the notebook there?"

Yes.

"Thanks," I said not sure whether to be pleased or discouraged.

Getting into Alyce's locker would be easy because I knew the combination, but it would not be so easy to get into the school over spring break. Security had been tightened a few years ago after repeated vandalism. Given the locked gates, high fences, surveillance cameras, and security guards, it was impossible to enter Halsey High.

Frustrated, I stared at the GEM even after the words vanished. So I couldn't get the purple notebook—but I might not even need it. What if I'd jumped to the wrong conclusion? Maybe Alyce's crisis had nothing to do with her trip to Green Briar. Temp Lifers only replaced people having emotional crises. The key to helping Alyce was figuring out why she'd needed a time-out from life.

So I asked the GEM, "What is Alyce's crisis?"

An answer spiraled across the page in red flowery ink:

Love.

I stared until the word faded to pink, then vanished. But it lingered in my head, pushing away thoughts of a stolen file and graveyards. I thought back to my last conversation with Alyce. She was having a meltdown, depressed and frantic as she begged me to come see her. "I need to talk," was all she'd say for explanation. I told her I was hundreds of miles away and asked her what was wrong, but she said she'd only explain in person. Her tone had challenged me to prove my friendship, to drop everything and come right away. And I'd failed her.

At first I wasn't too worried because it was normal for her to periodically shut everyone out, saying she was taking a "mentalscape" (her combination of the words "mental" and "escape.") Although sometimes I sensed a sadness in her that was beyond my reach... like last Father's Day, when I invited her to come along with my family to a movie and she made a snarky comment about sappy movies making her barf. Or when the freshman boy I'd welcomed with a Halsey Hospitality basket asked me to the Valentine's Dance, and no one asked her. The guy was too young for me even if I'd been interested, so I'd skipped the dance and invited Alyce to sleep over at my house. We'd had a great time, but I'd noticed whenever the topic of the dance came up, Alyce changed the subject.

During our last phone conversation, she'd been unusually stressed and sounded like she was crying—something she never did—as if her heart were breaking. If she had a boyfriend, this would make sense, but there wasn't any guy, unless she had a secret crush that I didn't—

A burst of music interrupted my thoughts.

Alyce's phone.

Glancing at the caller ID, I almost burst into song myself.

"Eli!" I cried as I cradled the phone to my ear.

"Amber? Is it really you?"

"Yes. But I know I sound like Alyce."

"You already told me... well, your grandmother did." He sounded tired as he explained that he'd called "Amber" first and thought I'd answered, but the more he talked to me, the more he realized something was wrong. When he'd accused Grammy of being a Temp Lifer imposter, she'd been surprised enough to admit the truth.

"Ooh, Grammy is a rule breaker," I said, smiling as I leaned back against black-laced pillows on Alyce's bed. "I broke rules when I told you about my last TL assignment and didn't want to do it again. Grammy did it for me this time, bless her."

Eli laughed—a sound so nice and wonderful.

"So what's it like being Alyce?" he asked.

"Weird."

"Weird freaky or weird interesting?"

"Both. She's taller than me and her hair is so long that I sit on it if I don't remember to push it back. And living with Mrs. Perfetti is even weirder." I told him about having to cook dinner, which made him laugh again.

"At least no one died of food poisoning," he joked.

"Your confidence in me is underwhelming."

"I'm just being honest—a trait I appreciate more than ever now that I'm living in the land of the fake and the famous."

"Already tired of being a big Hollywood star?"

"I'm not a star." His chuckle sounded tired. "This isn't *American Idol*. It's only shown on a cable channel that most people have never watched."

"But you're doing really well and might win. How cool is that?"

"It's okay." He said this casually, but underneath I could tell he was proud. "But if you need me, I'll ditch it all and come home right now."

"I'm fine," I insisted, warmed by his offer. "You stay

there and have fun singing. If you win, I can be your entertainment agent."

"You'd be great at it, but I'm not superstar material. This isn't the career I imagined," he admitted. "I'm more the guy who works in accounting or engineering, not the one standing on a stage with girls screaming my name like I was a rock star. Can you believe this little girl no older than ten pulled off my shoe?"

I laughed. "I hope your sock was clean."

"You could try being a little sympathetic."

"I could, but it wouldn't be as fun."

"This isn't all fun, you know. My schedule is insane with almost no time for sleeping. It's hard, too, being here without any friends or family."

"Isn't your sister still there?"

"Sharayah offered to stay but I knew she'd have more fun spending the rest of spring break with her friends, so I told her to go."

Just the other day I'd *been* Sharayah. My brain buzzed with questions about what had happened to her after I left her body—but those could wait.

"My competitors are great and we get along fine," Eli added. "Still, it's not the same as when you were here. I miss you, Amber."

"I feel the same way. It's hard being in the wrong body without the people I care about."

"I know what you mean. The loneliest place is when I'm in a crowd of strangers and I'd rather just be with you."

I warmed deliciously from head to polished black toe

nails. "I'd rather be with you, too. I don't know why I volunteered to be a Temp Lifer."

"Because you care about people. You really helped my sister and you'll help Alyce, too."

"I want to, but I don't know what's going on with Alyce. She's been doing some odd stuff."

"Considering she drapes herself in black and photographs gravestones, being odd is her normal. And I don't mean that in a bad way," he added quickly, as if worried I'd misunderstand. "I respect anyone who does their own thing and doesn't care what anyone thinks."

"But maybe she does care," I pointed out. "I keep thinking how upset she was the last time we talked. I hate myself for brushing her off."

"Don't beat yourself up over it. You had things going on, too, but now you're helping out. Alyce couldn't have a better friend. I should go." Eli yawned. "They have me in a room with three other guys and they'll be back soon. We have a photo shoot on the beach at six A.M. I have to pose like I'm surfing even though I've never surfed. It's going to be another crazy day."

"The perils of fame," I said teasingly. "When will you be home?"

"If I get eliminated in the next round, I'll be at school on Monday."

I pressed my lips tight so I wouldn't confess how I secretly hoped he'd be eliminated. I shouldn't be so selfish. "I hope you win," I told him.

"I'm not sure what I want. Winning would be cool, but it would mean missing school and going on a road tour."

"You'll get more of an education living life than study-ing about it." *But I may die from missing you too much*, I thought.

"I'd rather be with you."

"I feel the same way."

"And it's more than ... well, Amber, I—"

"You what?" I asked breathlessly.

"That I ... Amber, I think maybe ... well ... I love you."

He spoke with such sincerity that tears blurred my eyes. I said those words back, and suddenly we were both talking excitedly, sharing thoughts and feelings and dreams. After a while, with the reluctance of a million aching hearts, I let him go.

Back to his Hollywood world of fame and fans.

To ward off self-pity, I kept replaying his "I love you" in my head. We'd only been together a few weeks and had never even kissed (at least not when I was in my real body), but I wanted to be with him so much. I could imagine his face and feel his touch. No denying it any longer—what I felt for Eli was like a giant blanket holding me warm and tight.

Love, love, love! His words had wings that flew me to a place happier than anywhere I'd ever been. I wanted to soak in his memory, lather myself in the hopes for our future, and sink into dreams for all the amazing things we'd do together. Once I returned to my real body, going out in public would be great, but staying in would be even better. We'd be a real couple, holding hands at school and sharing lunch and whispering sappy things just because we could.

We'd talk, touch, and share until we were practically the same person.

This wonderful, fabulous, beyond-heaven emotion was too amazing to keep to myself. Love was the whole meaning of everything—the reason to breathe, a universal fabric uniting humanity, a solution to all the problems in the world. I only wished everyone I knew could feel this way, too.

Of course! I thought with a snap of my fingers. That was it!

The GEM said Alyce's crisis was "love." Maybe she was worried that I'd be too busy with Eli and she'd be left out. That wouldn't happen, of course, but Alyce had kept her feelings to herself without giving me a chance to reassure her. She didn't have many friends—maybe some casual "hey, how you doing?" friends in her classes, but only two real friends: Dustin and me.

What Alyce needed was a special someone all her own. *A boyfriend.*

I could hardly sleep that night thinking up ways to introduce Alyce to L-O-V-E.

No hooking her up with a random guy. He'd have to be someone really amazing, who accepted her unique style and wasn't easily intimidated by difficult mothers. He also needed to get along with Eli and me, too, so we could go on double dates.

Finding The Perfect Guy for Alyce would not be easy.

But I was up for the challenge, tossing and turning with whirling thoughts. I thought about the advice of a self-help book I had called *Perfecting the Art of Perfection*. The book advised accepting your imperfections; you're only limited by your own expectations, so aim for the best. Still, none of my books offered practical methods for matchmaking, and I wondered if I should stop by a bookstore to search for one. Finally, at 5:20 A.M., I gave in to restlessness and got up.

Remembering how annoyed I'd been when Grammy wore the wrong kind of clothes for my body, I was true to Alyce's creative spirit and slipped on a black ankle-length jacket over a dark-brown shirt, mid-length skirt, and knee-high, lace-up boots. As I turned toward the window to pick up Monkey Bag, my gaze drifted down to the front yard— to the driveway.

Something was wrong...and then it hit me.

Stupid, stupid! Why hadn't I noticed last night that there was only one car in the Perfetti driveway? And it wasn't Alyce's piece-of-crap dented station wagon.

Alyce bought her junker car after winning a local photography contest. She thrived on complaining that the car drank gas and made noises that sounded like farts, the tires were almost tread bare, and the crack in the side window looked like a smiling skeleton. Alyce really loved her car.

So where was it?

Unfortunately, I could guess the answer. Damn and double damn.

Alyce must have driven her car to Green Briar but parked it out of sight, which was why I didn't spot it. I needed to get Junkmobile back before her mother woke up and saw that it was missing.

But when I tried to call Grammy at my real house, I got an automated voice asking me to leave a message. So I tried a different number.

"Amber?" Dustin answered right away. Even at this insane hour of the morning, Dustin was manning his "Headquarters." I heard the hum of computers and a soft jingle from the keys he had dangling from his ceiling. He worked part-time for a locksmith and had a hobby of collecting unusual keys.

"Yeah, I'm still Alyce."

"What do you need?"

"I don't only call when I need something," I argued.

"So you're just calling to say good morning?"

"That, too. And I need a ride."

"Right now?"

"Please," I said with exaggerated sweetness.

"I haven't even eaten breakfast yet."

"You never eat breakfast."

"That's beside the point. I might have plans and leaving could be really inconvenient. You know, I do have a life too," he pointed out.

"I do know. But I thrive on adding drama to it."

"True. Should I thank you?"

"A ride would be enough."

"What's the hurry?"

"I think Alyce left her car near Green Briar and I need to get it before it's (a) stolen (b) towed away or (c) mistaken for garbage and hauled off to the dump."

He groaned. "Amber, sometimes you make me crazy."

"Only sometimes?"

"Continually," he amended. "All right, I'll be there in a half hour."

"Twenty minutes?"

"Don't push your luck."

Dustin was such a loyal friend that I'd be lost without him—literally. Not that I'd ever admit this to him. He already had a big enough ego and grand dreams of world domination.

After leaving a note for Alyce's mother on the table saying I'd be back in a few hours, I stepped outside, shivering at the cold, misty air. The sun was creeping up through trees, a golden hue shivering through branches and casting strange shadows that brought back memories of the face I thought I'd seen last night.

That face. Could it really have been Gabe?

In the light of morning, this seemed ridiculous. I was just being seriously paranoid. All I'd seen was a neighbor crossing the lawn or someone out for an evening walk. Even if Gabe were around, he wouldn't recognize me in Alyce's body.

Dustin showed up in less than twenty minutes. I knew he'd come right away, both because once he made a decision, he acted immediately, and also because of his secret passion for speeding. Fortunately he also kept some highly illegal police-locating equipment in his car, which saved him from expensive tickets. I waved him down before he even came to a stop and jumped into the car.

Within a half hour, we'd found Alyce's car, parked on a side street almost a mile from Green Briar.

Dustin leaned against the side of Alyce's car as I pulled keys out of Monkey Bag. "Should I follow you back to Alyce's house?" he asked. "Or are you off somewhere else?"

I hesitated, torn between the wants and the responsibilities of my assignment. I wanted to get started right away on finding a boyfriend for Alyce because I was sure this would solve her problems. But I couldn't forget the list of locations and dates. I had a duty to follow through on her plans—and she'd planned to go to someplace called Liberty today.

When I explained this to Dustin, he—as usual—had a solution.

"Let's go to my Headquarters," he said. "I'll do some checking on that list, find out if you're right about those places being cemeteries. I don't know of a city nearby named Liberty, but I think I've seen the name on a street sign or something. Then we'll tackle the matchmaking issue."

"Really think we can find someone great for Alyce?" I asked hopefully.

Dustin folded his skinny arms against his chest. "Do you want the truth?"

"Probably not, but you'll give it to me anyway."

"And you'll ignore my advice."

"Only the stupid stuff."

"Stupid stuff would be a fitting topic for your match-making scheme." He waved his hands expressively. "You may be inside Alyce's body but you're not thinking like her. If you set her up with some random guy, she'll kill you."

"But it's not going to be a random guy. I'll find the right guy."

"Should I point out the serious flaws in your plan?"

I sighed as I leaned against the open door of Alyce's car. "I'm not saying it'll be easy. But I know this is the right thing to do. Love is the answer to Alyce's crisis. She'll never be lonely again if I can hook her up with TRG."

"What if there is no Right Guy?"

"Pessimism is a hideous personality flaw and very unattractive," I said, giving him a scolding shake of my head. "Don't criticize unless you can offer a better plan."

"How can I when I don't know what's going on with Alyce?"

"I told you—it's all about love. Or lack of it. Maybe you should try it yourself, then you'd know all about love."

"Oh, and you know it all?" He was mocking me but since I needed his help, I let it pass.

"Sure."

"Ha!" He chuckled. "Okay, let's say that Alyce wants a boyfriend. How do you propose to find one for her?"

I stared pointedly into his eyes. "I have this really brilliant friend who can find out anything with the click of a mouse."

"He must be a loser if he doesn't have anything better to do than play matchmaker for you."

"Actually he's a genius."

"Never heard of the dude."

I laughed, knowing from his half smile and the thoughtful twist of his lips that he was already mentally downloading ideas.

A short while later I was following him into his "Headquarters"—a bedroom without a bed, where power cords lurked like snakes, slithering on the floor beneath tables and desks covered with computer equipment. He got to work right away, tapping keys on a central computer.

"What are you typing?" I asked, leaning on the back of his russet-brown leather chair.

He shushed me, his fingers flying over the keyboard.

Coding terminology meant nothing to me, so I didn't pay much attention until the name of my high school popped up with an official page demanding a password. Dustin stood up so abruptly I had to jump back so he didn't knock me over. He shifted to a different computer, typed on the keyboard, murmured to himself, then returned to the main computer. The Halsey High site opened up to lists of names and financial data—which I was fairly sure were off-limits to students.

"Eureka! Now I just need to hit…" His words trailed off as squares of colorful photos flooded the screen.

"What are those?" I asked.

"Yearbook pictures."

Bending to look closely, I saw names and squared photographs. "These are really current! But the yearbook isn't even finished yet."

"That doesn't mean the information isn't available…if you know how to sneak through the back door." Dustin grinned. "So we'll match Alyce's information with senior guys and find out if anyone is twisted enough for her."

I smacked his shoulder. "Don't talk about her like that. Just get to work."

"I am. But I'll need some data from you about Alyce."

I looked at him, waiting for him to laugh at his lame attempt at a joke. But he didn't even crack a smile. "You're kidding, right?"

"About what?" He blinked.

"Asking me for info on Alyce when we're all best friends and you know all about her."

He swiveled his chair slightly, glancing away from me. Then he cleared his throat. "Actually…no."

I gripped the edge of a scanning machine. "What do you mean, *no*?"

"I'm not as close to Alyce as you seem to think. I hang out with you and Alyce hangs out with you, so we're together a lot. But only because of you—you're the nucleus of our friendship. When you were in the hospital, Alyce and I barely talked even when we were in the same room. We just don't have much in common…except you."

I could not believe what I was hearing.

"That's how it's always been," Dustin went on. "You're so sure everything is how you see it that sometimes you don't see what's really going on. I'm not saying I don't like Alyce, because I do. I respect her individuality and she's an amazing artist. Whenever I see one of her baskets, I'm like WOW! And you got to respect anyone with the guts to wear a monkey backpack to school."

He laughed, but I didn't. I'd had no idea he and Alyce weren't tight. If I'd been wrong about my best friends, what else was I wrong about?

"So why aren't you and Alyce best friends?"

"I'm not really sure. We just never have anything to say to each other. Alyce puts out a vibe, like barbed wire on a fence, warning everyone to back off and not get close."

"No she doesn't."

"Not with you. But if you think about it, when the three of us are together, who's the one usually doing the talking?"

Answering would be self-incriminating, so I pursed my lips and glared.

"I'm just saying…" He shrugged.

"Saying that my best friend isn't who I think she is."

"Is anyone?" he asked philosophically. "Alyce is a cool person and I have her back if she needs anything, but I can't joke around with her like I can with you. For a long time now I've suspected there's something secretive going on with her. Maybe this is a chance to find out what it is."

"Maybe," I said thoughtfully, then gestured to his computer and said we should get back to work.

He seemed relieved to change the subject and for the next ten minutes, I answered as many questions as I could about Alyce. Things she loved, like black-and-white movies; her favorite color (purple); things she hated, like holidays (except Halloween), pink anything, girls who talked in baby voices, and poor dental hygiene. She scorned team sports and wasn't involved in extracurricular activities except the Halsey Hospitality Club that I started our freshman year. Alyce, Dustin, and I used to be the only members, but recently a bunch of volunteers had signed up. As president, I officiated at meetings and distributed "Hello Halsey!" gift baskets to new students. Dustin did paperwork, and Alyce worked behind the scenes creating these beautiful baskets.

When I was done answering questions, Dustin inputted everything and accessed some records for the school yearbook. After a few minutes, a printer started up.

"Got it!" Dustin announced when the printer was silent and a single sheet of paper fluttered in a tray. He scooped up the paper and held it out for me. "Here. The top three 'love' matches for Alyce."

With hopes fluttering, I read the names:

1. Zachary Hernandez
2. Kyle Mondovey
3. Taylor A. Pate

Oh. My. God.

Staring down at the printout, my throat went drier than a desert in a drought. I could hardly speak. No freaking way could Dustin be serious! This had to be a joke. Ha, ha, just messing around so he could mock me and prove my idea sucked.

Zachary wore neat, buttoned-down shirts and was always flashing a big grin like he was running for election—which could be the case, since he was on the Student Council and president of the photography club. While I didn't know Zachary personally, I knew enough to worry for his personal safety if he ever got too close to Alyce. She'd run him through the garbage disposal and feed his remains to her cat.

Kyle's rebel 'tude might intrigue Alyce: black leather, shaved head, piercings, and front teeth sharpened to dagger points. He was rumored to have a mob uncle and be only recently returned from his true alma mater, Juvie. And those weren't the worst rumors—his last girlfriend couldn't hide her bruises with makeup and, after showing up with a broken arm, she "coincidentally" transferred to another school.

"Amazing results, huh?" Dustin asked me.

"How can you possibly ask me that? Alyce could never fall in love with any of these people. Zachary is a total tool—she can't stand guys like him. And Kyle—well, he scares me. It's not safe to mess with someone with *family* connections."

"You know better than to listen to rumors. His uncle isn't in the mob. He works at a mobile phone company."

"That doesn't explain the bruises on his last girlfriend, Keesha, and I saw her broken arm."

"The computer doesn't lie," Dustin insisted as he scooped the papers out of my hands. "These three guys are the top matches for Alyce."

"Guys?" I snorted. "FYI, Dustin. Taylor isn't even a guy."

"What are you saying?"

"Taylor Ann Pate is in my gym class, and she's definitely female."

Biting his lower lip, he glanced down uneasily at the paper. "That's not possible. I couldn't miss such an important detail. Still, it's easily fixed. I'll delete Taylor from the list. That still leaves us two promising matches. Are you ready to proceed to the next step?"

"Next step?" I asked uneasily.

"Contact in a public setting."

"You mean ... dates?"

"How else will you select the best candidate for Alyce?"

"No, no, no way." I pulled over a chair and sank next to him. "I hadn't thought about that ... I mean ... How can I go out with other guys? I won't cheat on Eli."

"You won't be going out—Alyce will."

"With me in her body. Eww! What if Zachary or Kyle try to kiss me?"

"That would be a great opportunity to judge their compatibility. I suspect Alyce's body will let you know which guy she prefers. But you don't have to go through with this. I told you I think it's a bad idea. In my experience digging up dirt on politicians, love is never the answer but a mistake that leads to their downfall."

"That's lust, not love," I argued.

"Is there a difference?"

"That's the kind of comment I'd expect from someone who'd rather date strangers he meets online."

"It's only happened twice…well, three times if you count that one that lied about her age."

"You bragged about hooking up with an older woman," I remembered with a chuckle. "Until you found out she was older than your mother."

"A lesson learned and not to be repeated. I've sworn off romance until after college. I have too much to accomplish, anyway—like today I'm going to a protest. But before I go, I'll try to set up dates for you."

"Thanks…I think."

He gave me a deep look. "Sure you want to go out with these guys?"

I didn't want to—but this was for Alyce. And I owed her.

So I took the printout from Dustin's hand, studied the photos, then handed the paper back to Dustin. "Okay. Set up the dates."

6

Before I left Dustin's house, he Googled Liberty and Pioneer, discovering that they were (as I'd suspected) names
of historical cemeteries all within an hour's drive. But how
did lavish Green Briar fit on the list? Alyce went to a lot of
trouble for an old file. It just didn't add up.

Sighing, I looked up as Dustin's printer shut off.

"Here," Dustin said, holding out several printouts.
"Easy directions to keep even you from getting lost. On
second thought, I should go with you."

"And miss out on the chance for arrest?" I teased. "Go
kick butt at your protest. Don't worry, I won't get lost."

"You always say that."

"I always mean it."

"Until I get a SOS call," he teased. "I highlighted your route in yellow. Give me a call later to let me know how things go. By then I should have you set up for your first date. Which guy would you rather go out with first? Zachary or Kyle?"

"Neither."

"Should I remind you this was your idea?"

I stuck my tongue out at him and snatched the printouts from his hand. As the door thumped shut behind me, I wondered what would be a bigger waste of time:

1. Going out with guys Alyce would hate.
2. Going to cemeteries without knowing why.

This whole Temp Life thing would work better if Alyce's body came with easy-to-follow directions. Instead it felt like I was sinking deeper into "crazy." I envied Grammy for having such a simple assignment. No school, no obligations, just kicking back and having fun at my house.

Hmmm … what exactly was she doing?

Instead of starting up the car, I reached over for Monkey Bag and dug inside for Alyce's cell. Punching in my own number was so weird. The phone rang and rang and I was about ready to hang up when someone answered.

But it wasn't Grammy.

My mother!

"Just a sec," Mom said, in a rush as if she'd been interrupted (she was probably chasing Melonee, who always resisted having her diaper changed). "Amber!" she shouted.

Startled, I jerked back and smacked my elbow on the door handle, crying a sick-cat sound-combo of "Mom!"

and "Ow!" My eyes swam with tears but not because of my throbbing elbow. Mom had called me "Amber." Could I abandon all pretense and return home where I belonged?

"Amber!" Mom repeated, sounding far away, like she'd dropped the phone. "What's wrong with you lately? Didn't you hear me calling? Here, it's Alyce."

My soaring hopes crashed to earth like dead stars.

Mom hadn't been talking to me—and I missed her so much. It stung, worse than after the triplets were born and I wanted to stay with Mom in the hospital but was told to go home because the babies needed Mom more than I did. I needed her then and now, too.

I was ready to ditch my assignment and drive right over—until a voice from the phone yanked me back to reality.

"Amb—I mean, Alyce—are you there?" my own voice whispered.

"Yes," I told my grandmother with a rueful look down at my temporary body.

"Wait a minute while I take this in my room. You probably should call my cell next time."

"Your cell? But I don't have a cell phone."

"You do now. Probably because your parents nearly lost you after the accident and want to keep in touch with you." She gave me the number. "Okay, I'm in your room now so we can talk freely without Theresa overhearing."

"You're supposed to call her Mom," I said, a bit too sharply as I wiped a tear from my cheek.

"I've been trying, but it's so hard when I look at her and remember changing her diapers. Being my daughter's daughter is harder than I expected. Oh, and before I forget, you had a call from your beau last night. He's still in Los Angeles doing some singing contest. Nearly knocked my socks off when he knew I wasn't you, and since he knew, I told him who you were."

"Yeah, he called here." I warmed a little thinking of Eli. I wasn't able to be with my family, but at least I could talk to Eli. "Thanks for bending the rules and telling him what was going on."

"My rules, so I can bend them."

"Just don't bend too many—you *are* in my body."

"Worried I'll run out and get a tattoo?"

"Depends on the tattoo," I teased. I'd secretly wanted to get a tattoo but hated needles.

"I'll get a big pink heart surrounded by flowery words that say 'Grandmothers Rule Forever.'"

"Grammy!" I cried. "You wouldn't!"

"Sure about that?" She chuckled, sounding exactly like herself except with my voice. "Honey, you have nothing to worry about. I'm keeping busy here. Theresa was impressed with how I rearranged your bedroom furniture and organized your closet. I couldn't believe how much junk you crammed in there. I'm throwing out a huge pile of mismatched shoes, old clothes, and trashy magazines."

"They're not trashy! Don't throw them out!" I yelled, so loudly that a man walking his dog turned to stare at the "crazy girl" sitting alone in a car.

"Why keep old magazines?"

"How else am I going to study what's going on in Hollywood without being an insider? You know how serious I am about my career plans." I had *E-Buzz* magazines dating back five years, full of highlighted articles about entertainment agents and how these movers and shakers influenced Hollywood. With study and hard work, I planned to create my own style of influence someday. "I don't care about the old shoes and clothes, but return my magazines to the closet."

"Sure, honey. I've always been behind your ambitions one thousand percent. I'll take excellent care of your collection and I know the perfect shelf for them. Is there anything else I should do for you? I've already cleaned your room, washed dishes, dusted, and folded laundry. I couldn't find any homework."

"That's because it's spring break with no school until Monday."

"So what would you be doing if you were here?"

"Hanging out." I shrugged. "You know. Computer games, playing with my sisters, listening to music, talking to friends."

"That doesn't sound very productive."

Her critical tone, one she often used with Mom but seldom with me, made me bristle. "I don't always have to be doing something. But if you get bored, read my self-help books."

"I never get bored," she said firmly. "I'm going to help your mother by creating a daily schedule for the triplets, with meal times and educational activities. Theresa really is in over her head with the little girls. She has no organizational skills at all, but I'm doing my best to help."

I groaned. Mom hated anyone telling her what to do.

She believed in letting children discover themselves through non-structured play.

"Grammy, why don't you hang out with me? We're best friends, after all, so no one would think it was unusual. I can pick you up right now."

"Where are you headed?"

"An old cemetery."

"Why would you want to do something so morbid?" she asked. "It's not like any souls linger around; they go on to better things."

"I'm following Alyce's plans," I explained. "I found this list with dates and places she planned to visit. So I'll go even though I don't know what I'm supposed to do there."

"Did you ask your GEM?"

"It only said Alyce was searching for something that's lost—which isn't much help. Sure you won't come with me?"

"Count me not interested. I'll stay here and help your mother. I'm beginning to think that's my true purpose in being back here. Your mother and I didn't always get along and before I died we had—oh, she just called for you, I mean me. Bye!"

Abruptly, Grammy clicked off.

I wondered what Grammy had started to tell me about Mom as I tucked the phone back into Monkey Bag and fished around for the car keys. Movement on the street caught my attention. An elderly couple out for a walk stared at me, probably suspicious of a junky car loitering in their upscale area.

Time to get moving.

Alyce's car made a grinding sound when I started the engine, and I tensed, hoping her beloved Junkmobile wouldn't die on me. The car had been dirt cheap and for a good reason. Fortunately the grinding faded to a low roar and the car seemed okay. Glancing in the side mirror at myself and seeing Alyce sitting in her rightful place gave me an odd sense of connection with my best friend, as if we were sitting together.

Was she aware of her body? Did she approve of what I was doing? Or was she too depressed to care? If only I could have helped her before things got critical. I hoped she forgave me for not helping her when she needed me.

But I'm making up for it now. I sent thoughts out to her like a prayer. *Feel better and come back soon.*

Checking Dustin's map, I calculated where I wanted to go, tracing my finger along the yellow highlighted streets, then merging onto the freeway going north. But after driving a few miles, nothing looked right. Where did my turn-off go? I'd read every sign. There was no way I could have passed it.

Confused, I exited and read the map again. That's when I noticed that the word "Liberty" was upside down. Oops. As I turned the map around and got back on the freeway heading in the right direction, I made a mental note not to mention this small "detour" to Dustin.

When I exited at Liberty, I was surprised how close the cemetery was to the freeway. I'd driven by here a zillion times without noticing that the fence surrounded old tombstones. The land was rounded, dipping slightly then rolling upward, with oak trees shading the hard dirt and weedy ground. There was no formal parking lot, only a wide graveled area off the road.

After parking the car under an oak tree, I consulted my GEM. Or should I say, *attempted* to consult my GEM. When I asked for information about Alyce's reason for coming here, it only repeated that annoying *to find the lost* answer again.

Frustrated, I tossed the tiny book back into Monkey Bag and left the car. There was an elaborate, wrought iron double gate with the words "Liberty Cemetery" arched in a solemn welcome. I pushed it open. My feet crunched on rough grass as I entered the cemetery. I saw a pretty white gazebo and walked over to it, and found a sign containing all the names of those buried at the historical site. As I walked around, I read plaques dating back to the mid-1800s on gravestones that rose out of the ground like pale ghosts. Many were faded, made of rough-stone, but the area around them was well-kept and free of weeds.

I walked slowly from gravestone to gravestone, reading names and trying to guess what Alyce was looking for. Most of the graves were for pioneers and early settlers of the town of Liberty, which no longer existed. Some gravesites were adorned with real or fake flowers and bore inscriptions like "gone but not forgotten" or stating relationships like "mother," "father," or "son." There were a lot of small graves, many of the children the same age as my little sisters, which made me sad. And again I puzzled over Alyce's obsession with cemeteries. Was this idle curiosity or was she searching for that "lost" something?

If only I could tap into Alyce's thoughts. When I'd been

in a different body previously, I'd had unexpected flashes of their memories, like the body itself was trying to send messages. But I didn't know how to make this happen or if it was something that I had control over. Still, it couldn't hurt to try.

Sitting on a bench with eyes closed, I searched inside myself.

Alyce, if you're here, can you answer me? Why are you so interested in cemeteries? I always thought it was just because you like taking creepy photographs but now I think there's another reason. Does it have anything to do with your insisting I come see you when I was in Venice Beach?

Concentrating hard, I listened for any kind of answer—a shiver, a whisper, or even a strong feeling would help. But all I heard were cars, chirping birds, and a whooshing wind that shivered goose bumps up my skin.

No otherworldly messages.

Only the quiet of graves.

Maybe I was supposed to take pictures of unusual tombstones. I considered going back to the car for Alyce's camera but it wasn't like I actually knew how to use it. I'd watched her adjust the dials and buttons, but I never learned how to do it myself. I only knew how to use the point-and-click style.

So how long should I stay here doing nothing except staring at graves?

I glanced around one more time, wishing for inspiration, but there was nothing for me to do. Except leave.

When the gate clanged behind me and I returned to my car, I saw another car parked there, too. There was no one inside, so whoever was visiting graves must have gone on a different path. I liked imagining this unknown person paying solemn respects to an ancestor; that even the graves with fading names on their tombstones were still alive in the hearts of those left behind.

Cheered by this thought, I slipped back into the driver's seat. The engine sputtered a few times, then started right up. Good old Junkmobile, I thought, giving it a fond pat on the dashboard.

Keeping my foot on the brake, I waited for a slow-moving hay truck to pass and wondered what to do now. It was still early, and I should get something accomplished. But what? I could return to Dustin's for matchmaking plans. Except I got sick thinking about going out with Kyle and Zachary and wasn't sure what scared me more—a guy who might have beat up his girlfriend or one who was sure to bore me to death. Anyway, Dustin probably would be at his protest by now, so I couldn't go there even if I wanted to.

What I really wanted to do was go to my real home. A strong yearning grabbed hold of my heart and I could almost feel the car pull in that direction as I backed out of the graveled parking lot.

But if I saw my family, I'd never have the courage to leave again.

So it was back to Alyce's house. But I wasn't in a hurry to get there, so instead of heading back to the freeway, I opted for the long country route and made a left turn onto the main road. I could use the extra time to figure out a plan.

It was odd to be so close to a busy freeway yet isolated, with a panorama of crop fields stretching endlessly around me. An uneasy feeling struck me for no logical reason, and I shivered with a strong sense of wrongness.

Slowing, I looked around to make sure I wasn't being followed. But the road was deserted. Maybe I was going the wrong direction again—that could explain my bad feeling. Yet when I double-checked my map it showed I was going the right way.

So why did my heart thump with anxiety?

It had something to do with a smell, I realized. A sea-breeze scent wafted inside the car, so briny that I tasted salt on my lips. Yet there was no logical way I could smell the ocean, which was over a hundred miles away.

Panic stole my breath. I could hardly breathe. I didn't know what was going on, but I knew enough to listen to my intuition. Right now it was screaming, *Get the hell out of the car!*

I spotted a small country store ahead and sped up, eager to be around other people. Inside the store, I'd be safe and everything would be fine.

But before I made it halfway there, a hand clamped down on my shoulder.

"Keep driving," a familiar masculine voice ordered.

Too shocked to utter a sound, I looked in the rearview mirror, already knowing the face I'd see.

Gabe was back.

7

Questions tumbled like sharp rocks in my mind. How had he found me? The last time he'd seen me, I'd been in the body of Eli's sister, Sharayah. Now I looked like Alyce. Yet Gabe looked the same. If he was trying to elude the Dark Disposal Team, he should have switched bodies—since he didn't have to stay in the same body, why not steal into a new identity that no one would recognize? Even though he wasn't born into the face that loomed in my rearview mirror, there was a ruthless determination in his gaze that I recognized...and feared.

The brim of his navy blue cap rose above his dark-gold stubble; a strong jaw and hazel eyes stormy with intensity locked with mine in the mirror. I could have kicked myself for not checking the back seat before getting in the car. That was one of the first things I'd learned from my book on *The Savvy Girl's Guide to Self-Defense*.

"What the hell are you doing here?" I demanded.

"I had to see you … Amber."

He knew who I really was!

I could hardly speak with his Dark Lifer hand on my shoulder, tingling with a heat that drained my energy and made it hard to focus on the road. Chaotic thoughts raced in my head. It really was Gabe! I hadn't imagined him below my window last night. How had he found me? What did he plan to do? Was he angry because I'd sent the Dark Disposal Team after him? Obviously they hadn't caught him, but that didn't mean he wouldn't hold a grudge and want revenge.

"You shouldn't have come here," I managed to say, struggling to hide my fear. "The Dark Disposal Team will find you."

Gabe's hand sizzled as he pressed hard against my shoulder. "I never worry about the DDT. Keep driving."

"Where?"

"My usual destination—nowhere," he added with a bitter laugh.

"I can't just keep driving."

"So pull in somewhere we can talk."

"Talk?" I asked in a breathless whisper.

"You're not in any danger from me, if that's what you're thinking."

"I wasn't," I lied.

"Good, because I'd never hurt you. I've been thinking

about you since we parted on the boat. It's great to see you again."

I wanted to snipe back that it was hell to see him again, that his nearness and energy-sucking touch drained me. But it took all my strength to keep driving.

"Am I scaring you? Sorry, that's not my intention. It's just I couldn't find any other way to get you alone. So I followed you."

"Stalked," I spat out in a furious whisper.

"It was necessary so we could talk."

Times like this, a girl could really use an eject button to fling an unwanted passenger out of the car. It was hard to think straight, especially with the white lines on the road wavering like wiggling snakes. Fields and trees and paved road blurring, I drifted away, fading like smoke...

"Watch out!!" Gabe released my shoulder as he lunged over the seat to steady the wheel.

"I can drive just fine!" Without his heated touch, I could think more clearly. "Keep your poisonous hands off me."

"Sorry—I forgot how my touch affects a Temp Lifer." He sucked in a deep breath, then blew it out and leaned away from me. "I promise I won't touch you unless you want me to."

Like that would ever happen—*not*.

I kept my gaze on the road and spoke coolly, "What's this all about?"

"You have every reason to hate me, and I don't blame you. I simply want to talk."

"So talk."

"Not in a moving car. Find somewhere to stop—choose a public place if that will make you feel safer. You can trust me."

Trust him? Never. But I was all for going to a public place where I could yell for help. I thought fast, knowing that his Dark Lifer touch was as deadly to me as a loaded gun. Playing along with him seemed like the best idea for now—until I could sneak to my GEM and report him to the Dark Deposal Team.

"I'll pull over in that park." We'd driven into a suburban area with large homes that practically bumped into each other. There was no space left for yards, but it offered a few acres of lawn and shade trees in a community park.

He didn't argue, so I took that as acceptance.

I was relieved to see little children swinging and whooshing down a slide while parents sat nearby on benches. If Gabe pulled anything, a shrill scream would activate the mother-warrior instinct and playground moms would punch 911 on their cell phones.

As I pulled into a parking spot between two SUVs, I kept a hand poised on the door handle, debating on whether I should give into my curiosity and listen to him or try to escape.

But Gabe must have guessed what I was thinking because before the car even came to a complete stop, he sprang from the passenger seat, coming around to my side to open my door. With a sweeping gesture, he said, "Allow me."

I didn't thank him.

I pocketed Alyce's car keys and stepped out of the car.

"This way, please," he said, with such gentlemanly

charm that anyone listening would think we were on a date.

Now that I could see him better, his body was still hot looking: long, muscular legs in snug blue jeans; a dark-blond ponytail; and a golden tan that I knew was sprayed on to hide the Dark Lifer grayness of his hands. He had a subtle style, too, which seemed modern at first—jeans, a button-down shirt over a T-shirt. But a closer look revealed that the large silver watch he wore was obviously an antique and his boots were heavy leather, more suited for sailing than hanging out at a mall.

"What's this about?" I insisted, facing him with my hands on my hips.

"It's complicated." He pointed beyond the playground to a rose garden. "Let's go over there."

"Why?" I demanded. "Because it's remote and deserted?"

"No, because flowers are beautiful—I've always been a great admirer of beauty." He gave me a significant look.

I felt myself blushing and had to remind myself that I was talking to the enemy. "So why go to all this trouble to talk to me?"

"Would you have met with me otherwise?"

"No."

"My point exactly." He moved slowly and I fell into step beside him, walking down a worn dirt path between rows of brilliant blooming and budded roses. "Aren't you going to ask how I found you?"

"Why bother? You'll eventually tell me."

He chuckled. "You're right, of course, but then I expected no less from you. You're unlike any girl I've ever met."

"Nice line, but it won't work on me. I know your history of leading girls on, then breaking their hearts. I know better than to believe anything you say."

"Aren't you curious why I still wear this body?"

Well, duh. Of course I was, but I wasn't about to admit it to him. With a shrug, I stepped ahead of him over a green hose stretched across a dirt path between the roses. Inhaling soft flowery scents mingled with damp earth, I pretended nonchalance as I reached out to brush my fingertip across a lavender petal.

"Who can resist a rose?" he said with a wry twist of his lips. "As D. H. Lawrence said, *I am here myself; as though this heave of effort at starting other life, fulfilled my own: Rose-leaves that whirl in colour round a core of seed-specks kindled lately and softly blown.*"

"I have no idea what that means."

"It's about appreciation and living life to its fullest." He sighed. "But no matter how many lives I live, I'll never regain my own."

He spoke in a voice raw with emotion; the dark hopelessness in his eyes made me feel as if I was staring into his soul. I could imagine his endless cycle—stealing a body every moon, decades passing in a whirl of wars and technology. Yet he'd chosen to live as an outcast.

"I should have already moved on. I need to find a suitable host to inhabit before the full moon next week." He stared wistfully at the roses. "But I wasn't ready yet."

"Why not?" I asked quietly.

"Because of you."

"Oh, please. You don't even know me," I pointed out.

"Most of the time we were together, you thought I was someone else."

"Appearances mean little. It's your soul essence that sparked emotions in me I thought were long dead—curiosity, interest, and a longing to see you again. I stayed in this body so you'd know me when we met again."

"That's a dumb move. Aren't you afraid the DD Team will find you?" I thought of Monkey Bag tossed casually on the floor of Alyce's car, with the GEM zipped inside. All I had to do was get to the car, open the book, and report him to the DD Team.

"You were worth the risk," he said simply.

"That's crazy."

"No crazier than discovering you're a Temp Lifer—only one of the intriguing things about you. And the way you stood up to me, fearless. I've thought of nothing else but finding you since we last met."

Had that only been a few days ago? I could hardly believe so little time had passed since the drama on his boat, where he'd barely escaped the Dark Disposal Team.

"You should never have found me," I told him. "It's my duty to turn you in again and I will, if I get the chance."

"I know … and I find it strangely exciting. You probably have a GEM in the car. If you want to report me, go ahead. I won't stop you."

"Why not?" I asked suspiciously.

He arched a dark brow, studying me. "Perhaps I have more trust in your good nature than you have in my bad nature."

"Doubtful."

"Would you really turn me in?"

"Yes."

"Then do it. Your car's not far away."

I turned to look at the car, then back at Gabe. I couldn't figure out what sort of game he was playing. Was he trying to con me into believing he was a friend? I wasn't that naive. Still, he could have hurt me and hadn't...yet.

"First tell me why you're here," I said.

"Curious?" He smiled, amused.

"I'll listen to what you have to say before turning you in."

"Ah, being fair-minded. I'm grateful."

"You're mocking me," I accused, irritated by his smug smirk. "You may not respect Temp Lifers but I do, and it's important to me to do a good job."

"It was important to me too...once upon a time." His face tensed into hard lines, but otherwise he showed no expression. He just stood there, surrounded by blooms of new life which seemed like an ironic background for someone who stole lives and should have died naturally decades ago. I should have run to the car and grabbed my GEM. But I stood still, too.

"Aren't you afraid of being captured?" I asked.

"The DD Team has been trying for over a century with no success," he said wryly. "The only way they'll catch me is if I let them."

"They came close on the boat."

"I was gone before they even touched Earth. I have powers far beyond the average Dark Lifer. Most of them think the only way to gain energy is to steal glowing light from someone who has recently contacted the other side. But powers mean little to me anymore. This existence is meaningless and boring." His shoulders slumped and he stared down at his hands. "I'm tired of always running, only living borrowed lives. That's why I've decided to change ... if you'll help me."

"Why me? We're not exactly friends! You threw me in the ocean and then tied me up with duct tape."

"That's all in the past."

"Only a few days!" I argued.

"Mark Twain said, *Forgiveness is the fragrance the violet sheds on the heel that has crushed it.*" He gestured to a small lavender rose bush that was past its bloom and hung heavy with withered pedals. "A purple flower represents forgiveness. I'd offer you a bouquet if you'd accept it."

"Are you trying to apologize?"

"If I was, would you accept?"

"No. I doubt you went to all the trouble to track me down just to say you're sorry."

"It wasn't that difficult to find you." We turned down a row of miniature roses, most still full with buds and ready to bloom. I had to hurry to keep up with his long-legged stride. "Once I've met someone, I know not only their face but also their unique aura, which is like a soul fingerprint. When I found the imposter in your body, I knew she wasn't you."

"You met her!" My breath caught nervously. Grammy hadn't said a word about meeting a Dark Lifer—especially one that was #1 on the *Wanted, Dead and Alive* list.

"I was suspicious at first to find a Temp Lifer in your

body. I thought this might be a DD Team trap until it was obvious she believed I was a friend from your school—she didn't recognize me. Her glow, though, was surprisingly bright, almost as sweet as yours. Who is the Temp Lifer in your body?"

I shook my head, determined not to give Grammy's secrets away. "I don't know. I only do what I'm told."

"But you're a living girl, so why leave your body? It doesn't make any sense ... unless this is an elaborate trap to catch me."

"Not everything is all about you."

"You're avoiding the question," he said, his eyes narrowing.

"If you must know, I'm doing this because I care about people—something you obviously know nothing about."

"I know too much about people—most of it unpleasant."

"*Negativity equals a bad attitude.* You aren't the only one who knows quotes. That's from a self-help book called *Pollyanna's Rules for Gladness.* You could really learn from self-help books."

"I'd rather learn from you." He reached out, taking my hand, his touch sizzling hot, tingling dangerously.

"No!" I pulled back. "You promised not to touch."

"Right," he said. "I apologize and hope you'll listen to what I have to say without judgment. You see me as a villain but once I was like you, a new Temp Lifer eager to do a good job and improve lives."

"Improve by lying, being cruel, and betraying trust?" I scoffed, folding my arms across my chest.

"You made me realize I've made grave mistakes. That day on the boat, I wanted to stay and get to know you—the real you. I regretted having to leave so abruptly, before I could confide in you. I sensed you would never betray a trust."

I knew he was referring to the great betrayal of his human life, back in the late 1800s, when he confessed to a crime he didn't commit to save the woman he loved, but she left him to the gallows while she went off with another man. I felt sorry for him...but was wary.

"What do you want from me?" I asked softly.

"Only that you listen to me as you would a friend." He frowned, staring beyond me out the window. As his gaze shifted back to me, I sensed tenderness. "I've been alive for over a century yet don't have one true friend."

"You must have had some friends."

"Only sweethearts...and that always ends badly."

"Your fault," I said. I thought of girls like Eli's sister, who had fallen in love with him only to have their hearts broken.

"If I'd met you sooner, things might be different."

"I doubt that," I said, leaning slightly toward him as I studied his sad face. His salty ocean scent stirred my sympathy. It was dumb to feel sorry for the guy who'd carjacked me. I didn't let down my guard but nodded for him to continue.

"No one else has talked to me like you did that night in the boat," he told me.

I tried to remember what I'd said. After we got past the whole kidnapping thing, he'd explained about his past and how he'd gone to the gallows for the girl he loved. I'd told him a few things about myself, too. I'd admitted to being a Temp Lifer but only because I wanted to convince him to let me go.

"You said some things that made me realize I'd been living my lives wrong. I wronged you, too, yet you didn't hold a grudge and showed unusual compassion. That's another reason why I sought you out."

"I can't do anything." I shook my head. "I'm just a typical human girl."

"Typical?" he asked with a hint of a smile. "I think not. You've changed the weather of my soul like a force of nature. You're my only hope for forgiveness so I can end this half-life of stealing bodies."

I gasped. "You want to end your life?"

"No—I want to begin it again, where I belong. I'm ready to go home."

"You mean ... to return to the other side?"

"Yes." He bowed his head in a solemn nod.

"I don't believe you. This is some kind of trick."

"No, only the truth."

I doubted him ... yet he sounded so sincere, and I couldn't think of any other reason why he'd risk coming here. "Well ... that's easy enough," I said. "I'll contact the DDT with my GEM and they'll come ASAP."

"No!" he protested with a shake of his head.

"But you just said you wanted to go back."

"Not by force with the Dark Disposal Team. If they take me, my future will be hell. They'll lock my soul away in such a dark pit of horror that I'll never see light again. I won't be able to prove that I've reformed and that I'm ready to make amends for my mistakes. You're my only hope for a second chance."

"Me?" I shook my head. "You can't be serious."

"But I am. Deadly serious." He stared deeply into my eyes. "Amber, will you help save my soul?"

"I can't help you," I insisted.

Walking among rows of flowers, shrubs, and trees with a dead guy who spouted poetry and stole bodies was weird, but finding out that he wanted me to save his soul was weird squared to infinity.

"I beseech you, Amber, give me a chance."

Gabe's mix of old-styled and modern language, spoken in such a deep refined voice, made me feel like following him to the ends of the universe. He looked so vulnerable, like a lost child trying to find his way home, that my heart ached for him.

"I don't have any special powers, and I don't know how to help you."

"Use your connections to the other side."

Connections? This was a word that came up a lot whenever I researched becoming an entertainment agent. Knowing the right people in influential places was like an "open sesame" spell that magically unlocked doors. If Gabe had asked me to help him get into an audition or how to become a Hollywood star, I'd be right there offering advice. But this was beyond my knowledge—especially since my only "contacts" on the other side were my grandmother and my dead dog Cola.

"Sorry." I shook my head. "You're looking at the wrong Temp Lifer if you expect connections. I'm a newbie without any influence."

"Your grandmother is head of the Temp Lifer program."

"So?" I asked warily, wanting to kick myself for telling him about Grammy Greta's job. It had slipped out when he'd trapped me on a boat and I'd been desperate to escape.

"I hope you'll convince her to see me. If I can explain that I'm sorry and want to return, then I could go back without interference from the DD Team."

"I can't just pick up my cell and call her," I lied.

"Leave a message through your GEM." He rushed on before I could interrupt. "Don't look so surprised that I know how GEMs work. Remember, I was a Temp Lifer."

"Until you turned Dark," I accused him, wondering if I was crazy for talking calmly to the most-wanted dead criminal alive.

"I had a good reason." He glanced around as if to make sure no one was close, then gestured that we sit on a bench in the shadows of shade trees and roses. "Despite all the injustices in my Earth life, when I became a Temp Lifer I excelled at my job. I'd thought I'd found my purpose in death. Everything was going great—until they assigned me the body of a shy young gentleman."

"How long ago was this?" I sat a safe distance from him on the bench so that he couldn't touch me.

"Around the turn of the century."

"Really? I thought it was much longer, like before I was born."

"The *twentieth* century," he clarified. "My Host Body lacked the courage to approach the girl he loved and was going to lose her to another suitor. I was prepared to woo her with sweet words and romantic bouquets. Flowers always win a young lady's heart." He gestured over to a garden of brilliant blossoms in red, yellow, pink, and lavender. "But when I met his young lady, everything changed."

"Why? Did you fall in love with her?"

"Quite the opposite." His eyes narrowed. "She was the daughter of the woman whose betrayal sent me to the gallows."

"No way!"

"Unfortunately, it's true. But I had no alternative but to perform my job. A Temp Lifer must always follow through on his Host Body's plans," he added with a bitter snort. "I recited Barrett and Lord Byron, and wrote a love sonnet for my host's sweetheart. When I proposed marriage, she eagerly accepted. I gave her a ring—but I couldn't go through with it. All I could think about was how her mother had destroyed my life. So I yanked the ring off her hand and told her she was a fool to believe in love."

I gasped. "No!"

"It was the only way to toughen her foolish heart and to save my Host Soul from marrying into a murderous family."

"You wanted revenge," I said.

"Justice," he insisted. "Afterwards, I knew no one would understand and I could never go back to being a Temp Lifer, so I switched into another body. It was amazingly easy. I quickly discovered there are more freedoms to being in a temporary body. No rules, and powers that you won't find in your precious GEM."

"What sort of powers?"

"Mind connecting, memory manipulation, and astral transporting. You've been told you can't leave your Host Body until they decide to call you back—but that's not true. You could leave that body any time."

I shook my head. "I've tried and it didn't work. The only way I can switch is when my assignment is over."

"That's what they want you to believe—but it's not true. Help me meet with your grandmother, and I'll teach you the secrets of tapping into your power."

"I don't want to learn *your* kind of secrets."

"Not even how to mind-blend with your Host Soul? You could go to your friend right now and ask her anything. Don't you have questions you'd like to ask?"

Of course I did—but I wasn't about to admit that to him.

"It's unfair how Temp Lifers must figure out their missions with so little information," he went on. "Especially since those who run the program are aware of these useful skills."

"You mean my grandmother?"

"Of course. She's privy to many secrets that she'll never reveal. But I can show you, and you'd never have to rely on a GEM again." His voice was so sultry, so tempting...

I didn't want to believe him. Yet Grammy had joked about not using a GEM. She'd said they were annoying (which was true), but maybe she had another reason. Did she know how to pluck memories from her Host Body? Is that why she seemed so comfortable doing her job without the stresses I was going through? But wouldn't it make more sense to arm me with more powers, too? It wasn't fair to leave me stuck in confusion while I struggled to make sense of my assignment.

I thought back to the rare moments when I'd picked up memories from the bodies I'd temporarily inhabited. It had always happened randomly, without any warning. I'd assumed it was a gift from the other side to help my assignment. But if what Gabe was saying was true, I'd accidentally tapped into my own powers.

Still, if I was supposed to know these things, Grammy would have told me. I trusted her far more than I trusted a Dark Lifer.

"I'll pass on the lessons," I told him, running my hand idly over a rough edge of the bench. "I'd help you without any bribes, but there's nothing I can do. You can't meet with my grandmother."

"Why not?"

"She's not there." I gestured to the sky as if the clouds floating overhead hid a portal to the other side. "Grammy's away... on vacation."

He knitted his brows, regarding me skeptically. "No one vacations from the other side."

"I can't contact her, but I can get a message through my GEM to the DD Team and ask them to give you a second chance."

"No!" He jumped up from the bench, nearly tripping over another hose that snaked across the path. "If I go back, it will be on my terms—not captured pitifully by the DDT. They hate me."

"Grammy says hate isn't allowed where she lives now."

"Neither are vacations, but as you said, she makes her own rules. And she's not the only one. The DD Team can't wait to toss me in a dark pit and doom me to eternal hell. I won't get the chance to make up for my mistakes and see the light of auras again—unless your grandmother could talk to them first."

"Talking to my grandmother is impossible."

"When will she return?"

"Um... I don't really know." I looked down at my temporary body and shook my head. "But when I hear from her, I'll tell her you're sorry and ask her to go easy on you. I'm sure that when I explain everything, she'll help you. Being banished to a hell pit isn't fair. I'll tell Grammy that I think you should have a chance to make up for your crimes."

He bent close to my face, not touching me but so near

that warm tingles sizzled through me. "There's a light in you that makes me want to be better, to do good things."

"I hope you get the chance."

"A chance is all I ask for." He closed his eyes, grimacing as if haunted with dark thoughts. "It's like I've been lost forever and suddenly I can see the right doorway ahead, but it's blocked and there's no time to find my way."

"Grammy says time doesn't run the same on the other side."

"But it's running out for me here. I'm weary of going from body to body and all the pretense. It's time to stop. When my time in this body expires, I won't find a new one."

"What if I can't talk to my grandmother before then?"

"My soul is already heavy with my crimes. I won't add any more."

"But if you don't switch, the DD Team will find you."

He sighed. "Yes, the worst may happen."

"So you should escape now, while you have the chance."

"I should, but my soul is so weary of hiding."

"I really will talk to my grandmother for you."

"While I appreciate the offer, I need to talk to her personally."

"You can't—not now, anyway. But maybe there's someone else you can talk to."

"There's no one else. If I can't talk with your grandmother, I might as well give up now and turn myself in."

"You don't mean that! Fight for your life … or lives … or death." I wasn't really sure how all the worked, but I hated to see anyone give up.

"I didn't beg for mercy when I was walking those final

steps to the gallows, and I won't beg now. All I can hope for is your grandmother's sense of fairness and mercy. I'm not asking you to defend me to her, just to set up a meeting so I can plead my own case."

"I would if I could…" I glanced down at the damp ground and a smudge of dirt on my sneakers. With a shake of my head, I lifted my gaze back to his. "Like I said, it just isn't possible. She can't meet with anyone now."

"So be it," he said, with such agonized resignation that my heart crumbled. "I'll leave now, so you'll never be burdened by my problems again."

A half hour ago I would have jumped for joy if he'd offered to leave, but now it felt all wrong. By refusing to help, I'd signed his death sentence. "Don't go, Gabe. Let me help—"

I thought about his story of the betrayal that ended his life. He hadn't been much older than me, yet his life was over. Stealing bodies and breaking hearts was wrong and I couldn't forgive him that easily. But I couldn't forgive myself if I didn't at least try to help.

So I agreed to set up a meeting with my grandmother.

Heaven help me.

The drive back to the cemetery was surreal.

Along the way, though, the fear I felt toward Gabe started shifting into something I couldn't define. Although he made no move to touch me, I was very aware of his arm casually resting on the compartment separating our bucket seats. Not his arm, I reminded myself, but a borrowed arm from a stolen body. I may feel sorry for him, but that didn't suddenly make him a paragon of virtue. His personality was closer to a devil than an angel, and I had no business sneaking glances at him and inhaling his salty sea scent. If the light touch of his hands electrified me, how would it feel to be in his arms...

Down, evil thoughts! What was wrong with me? It was wrong to think these kind of thoughts about anyone except Eli. He was the only guy I cared about—not someone who'd died over a century ago.

What I should be thinking about was how to set up a meeting with my grandmother. If I explained everything to her, would she understand? Would she agree to talk to him? I'd like to think so...but I doubted it. More likely she'd be furious I'd broken rules in such a big way and kick me right out of my temporary body.

As we parted and Gabe slid into his own car, I kept my expression calm but inside I was quaking. Damn. Why had I promised to help him? It was almost like I'd been under a spell.

Resisting the urge for one last look at him, I shifted into reverse and got the hell out of there. I should have driven straight to my real home and talked to Grammy. Except if I saw her and explained about Gabe, she might get angry that I didn't report him. Even worse—I might start blushing, which would lead to lots of awkward questions. It was confusing how Gabe made me feel, and I didn't want Grammy to get the wrong idea. Eli was the guy I cared about; Gabe was just someone who needed help. I needed to make careful plans for how to approach Grammy about Gabe.

So I headed back to Alyce's. Her mother would be at work and I'd have the house to myself. I'd make some lunch, maybe watch some TV, then get on with my plan to save Gabe's soul.

When I reached Alyce's, the door was locked and I had to dig down to the bottom of Monkey Bag to find a key.

That's when I heard Alyce's cell phone beeping.

Picking it up, I saw a text from Dustin.

Hoping he hadn't been arrested at the protest and needing a lawyer, I tapped a button and read the short message.

GOOD NEWS!
Z WILL MEET 2NITE.
YOU'VE GOT A DATE!

9

Convincing Grammy to meet with a Dark Lifer would be hard, but going out on a date in the wrong body with someone I was sure was the wrong guy was seriously scary. How had Dustin arranged this so quickly? He was too damned efficient for my own good. I really, really did not want to do this...

At least Zachary was an okay guy—his rep was for being boring, not for beating up his girlfriend like Kyle. Still, I couldn't imagine him and Alyce as a couple. Popularity-wannabe Zachary matched with anti-everything Alyce? Ridiculous! What could they possibly have in common?

But the more urgent question was—what was I going to wear?

Even though I had a key and the legal right to enter Alyce's house, I still felt like a trespasser. There were no sounds of life, only echoes of emptiness that shivered up my skin. Smoke and a scent of candle wax lingered in the air, and the only sound came from my footsteps and a steady ticking, like a heartbeat, from the wall clock over the TV. Peering around nervously, I half-expected Mrs. Perfetti to suddenly jump out and demand to know what I was doing here.

I bypassed the kitchen (despite growls of protest from my tummy) and headed straight to Alyce's closet. I'd already seen most of her clothes, but it still felt strange to view them through her eyes. She rebelled against popular brands and trends by wearing only natural fabrics in bruised shades of blacks, blues, and browns—except when it came to shoes. Blessed with model-perfect feet, Alyce sought out stylish vintage shoes at antique shops: gold sandals, knee-high patent-leather boots, 70s platforms, etc. At school, kids would walk by with snooty expressions denouncing her as a "Goth Loser"—until they noticed her shoes. Then they'd slow down to stare, maybe even drool a little; scorn was replaced with envy. Once even Miss Popularity-Plus, Jessica Bradley, stopped to ask where Alyce had brought her 80s leather-slouch pirate boots. But Alyce ignored the question and strode past Jessica, her own scorn intact.

I had to embrace my inner scorn to think like Alyce, I told myself. But I also needed to open up to the possibility that Zachary could be her Mr. Right. If so, I had to show him the authentic Alyce; the quirky, caring, thoughtful side of Alyce that only a trusted few ever saw. This meant putting my personal opinions about Zachary aside.

If only I was more experienced with dating! Then I could just relax and go out without getting all nervous and overthinking everything. I hadn't officially gone out on a date since...well, ever. Not even with Eli due to the whole body-switch thing.

Staring hopelessly into Alyce's closet, I knew I was in over my head. How could I get through a date when I couldn't even decide what to wear? It would help to know where Zachary was taking me. Should I dress for dinner, an outdoor concert, or disco bowling? Why hadn't Dustin included that in his message? When I tried calling him back, he didn't pick up—not a good sign, considering his radical behavior at protests. If he'd been arrested and his phone confiscated, I might not hear back for hours.

I chose two potential outfits: casual chic with bleached jeans, or a pleated, gypsy-styled shirt under a velvet jacket. Both were on the tame side of Alyce's personality, but it was the best I could do without actually asking her.

Unless I *could* ask her...

This traitorous thought snaked through my mind as I remembered my conversation with Gabe. Before he'd left, he'd given me his cell number. If I told him I'd changed my mind about wanting to learn his secrets, I could mind-connect with my Host Soul and have a real conversation with Alyce.

That would be sooo great.

But wrong.

Only how wrong could it be to want to help my best

friend? If I talked to Alyce, she could tell me which guy she preferred. This was her love life, after all, so it was only fair she had a say in what happened. Then I'd solve her crisis and become the best Temp Lifer ever ... or get kicked out of the program for breaking the rules.

What I couldn't figure out was why, if contacting Alyce was so easy, Grammy hadn't told me how to do it. She must have a good reason—although I couldn't think of one. What it came down to was the question of who I trusted more. A fugitive Dark Lifer I'd just met or the grandmother who'd loved and supported me my whole life.

A no-brainer.

With this decision made, I left Alyce's room and finally headed for the kitchen to get some lunch. (I'll admit it— I'm a foodie, no matter whose body I inhabit.) And a short while later, I carried out a steaming soup dish, a grilled cheese sandwich, and a glass of milk, arranging everything on the coffee table that often doubled as a dining table.

Glancing at the clock, I calculated that I had at least three hours before Mrs. Perfetti returned from work. I knew she wouldn't like the idea of Alyce going out on a date, so I wouldn't tell her. I'd leave a note saying I was helping Dustin with a project. Mrs. Perfetti actually approved of Dustin while she only tolerated me (Amber). Go figure.

Before things got crazy (which I was sure they would), I figured I might as well relax. Turning on the TV, I surfed channels, eager to catch up on the latest Hollywood buzz.

I listened to the latest on Angelina, Brad, and Britney, always impressed at the job their "people" were doing to make them newsworthy. Bad behavior scored way higher in the ratings than sainthood. I could learn so much from those master agents, wishing for the umpteenth time they taught Hollywood 101 subjects in high school. Instead, the best I could hope for was an internship while I went to college. I'd already been accepted, with scholarship, to a California State University of my choice, and Alyce and I were planning to share a dorm room if we got into the same schools. Alyce's grades weren't always the best, since she only bothered with assignments from classes she liked, but she had a lot going for her. I was confident she'd receive acceptance letters soon.

Abruptly, my daydreams were jerked back to reality—reality TV, to be exact.

Ryan Seacrest was making a lame joke about *American Idol* copycats. The scene cut to a stage, and there on the TV screen was Eli. He looked so wonderfully the same, yet different, too. His hair, which was usually unruly with a strand falling across his eyes, was jelled and spiked like a hardcore rocker. He wore a black leather jacket over a ripped white shirt, along with a heavy belt of chains, gold studs in his ears, and glitter eye shadow. My boyfriend was wearing makeup! OMG!

A twenty-something reporter wearing a formal blazer over western jeans shoved a microphone in Eli's face. "The *Voice Choice* competition is heating up and only the final three will be left after tonight!" the reporter exclaimed, with a huge smile for the camera. "Anything you care to say to your fans?"

"Not really … just thanks … I guess." His shy smile broadcasted straight to my heart.

"So Rocky," the reporter asked. "Who do you think is going home?"

It was weird hearing him called "Rocky" but kind of funny, too, since he looked more like the boy next door than a rugged Rocky.

"Me, of course," Eli answered. "My competitors are all so talented, I can't imagine any of them being eliminated."

"Humble is today's cool! You're one rockin' dude." The reporter flashed his pearly whites at the camera again, then returned to Eli. "You're doing great and are developing quite a fan following. Let's give a shout-out to your fan club—the Rocky-ettes!"

At this question, the camera panned to an audience of girls who jumped up waving signs. They read: *ROCKY ROCKS! LOVE YOU ROCKY!* and *NICE GUYS FINISH FIRST!* Then riotous shouting erupted—girls screaming and crying like they were in pain. I might have been jealous if Eli's adoring fans looked old enough to be in high school, but since they weren't, I thought it was sweet.

"Rocky, what song will you be singing tonight?" the reporter continued.

Eli shrugged. "We haven't decided."

"We?" I wondered at his use of plural—like he wasn't thinking for himself anymore but had "people" who did it for him. But he couldn't possibly have "people" yet—and when he did, I was the entertainment agent for him.

"So tell me honestly, Rocky, are the rumors about you

and a certain young lady true?" The reporter's black brows arched up into sharp points like little temples of curiosity.

"Don't answer!" Jumping off the couch, I shouted at the TV screen. "Don't say anything about us!"

Eli shook his head. "There's nothing to tell."

I blew out a huge sigh of relief. My life—or Grammy's, depending on the body situation on Monday—was complicated enough without being the buzz topic when I returned to school. While I wanted to have a famous reputation as a top agent someday, I did not want my love life broadcast in public.

"That's not what I hear," the reporter wheedled. "Come on, Rocky, just between us"—and thousands of viewers, I thought—"tell me about her."

Eli shook his head again, his blush so bright that his ears looked like they were on fire. "I really … um … can't."

"Don't be modest—you can brag a little! From what your friends tell me, you have the real thing going on. It's not often you meet a gorgeous girl with talent and brains."

Now I was blushing. What had Eli told his new friends about me?

"I don't really … " Eli tried to back away but the predatory reporter aimed the microphone like a loaded weapon.

"Come on, I already know who she is and your fans suspect—it's impossible to keep a showmance a secret for long." The reporter turned as if he'd heard someone call his name. When he swiveled back toward Eli, there was a triumphant grin on his face. "And here she is now! The beautiful and talented Miss Mila Monroe!"

The camera spun, then focused on a petite girl with

an unnaturally mega-white smile and thick, honey-blond hair that tumbled around her shoulders, waving down to her very ample cleavage. She flew toward Eli like a female cyclone, wrapping an arm around his shoulders and placing an enthusiastic kiss on his cheek.

"Oh Rocky, you are just so adorable and honorable, protecting me when there's just no reason at all to keep our feelings a secret," she said, in a rush of sexy that reminded me of a Marilyn Monroe wannabe. If her last name was truly Monroe, I'd eat a microphone.

I could only stare—at her arm around *my* boyfriend's neck, the faint pink smear of lipstick on his cheek, and her way-too-low and way-too-tight dress. What the hell?

"The rumors are true," she announced into the microphone. The reporter shifted eagerly to her side. "Rocky and I are going out—well, to be exact, we're staying in a lot. We don't get much free time with the crazy practice schedule."

The reporter laughed. "But I'm sure you manage to sneak away ... for some private time."

"You are so bad! Rocky and I are just fine and that's all I can say on national TV," she said with a sly wink that clearly hinted he was right.

"What about you, Rocky?" The mic was shoved back in Eli's face. "Care to add anything about your feelings for Miss Monroe?"

"NO!" he choked out, pushing away from Mila and looking sick enough to puke all over the reporter's nice pressed suit and tie. "I got to go!"

Then the camera panned back to Mila, or as I shall refer to her always, The Slut Who Stole My Boyfriend. She had no shame, only smiles, for the reporter. "Don't mind Rocky, he's adorably shy. But I'm happy to answer any questions about the competition. I'm pretty sure who'll be eliminated tonight..."

I wanted to smash the TV, grab her throat, and personally eliminate her.

But I heard the musical ring and answered my cell phone.

When I read the caller ID, I felt hot, cold, and angry all at once.

"Amber, listen to me!" Eli said in a rushed whisper. "I don't have much time but I have to tell you something important before you see it on TV."

"What?" I glanced at the TV, where Mila was smiling like she owned the world. Grabbing the remote, I shut the TV off. I pressed my lips tightly together as I waited for Eli's news, bracing myself for the breakup words. I couldn't blame him, really, not after the weirdness I'd put him through. And now that he had a big chance for stardom, he could have any girl he wanted, so why put up with one who couldn't stay in her own body?

"You're going to hear some stuff about me and another competitor named Mila."

"I saw Mila on TV." I steeled my heart. "She's really pretty."

"Um... some people think so, I guess."

"You don't think she's pretty?"

"What does that matter? She's totally fake and... well... she's not you. So, if you hear anyone saying that Mila and I are having a showmance, it's crap."

"Why would they say that?" I asked cautiously.

"For ratings and publicity—not that I even care. When the show's publicist asked me to say I was going out with Mila, I refused. But Mila thought it was a great idea and acted like we were together when I was being interviewed."

I sucked in a raw breath, my insides twisting with a complicated mix of joy and jealousy. It was great to hear Eli say he preferred me but hard to get over the image of the girl hanging on him like cheap jewelry.

"I saw the interview," I admitted.

"Oh, crap." He groaned. "I'd hoped you weren't watching. It's not what you think."

"What do you think I think?"

"That I'm a lying, cheating jerk."

"Not even close." I shifted the phone to my other ear as I curled up on the couch. "I think Mila is trying to use you to improve her career."

"So you believe me?"

"You've believed some pretty outrageous things that I told you. Besides, that look of horror on your face when Mila wrapped around you was priceless."

"I couldn't get her off—she was pinching my arm." He let out a heavy breath. "Did I ever tell you that you're amazingly cool?"

"No, but feel free to say it often."

"How about I ditch this freaking contest and say it to you in person? Singing is fun but not worth all the other stuff—photographers, interviews, gossip. I'd rather be there with you."

"And I'd rather have you here." I sent my soft words

across invisible lines from my heart to his. I imagined Eli, not as I just saw him on TV with makeup and gelled hair, but the way he looked last time we were together—in casual jeans, with his unruly hair falling across his eyes as he leaned close to me.

"If I catch a flight tonight, I can be there before tomorrow. I'm not cut out for this lifestyle—hotels and interviews and wearing clothes picked out by strangers."

"You're not cut out to be a quitter, either. If you leave now, you'll regret it."

"Yeah," he said after a long pause. "I would."

"So do your singing thing and don't worry about anyone else."

"I really needed to hear that—thanks, Amber. It's cool how you don't freak out over dumb stuff like what happened on TV. The girl my brother was dating last year dumped him just because he gave a golf lesson to another girl."

From what I knew about Chad, I suspected he deserved to be dumped. He had a history of cheating on his girlfriends—which I'd found out personally when I'd been in the body of one of them. But I liked Eli saying I was cool, so I pushed all negativity aside.

"Trust is really important," I told him. "Relationships can't survive without it."

"Yeah. Trust is, like, huge. It's cool we've got so much between us."

I started to reply, then heard a beep. "Oh, I've got an incoming call ... it's Dustin! I was afraid he wouldn't call in time."

"In time for what?" Eli asked curiously.

"Dustin set up a date for Alyce."

"But you're Alyce."

"Exactly. I'm so glad you're not the jealous type or this could get really awkward."

"I'm not ... um ... who are you going out with? You won't actually do any—"

"I'll tell you all about it later. I really miss you, Eli. Bye!"

I clicked off and switched over to Dustin.

Then I sucked in a nervous breath.

And asked about my date.

10

"I would have called sooner but I couldn't get a signal inside the dumpster," Dustin said in a distracted tone, electronic noises buzzing in the background as if he was doing at least three other things simultaneously.

"So the protest didn't go well?" I teased.

"Au contraire, it went brilliantly! I just opted to skip the whole arrest-and-bail scene with a quick maneuver into a dumpster. Once the cops were gone, I zipped back to Headquarters and found a message from Zachary."

"Did he back out of our date?" A girl could hope, right?

"No. It's on for tonight."

"Oh." Hopes dashed.

"Zachary will meet you at 7:30 at the Neon Green Gallery."

"Isn't that the green cone-shaped building downtown?"

"Great spot, huh? Turns out Zachary likes surrealist art—and that's not all he likes. I think he has a secret crush on Alyce. When I suggested a date, he not only knew who she was, but said he'd been in an art class with her. He raved about her acrylic gothic paintings."

"Really? She never mentioned him to me."

"Do you expect her to tell you everything?"

"Well … yeah. I tell her everything."

"I doubt there was anything for her to tell," Dustin said. "It didn't sound like Zachary ever admitted his feelings to Alyce. He was surprised, then excited when I hinted that Alyce might want to go out with him."

"I've got to hand it to you. This matchmaking stuff could actually work out."

"Did you ever doubt the accuracy of my computer?"

I nearly reminded him that his computer also tried matching Alyce up with a girl, but I appreciated all he'd done for me, so I thanked him. I was relieved that my date wasn't going to happen at some cozy romantic restaurant or theater. Going to a gallery would be more relaxed. I'd heard that the Neon Green Gallery showed avant-garde works by local artists. Not my taste, but so very "Alyce." Maybe there was more to Zachary than good grades and an uptight attitude. The art show could turn out to be very interesting.

It also turned out to be near the downtown arena, where a mega concert had jammed the streets with pedestrians and traffic. I couldn't find a parking place near the gallery, so I ended up parking about a mile away. And walking in Alyce's three-inch boot heels was agony—how she managed not to fall in these shoes was a mystery to me. But they did look great under my swirling gypsy skirt, and I could tell by the way Zachary's black eyes lit up when he saw me that he liked how I looked.

He was waiting outside the gallery on a wrought iron bench, looking stiff and clean-cut in a navy blue jacket, a blue button-up shirt, and dark, pressed slacks. When he stood up, I realized Alyce was two inches taller than he was.

"Hi, Zachary," I said, a bit shyly.

"Hey, Alyce. Here." He offered me a small wrapped present.

"You didn't have to get me anything."

"I wanted to."

"Well…thanks."

"I didn't think you were the flower or candy type so I gave you—"

"Breath mints," I finished, as the wrapping paper crinkled. "That's really…um…thoughtful."

"You can never have too many breath mints. I always give them to my teachers, too. I hope you like spearmint with lemon."

"Sure." I almost made a joke about it being a "sucky" gift—but Alyce always groaned when I made puns. So I asked him if he'd been ever been to this galley.

"No, although I've always wanted to check it out." He shook his head, his black hair so short and slicked with gel that not a strand moved. "It has a great reputation with displays of surrealistic, 3-D, and neon art. But of course you know that."

"I do?" I gave him a startled look as he opened the Neon Green Gallery door for me.

"I heard you talking to Tobey."

Tobey, otherwise known as Mr. Toben, was Alyce's art teacher sophomore year. He had this open-door policy with students, so when she couldn't deal with crowds at lunch, she'd hang out in his classroom.

I knew next to nothing about art, so I wisely didn't say much as Zachary pointed out sculptures and paintings, most of it too strange for my taste. The paintings ranged from depressing images of despair and horror to colorful splashes of color that could easily have been splatter-painted by my little sisters. When I looked at a random price tag, I nearly gasped at the five figures. I mean, who in their right mind would pay that much? I could frame my little sisters' finger-paint art and make a fortune.

I struggled not to yawn as Zachary explained his theories on conceptual and visionary paintings—things like inner conflicts depicted in physical form represent suppressed longings. Blah, blah, whatever. Who cared about a bunch of globs that was supposed to represent an ailing planet?

My interest returned when Zachary led me to a room titled "About Face." Across the walls a world of photographs smiled, frowned, cried, rejoiced, and raged in full color, black and white, or sepia. I remembered that when Alyce experimented with black and white, an ordinary chair would turn into something fascinating. When I'd complimented her work, she'd frowned and said it was crap. I found out later that she'd burned the chair photograph.

I was studying a portrait of an old man, his eyes wide open yet lifeless, like he was dead, when Zachary called me into the next room.

The room reminded me of a cave with its low ceiling and dim lighting. The only illumination came from spotlights flowing across individual paintings. Zachary led me over to a painting titled "Bones." At first glance I only saw a never-ending void of nightmare black, until I looked closer and saw curves of white and silver, brush-strokes that blended together to form a single image—of a skull.

"I knew you'd like it." He mistook my gasp as appreciation. "Dark art isn't usually my thing but when I saw this I thought of you. It's like the style you used in class for the self-portrait assignment."

Well, it should, since Alyce probably painted it, I thought. I stared hard until I found a signature—not the name I expected, just initials that meant nothing to me.

"Who's SAM?" I pointed to the initials in the bottom corner.

Zachary shrugged. "No idea, but I could ask if you want to buy it."

I laughed. "At $1,700? Noooo. It just interests me."

"You know what interests me?"

"I hope it's not that picture," I joked, pointing to a painting of a giant glazed donut swallowing a man.

He didn't even look at the cannibal donut, shrugging like he had zero sense of humor. But then Alyce could take serious to the extreme, too.

"That's not what I meant," he told me. He reached out and grasped my hand, pulling me close to him. His face was so close to mine so that the smell of peppermint nearly made me gag.

OMG! He was going to kiss me!

But my push was quicker than his pucker. "Zachary! No!"

"Why not? I thought we were getting along...that you'd like to...but I guess I was wrong." He drew back sharply as if insulted.

"It's not that I wouldn't like..." God, I was so bad at this. "I mean...we're in public."

"We haven't passed anyone since that old couple in the neon room." He crossed his arms over his chest. "You're the one who asked me out."

"I did? Oh, yeah. I did."

"If you don't like me, why even ask?"

"I never said I didn't..."

"You pushed me away like I have some contagious disease."

"I like to take things slow. I barely know you."

"You sat next to me in art for a whole year."

"But we were never really alone."

He looked at the nightmare skull then back at me. "Alyce, what does it take to crack that shell you put up? You go around school like a hater, but I've seen your passion for art, and it's not about hate. When you work, you focus so intently that you shut out everything. Everyone. I wanted to tell you how I feel...but you always blew me off."

What would Alyce say to this? Would she care enough to explain herself or would she shut him out? Now that I thought about it, Alyce *did* keep people away. I was the only one she allowed to get close—but she'd even kept secrets from me. What if one of these secrets was a crush on Zachary? If so, I didn't want to blow this for her.

So I reached out for his hand, cringing as his warm fingers curled in my own because it felt like I was cheating on Eli. "Can't we just see what happens?" I asked him.

He stiffened a moment before his fingers relaxed in mine. Then he murmured "okay" and suggested we finish looking at the gallery.

I faked an interest in bronze monkey sculptures, all the while thinking about Alyce. We'd been friends for so long, sharing everything—or so I thought. Apparently she'd kept more than a few secrets from me. I thought back but couldn't remember her ever mentioning Zachary. She'd talked about her teacher, Tobey, but nothing about a guy who admired more than her art talent.

So maybe she was clueless about Zachary's interest. But she should have told me about the "Bones" portrait—*her painting*. She had a similar skull sketched on the back of her purple notebook. Why had she made up the name "SAM" for her signature instead of using her own name? Why hide her identity when she should be proud? She had her work displayed in an important gallery and had never told me. What did I really know about my best friend?

Not much, obviously.

What else hadn't she told me?

As we came to the last exhibit in the gallery, I sensed a

change in Zachary. He kept sneaking glances at me, as if I was on exhibit and he was searching for hidden meanings. Was he deciding whether to ask me out on a second date? Was he wondering if I'd let him kiss me good-bye? Or was he considering switching schools to avoid any future contact with me?

I might have found the nerve to ask him if my cell phone hadn't picked that moment to burst with music. Expecting Dustin, I looked at caller ID with puzzlement. Who was Edna Charles? I didn't know anyone named Edna, but when I answered, it was clear that Edna knew Alyce.

"Alyce!" said a woman with a slight Indian accent.

"Uh … yeah?"

"You must come … now!"

"N-Now?" I sputtered. "What's going on?"

"You asked me to call if it happened again—and it's worse than last time!" The woman's voice rose with agitation. "I can't stay much longer, so you better get your ass over here before your mother gets hurt."

"My mother!" I cried, glancing over at Zachary, who came to stand beside me with a concerned look. I was visualizing my real mother sick or injured until I realized that Edna meant Alyce's mother.

"She was lucky I'm the only one working late," the woman continued. "If the boss saw her like this … well, you know."

The problem was I didn't know, but it had something to do with Alyce's mother. She must still be at her job. I knew she worked at First Trust Insurance, but I didn't know the exact location. Alyce wouldn't need to ask directions to her mother's office. How could I ask without raising suspicions?

"I'm not sure I can get there...uh...to the insurance company?" I added uncertainly. "I'm not at home."

"Where are you?"

"Downtown."

"That's only a ten minutes drive. You do have a car, don't you?"

"Yes."

"Ten minutes," she cut in. "I won't wait any longer." The line went dead.

"Damn!" I stared at the phone, snapping it closed. It would take me more than ten minutes just to hike back to Alyce's car.

"Did something happen to your mother?" Zachary asked with concern in his dark brown eyes.

"I'm not sure," I said.

"Is she at a hospital?"

"No, at her job. She works at First Trust Insurance."

"An insurance office is open this late?"

"She stays late sometimes, after it closes. She should have gone home by now." I bit my lower lip. "I don't understand what's going on—just that I need to go to her and I don't know the way."

"You don't know where your own mother works?"

"Uh, she helps out at different branches." That sounded so lame, no wonder Zachary was giving me such a weird look. "All I know is that she's at a branch ten minutes from downtown."

"I'll find it with GPS," Zachary said, pulling out his

BlackBerry. "My car is right over there, so I can get you there quick. It's not far. Come on."

I didn't need to be asked twice, and followed Zachary to his car.

When we reached the insurance company, it was dark except for a light in the lobby where a petite woman with black hair piled on her head peered through a crack in the door. As soon as she saw me, she waved frantically for me to come in.

Before Zachary could offer to come with me, I thanked him for the ride and said I needed to do this alone. But suddenly, he switched to this macho attitude and insisted on coming in. I didn't have the energy or time to argue, so I took off through the door and hoped he wouldn't follow.

No such luck.

The woman, Edna, recognized me immediately, which felt weird since we'd never met. "Alyce, hurry!" she exclaimed, taking my arm.

"Where?" I asked.

"My office," she said, in a tone that hinted I should know where she meant. But I didn't, so I hurried to keep up with her. Behind me, I was aware of Zachary following, which probably wasn't a good idea. But I'd deal with him later.

I followed Edna away from the lobby doors and down a side hall. When we reached the end of the hall, she turned and opened the last door.

At first all I saw was a typical office, with a desk, shelves stacked with files and books, and metal cabinets.

"Where's my mother?" I asked, looking around but seeing only an empty desk chair and some papers and random objects scattered on the floor.

Edna pointed underneath the desk, and that's when I saw Mrs. Perfetti huddled into a ball. Her hair, usually held back in a tidy bun, was loose and tangled around her wide-eyed face.

"Alyce!" she cried shrilly. "I'm so glad you're safe!"

"Why wouldn't I be?" I moved closer, bending toward her.

"They might get you! Come under here or they'll find you!"

I glanced uncertainly at Edna, who just shook her head at me. "Mrs...Mom, what's going on?"

"Shssh!" She put her finger to her lips. "Don't speak too loud, you never know who's listening. They're watching and now they'll get you too, like last time. Hurry and hide with me! I won't let them take you!" Her voice rose hysterically.

I glanced around, for a moment expecting a Dark Lifer to grab me with shiny gray hands. But I only saw Alyce's mother, Edna, and Zachary.

Zachary came up behind me and whispered. "Is she on drugs?"

"No!" I said, a bit too sharply because I felt guilty for wondering the same thing.

"Then what's wrong with her?" he asked.

"She's had some panic attacks before, but nothing like this," Edna said. "One minute she was fine, helping a nice young family open an account, then suddenly she rushed out of the room and locked herself in the bathroom. I calmed her down enough to get her to come in here, but that was over an hour ago. If she doesn't get herself together quick, I'm calling 911."

"Please don't!" I cried, glancing anxiously at Alyce's mother, who was rocking back and forth in a pitiful ball underneath the desk. I had no idea what to do, but I knew Alyce would never abandon her mother. So I said that I'd handle this. Then I reached out a hand to Mrs. Perfetti. "Everything will be okay," I told her. "I've come to take you home."

"Home?" She blinked.

"Yes. Just take my hand."

She shifted her legs, rising slowly to grasp my fingers. Her hand felt so warm and small in mine that I felt strangely protective toward her.

But suddenly she jerked away, her hands flying to her chest.

"No!" she screamed at me. "Keep away!"

"What's wrong?" I cried.

"Evil is here with us!" She turned chalk pale and stared at me with terrified eyes. "He'll steal your soul and take you away!"

"Don't be afraid. You're completely safe," I said in my calmest voice.

"But you're not! You can't trust him!" Mrs. Perfetti rose her arm like a sword with sharp accusation and aimed it directly at Zachary. "He's the devil!"

Zachary may be a lot of things ... but the devil?

This was so absurd, I almost laughed—until I saw Zachary's scowl and realized that he was *not* amused. There was nothing else to do but end the date ASAP, so I told Zachary to leave. I expected him to argue, or at least ask if I needed a ride back to my car, but sadly, no. He'd had enough—too much, in fact—and I couldn't blame him.

My first date as "Alyce" was a total failure.

Her mother wasn't the same "Mrs. Perfetti" I knew and avoided. Her eyes had an unfocused glaze and she spoke all whispery, like a little girl. When I asked for her car keys, she obediently handed them over.

Then I turned to Edna. "I'll take her home now. Thanks

so much...you've been great to my mother. She's lucky to have a loyal friend like you."

"I am her friend, but..." Edna's wrinkles deepened as if she was struggling with her own emotions. "But it's hard when she gets like this. Please convince her to see someone. To get help."

"I'll do my best," I said, although I wasn't sure what kind of help she needed—a doctor, a shrink, or an exorcist?

I'd known Alyce more than half my life, yet had never seen her mother so out of control. I mean, Mrs. Perfetti was all about control—from the spare cleanliness of her house to the tight leash on her daughter—yet according to Edna, this wasn't the first time she'd gone freaky. What was going on? Was it some sort of mental breakdown? Or was Zachary's guess right and Mrs. Perfetti had a drug problem? That would explain the paranoia and devil hallucinations. I didn't think she was an alcoholic, because she preferred tea to wine and I hadn't smelled liquor on her breath. Then there was another possibility—darker and scary.

I led Mrs. Perfetti out to her car because no way could she drive—not when she kept murmuring about "the devil" and moving like a zombie. I hated to leave Junkmobile on a downtown street, but it was more important to get Alyce's mother safely home. I could get the car later.

Mrs. Perfetti fell asleep on the drive, and I had to lead her by the hand into the house like I was the adult and she was the child. Seriously weird. After years avoiding any contact with Alyce's mother, I was now her caretaker. I eased her onto the couch and handed her the remote control. I hoped she'd fall asleep watching CNN so I could go back to my room and consult the GEM.

"Alyce, what's for dinner?"

I stopped mid-step, turning back toward the couch with a sinking feeling. "Um ... dinner?"

"Can you heat up tomato soup and grill a tuna melt for me?"

Her request wasn't issued in the commanding tone from last night; she was still using a whiny, little-girl voice—like she was literally someone else. I didn't want to believe there were supernatural reasons, yet I found myself staring at her suspiciously, searching for telltale grayness around her hands or fingernails. But I couldn't find any hint of a Dark resident lurking inside her, only a sadness that lingered around her like a gloomy fog.

As I smoothed mayonnaise on wheat bread and slapped on cheese, I kept sneaking peeks into the living room, puzzling over Alyce's mother. She'd turned on the TV, but instead of flipping to CNN, she watched the cartoon channel. Not really watching, though, since her gaze was fixed on the closed window blinds.

Sighing, I flipped the sandwich over, worrying that I couldn't handle this Temp Life assignment. Finding a boyfriend for Alyce seemed simple enough and while the gallery had been a little boring, I'd sensed a connection between Alyce and Zachary. I'd even started to imagine Eli and I double dating with Alyce and Zachary. But Alyce couldn't exactly date someone her mother thought was the devil. Either Mrs. Perfetti was completely off her rocker with hallucinations or she could see something that no one else could...was Zachary a Dark Lifer, too?

But I'd touched his hand, and there wasn't any gray glow or tingling heat. Maybe I was the one hallucinating, imagining that Dark Lifers were everywhere. Besides, from what Edna said, Mrs. Perfetti's problems had been going on for a while, and this wasn't the first time Alyce had had to come for her mother. It was just the first time I'd known about it.

Bending to turn off the stove, I caught my reflection in the glass oven door. "Who are you, Alyce?" I whispered sadly. "Did I ever really know you?"

There wasn't an answer, although my stomach did grumble. But it would have to wait a little longer. I placed the tuna melt on a dish, the cheesy smell making my stomach growl louder.

The cartoons were still on, and Mrs. Perfetti seemed mesmerized by Bart Simpson mouthing off to his sister Lisa. When I set her plate on the coffee table, she smiled up at me in a vague way, gesturing that I should sit beside her.

I shook my head. "I have other things to do."

"Don't leave me...please." She pointed to the windows. "They're out there, waiting to take you away."

"No one is going to take me away."

"They already did." She looked at me with a strange expression. "Who are you?"

Ohmygod, how could I handle this? She was completely crazy!

"You know who I am," I said softly. "I'm your daughter."

"No, no! My baby girl is...is gone."

"I'm right here."

She put her hands over her face as if she hadn't heard me. "Don't lie to me … why does everyone lie to me? Doesn't anyone understand that I just want her back … where is she? Why can't I find her?"

With an anguished cry she jumped off the couch, jarring the coffee table so some soup spilled. Her feet pounded down the hall, then stopped. A door slammed. I guessed she'd gone into her bedroom. Now what was I supposed to do? If I left her alone, she might hurt herself. Nervously I went down the hall, pausing at her door. It was slightly ajar and, through the crack, I saw her lying with her face buried in a pillow, her shoulders quaking with sobs.

"Are you okay?" I called out.

No answer.

"Can I get you anything?"

I heard a muffled, "Go away!"

Shutting the door, I gave myself a big fat red *F* for Failure.

I was totally in over my head as a Temp Lifer—and as Alyce's best friend. I should stop now before I messed up everything. I owed it to Alyce, her mother, my family and the entire Temp Life program to quit my assignment. Grammy could replace me with someone experienced. Before I lost my nerve, I went into Alyce's bedroom to call my grandmother.

The phone flashed with messages. A missed call from Grammy and texts from Eli, Dustin, and Jessica Bradley. Jessica? What did Ms. Popularity-Plus want with Alyce, anyway? Curious, I read the text:

RE: BASKET CLUB MTG. MON-LUNCH. C YA!

Huh? I was President of the Halsey Hospitality Club and hadn't scheduled a meeting on Monday. But knowing Jessica, a new member of what she fondly called the "Basket Club," I wasn't surprised to see her taking over. Jessica was a do-gooder with more fashion sense than common sense. It had been her idea to celebrate my (assumed) death by holding a canned food drive/memorial service. She clearly had a big future as a corporate pirate, stealing companies with a sweet smile and worthwhile goals.

I deleted Jessica's message, then read Eli's text:

MY SONGS R 4 U. LUV E.

I read this over and over, loving him, missing him, wishing he were with me instead of singing duets with the Showmance Bitch. I nearly made the huge mistake of calling him back, until I realized he'd want to know everything and I couldn't tell him about Gabe. So I sent a text (too private to repeat) and signed it *Luv A.*

Then I clicked on Dustin's text:

HOW'D IT GO?

This question struck me as so ridiculous that I laughed out loud. As if my date was a normal evening that ended with a kiss, not with a crazy mom calling my date the devil. It would take hours to describe my disastrous night and I didn't have the energy to go into that now. So I replied with a symbol of a frowning face.

PROBLEMS? he texted back.

I sent three frowning faces this time. Then I added *TTYL*, sure he'd understand that I wasn't ready to talk yet. I'd fill in him tomorrow. He might not know it yet, but he was going to drive me downtown to collect Junkmobile.

Then I stared down at a missed call message from Grammy. No text or voicemail, so I didn't know why she'd called. I wanted to call her, yet dreaded it, too. While she always knew the right things to say so I felt better, talking to her would be tricky because of my promise to Gabe. You'd think arranging a meeting between them would be easy. Far from it! Grammy would be angry that I'd broken serious Dark Lifer rules.

Instead of calling Grammy, I shut off the phone.

Why did everything have to be so complicated? I sank on the bed and hugged a pillow to my chest. Guilt and confusion swamped me like a tidal wave. And I missed Alyce sooo much. I could look at her face in the mirror but I couldn't talk to my very best friend, and that made me feel more alone than ever.

She'll come back sooner if you do your job, I reminded myself. So with a firm resolve to ditch the self-pity, I shifted into action mode. Planning is what I'd always done to keep myself focused and not dwell on sad emotions. I'd find a notebook and create a plan of action. Things always seemed clearer when I could strategize a solution on paper. Alyce, on the other hand, channeled her emotions into creative brilliance: amazing gift baskets, photographs, paintings. But even with those outlets, she'd spiraled into a crisis—a crisis about "love," according to the GEM. Maybe I was going about this all wrong. What if her crisis wasn't about romantic love but about her love for her mother—her unpredictable, unstable mother?

I dug into Monkey Bag and pulled out the GEM. Staring down at the tiny book, I flipped to a random blank page.

"Would a boyfriend for Alyce solve her crisis?"

No.

"No? But when I asked what her problem was before, you said it was love."

There are many different loves.

"Does that mean I should go out with a different guy?"

Find the missing.

"What's missing for me is a GEM that gives helpful answers. I went to all the trouble of going out with Zachary because of what you told me. And now there's the drama with Alyce's mother. What's wrong with her, anyway?"

A broken heart begins a chain of sorrow.

"Am I supposed to help Alyce's mother, too?"

Hope cannot be restored until the lost is found.

"The lost WHAT? You said that before and it still doesn't make any sense. What am I supposed to find?"

Not what—who, the smart-ass book corrected.

"Okay then." Grinding my teeth and reminding myself I was talking to a tiny book, not a real person, I tried another question. "Can you tell me *who* is lost?"

Yes.

"Then do it! Tell me who's lost!" I cried, losing my temper. "No more confusing answers. I want a name and I want it now."

SAM.

"And who the hell is Sam?"

Four-letter words are rude.

The book slammed shut.

Just great, I thought, tossing the worthless bundle of pages on the bedroom floor. Stupid book had too much attitude. Twice in one night, I'd heard the name Sam. It was puzzling enough to see it signed on a painting I knew Alyce had painted, but according to the snarky GEM, Sam was a person who was lost. Yeah, like that made sense.

What would happen if I marched into Mrs. Perfetti's room and asked about Sam? Would she tell me the truth? Or would that only upset her?

Determined, I left Alyce's room and went to her mother's closed door. Leaning my head against the wood, I listened for sounds but heard nothing. Slowly I turned the knob and peeked inside. Mrs. Perfetti was sound asleep.

Still, I was stomping angry at the unfairness of having an assignment without knowing all the circumstances. Why wasn't I given more information before being thrust into Alyce's body? When I'd complained about this, Grammy said my job wasn't to solve Alyce's problem, only to live her life so she could ultimately solve her own problem.

Humph! If Alyce could solve her own problem, neither

of us would be in this mess. So it was up to me to tackle her problems. Only how could I without knowing more? I had a feeling Sam was the key to Alyce's crisis.

Find Sam = Save Alyce.

GEM and Grammy hadn't helped, so I'd turn to someone who could.

Digging deep into my pocket, I pulled out a piece of paper and stared at seven numbers scrawled in dark, masculine writing.

I hesitated, biting my lip. Should I? Shouldn't I? Would I regret it?

Maybe, but helping my best friend was worth the risk.

Before I lost my nerve, I grabbed the phone.

And called Gabe.

Gabe answered before I even heard a ring, as if he'd been holding the phone, waiting for a call he knew would come.

"Amber?" His voice was low and sexy.

"Gabe, did you mean what you said earlier?" I asked, the loud pounding of my heart muffling my voice.

"I always mean what I say."

"What you told me ... about powers I could learn ... could I really contact Alyce?"

"Yes."

"Could you show me how and could I learn quickly?"

"Yes to both."

I sensed mysterious undercurrents in his answers; deep

rivers of secrets that could sweep me over the edge of danger. His simple "yeses" were so not simple and my hand tightened around the phone, aware of the depth of that huge small word.

"All right then." My pulse raced. "When can we meet?"

"When can I meet your grandmother?" he countered.

"Oh, yeah … about meeting Grammy …" I fidgeted, tapping my finger against the phone. "I haven't managed that yet."

"Is there a problem?" he asked, a sharp rise in his tone.

There will be when she finds out about you, I thought. I shook my head. "No. I'll talk to her, but I need to talk to Alyce first. Once I find out some things from Alyce, it'll be easier to talk to Grammy."

"All right then." He paused. "Let's do this, but my moon cycle in this body ends in three days, so it has to be soon."

"How soon?"

"Tonight would be good for me—how about you?"

A glance at the digital clock on Alyce's dresser showed me it was almost midnight. I should be in bed, asleep … but I was too hyped up to relax. Anxious energy pumped through my veins and sleep seemed like a concept for average mortals. With Alyce's mother safely in her room, I could easily sneak out.

"Okay." My answer was a leap off a high cliff into a bottomless canyon. "I'll be waiting outside."

The car light flashed on Gabe's ruggedly handsome face and hazel-green eyes as I slipped into the passenger seat. The door shut, light fading into a fog of darkness. The only illumination came in muted yellow and red glows from the car's dials and buttons.

"Where are we going?" I asked, my wildly thumping heart making me dizzy. Or maybe my light-headedness came from being so close to a Dark Lifer...and not just any Dark Lifer, either, but a dangerous fugitive. I had to be crazy to go off with him like this. He had a history of lying, deceiving, and cruelty. Yet it wasn't fear I felt—it was excitement.

"We'll go somewhere we won't be disturbed," he answered.

A tremor slithered up my spine. "But I can't be gone too long because Alyce's mother might wake up and need me. I don't want to go too far."

"It's only a few miles." He started the engine and drove away from my last connection to safety.

We pulled into a strip mall with specialty stores, banks, and restaurants. The only business open was a twenty-four-hour grocery store, but we drove past it and parked in front of a small store called Wet Pets.

"Come on," Gabe said, killing the engine and reaching into a compartment and pulling out a set of keys.

"Where are we going?" I asked, gesturing to the darkened buildings.

"Inside." He nodded toward Wet Pets.

"But it's closed."

"Closed means privacy."

His keys jingled softly, reminding me of the warning rattle from a snake. So many reasons to turn around and run before it was too late—yet I followed.

He walked up to Wet Pets, ignoring the *Closed* sign as if he owned the place. He reached for a side control panel, which lit up when he punched in some numbers. *Beep, beep*, and a red light flashed to green. Gabe splayed out the keys and chose a small gold one to fit into the lock. Click. The door fell open into a dark cavern.

"This way," Gabe told me, crooking his finger in a "follow" gesture.

I followed into a shadowy world of fish.

"Are we allowed in here?" I asked in a hushed voice. My eyes adjusted to the dim light, which illuminated the rows and rows of large glass tanks full of many species of fish in amazing colors. There was a low electrical hum and echoing, bubbling sounds.

"It's perfectly all right," he said with a shrug. "I used to work here."

"You worked?"

"Don't look so surprised. I earn an honest wage when it suits me, and managing a fish store suited me well. The owner, an odd little man with a glass eye, trusted me completely."

"Trusted *you*?" I raised my brows skeptically.

"I was the best employee he ever had."

"Then why did you leave?"

He gave a bitter chuckle. "Why do I always leave? But I like to think my boss noticed a change, perhaps a lack of efficiency, in his employee after I left. He became merely an ordinary human."

"Why do you still have keys?" I pointed to the faint lump in his jacket pocket.

"I keep souvenirs of my lives—at least the more memorable ones—and tonight the keys came in handy. Luckily, the manager was too lazy to change the security code." He walked over to a tank of colorfully striped fish and leaned close to the bubbly water. "Isn't that the most amazing scent?"

"Fish?" I crinkled my nose, a little grossed out.

"Seawater. Even though it's not pure seawater—stores that sell fish use bags with a salt mix to create seawater—the scent of salty water energizes me. I always try to choose bodies that work or live near the ocean, but sometimes I end up miles away and have to improvise."

"Why does the ocean mean so much to you?"

"It's my life...or it was before...well, you know. No matter what body I move into, I feel the sway and pull of the ocean. It's the beat of my heart, the rise and fall of the tide. Where I get my soul energy."

"Soul energy?"

"It's hard to explain when we're stuck in these heavy earth bodies, but it's how souls without a permanent body draw strength. It took me many decades to learn that my energy increases when I can breathe in the ocean air or swim in the sea."

"Will I gain energy by touching seawater?" I gestured to the nearest fish tank.

"No."

"But if it worked for you, why not me?"

"As Alexander Pope said, *On life's vast ocean diversely we sail. Reasons the card, but passion the gale.* The ocean is my passion, not yours." He moved down the row of aquariums and stared wistfully at the eels slithering across the glass. "All souls have something important to them, passions that bring joy and heighten the emotions. During the hippy era, they would have called this finding their nirvana. It's different, though, for those of us shifting in and out of borrowed bodies. This essence of ourselves is stronger because we aren't restricted by a jail of flesh and bone."

"You're confusing me," I said.

"Not surprising since humans only use ten percent of their brains. You'll understand much better in a pure energy state."

"We're already in California." I couldn't resist joking.

"Not that kind of state." He turned toward me, sly amusement mingling with the glow of yellowy fish tank lights. "*Most people are other people. Their thoughts are someone else's opinions, their lives a mimicry, their passions a quotation.*"

"Who said that?"

"Oscar Wilde."

"Don't tell me Oscar Wilde was a Temp Lifer, too."

"Doubtful. That quote isn't about literally living other lives; it's about people following others rather than seeking their own passion. Soul passion is the key to power."

I still didn't understand, but I was mesmerized by the lyrical lilt of his so-very-masculine voice. I found myself leaning closer, inhaling his scent of sea and mystery, eager to learn more.

"These bodies are vessels for life yet they are prisons, too, much like these aquariums are to the fish inside," he went on. "But since you and I aren't the true owners of our bodies, only visitors, we aren't bound by the same rules of nature. To connect with your friend, you'll need to free your soul."

"Huh?" I said oh-so-brilliantly.

"Amber, listen carefully and do exactly what I say." His tone deepened, somber and serious. He started to reach out for me, but then pulled back, obviously remembering our "no touch" agreement.

"Just tell me what to do," I said, my voice softer than the bubbling hum from the surrounding fish tanks. "How do I reach Alyce?"

"Tap into your innermost passion. What do you love more than anything?"

"My family." And Eli, I thought privately.

"Not human attachments—your personal passion. For a pianist it might be playing at a concert, sports for an athlete, and for my ex-boss it was buying exotic fish."

"Fish leave me cold. I don't play an instrument or do athletic anything."

"Dig deep into yourself—what brings you great joy?" Gabe persisted.

I thought of something but hesitated, embarrassed. "Promise you won't laugh."

He pantomimed crossing his heart. "I shall resist laughing."

"Okay…" I clasped my hands. "I've got a thing for … um … chocolate."

He burst out laughing.

"You laughed!" I accused, scowling.

"I did resist … briefly. You continue to surprise me."

"I'm not a choco-pig." I lifted my chin, striving for dignity. "I just enjoy the smell, texture, and taste of chocolate. But it's not like I go crazy and eat tons of chocolate. I know how to use restraint."

"No restraint tonight—not when we need to tap into your power. It's much easier to find chocolate than a piano." Then he walked over to a display shelf behind the checkout counter and offered me a Milky Way candy bar—king size.

Immediately my mouth watered and the choco-pig inside me snatched the candy bar from his hand. I ripped the wrapper and then slowly tore the rest of it off, revealing the chocolate bar. The smell … the smooth, rich, creamy milk chocolate layer … the gooey spurt of caramel … then the decadent sweet taste spilling into my mouth.

"Wait!" Before I could take a second bite, Gabe pulled back my arm—his touch shocking me like an electric jolt. "Don't eat it all yet … stop and think about everything you're feeling."

"Your hand. On my arm," I accused.

"I apologize." When he pulled back, my skin was warm where he'd touched it. "But we'll need to be close during these lessons, so while I can promise not to drain your energy, I can't promise not to touch you. You do want to learn?"

I nodded.

"Then close your eyes." His voice washed over me, compelling, hypnotic, and impossible to resist. "As chocolate melts over your tongue, allow yourself to feel the happiness and let it fill you up like air inside a balloon. Happiness creates energy that lifts the soul."

It seemed odd to hear him talk about happiness, considering he'd spent a century causing tears and heartbreak.

"Stay focused," he said sharply, as if he could see inside my mind. "Keep your eyes shut and wrap all your senses around your emotions for chocolate. Feel power surging through you."

I focused inward, but didn't notice any sudden influx of power. Still, what I was feeling was nice. My negativity was melting away, leaving only calmness, peace, and trust. There was a little dizziness, too, which probably had more to do with his energy than mine.

"You're doing well, Amber," Gabe's voice guided me. "Gather your most intense feelings and imagine them spreading through you. Yes! I can see it in your aura—it's brightening as if electrified. Keep visualizing. Your power heats like melted chocolate and fuses with soul energy."

I did feel an electricity, but it wasn't shocking; it was warm and so delicious that I could taste sweetness. Energy sparked as if lightning, not blood, surged through me. And it felt good, like I could reach out and hold the entire world in my powerful hands.

"Now think of your Host Body."

"Alyce," I whispered.

"Visualize her, not how she looks but who she is. Can you see her?"

I tried but all I could manage was the memory of looking into a mirror at Alyce's face. "No."

"Dig deeper into yourself. A part of her is attached to this plane, so she's never really far away. Spread out until you feel her...find her."

And just like that, I saw Alyce, or at least how I imagined her, lying on a beach with the surf lapping close by like a lullaby. She wore a gold bikini and glowed with a tan that never burned. Her eyes were closed and she looked so peaceful that I felt reluctant to invade her paradise.

"Go to her," Gabe urged.

"I can't...I don't belong there. I'm afraid I'll hurt her."

"You'll hurt her more by doing nothing. As Plato said, *Courage is knowing what not to fear.* Alyce is your friend, so there's no reason to fear talking to her. Take her hand and think of the questions you want to ask. She won't be able to resist, and you'll see what you seek in her thoughts."

"But she's sleeping...it wouldn't be right."

"It's your right to have questions answered," Gabe said forcefully. "Go. Now."

So I went, surprised at a rough warmth of grainy sand under my feet and sunrays warming my skin. Still, prickles of fear made me shiver because I felt like an intruder. But I'd come too far to leave now. I had to help Alyce...no matter what happened to me.

"Alyce," I whispered, taking another sandy step. My fingers, an unearthly shade of gray, hovered over her shoulder.

She gave a low moan, shifting on the beach blanket, one hand clutching tight to a beach towel as if it were a child's blankie. She seemed so vulnerable that my heart twisted in guilt for what I was about to do.

"Touch her," Gabe told me.

"I can't."

"You must!" he ordered. "Put your hand on her now."

Standing over Alyce, I whispered her name and waited for a sign from her that I was doing the right thing. But her eyes stayed closed and I could hear Gabe's voice urging me to touch her ... so I reached down and placed my fingers on her skin.

Electricity exploded under my fingertips and my world reeled into a spinning vortex of sand, beach, and waves. And I fell, fell, fell into Alyce's thoughts.

Whirling deep into her memories, I lost almost everything of myself ... except a lingering, sweet scent of chocolate.

13

I was more than Alyce, more than myself, more than human.

Everything was different, as if I'd left a well-marked highway for uncharted roads with unknown destinations. But there was also a sense of homecoming, too.

When I'd stepped into Alyce's body yesterday, adjusting to ordinary things like brushing my hair and putting on clothes made me feel like a toddler taking first steps. But this experience wasn't bound by flesh or gravity. I wasn't sure whether I was beside, above, or inside Alyce as I was swept inside her memories—part voyeur, part companion.

Her long black hair danced in a thick braid, like a wild snake trying to catch us as we ran through the kitchen and hid under the table. It was strange how this table seemed so large, as if it had doubled in size since that afternoon.

"It's not the table that grew," I realized as a new awareness of self settled over me. Alyce and I were together in her little girl body, giggling with impish delight. She was much younger, maybe four. This memory must have happened before we met.

"I see you!" a man's voice rang out, laughing.

Then I heard a chair being moved and felt myself lifted into strong arms.

"Daddy! You cheated!" Alyce cried, pretending to be mad, but her giggles gave her away.

"You always hide under the table," he said.

"Next time I'll hide in my closet and you won't find me."

"It's a deal," the stocky man with sideburns and a nice smile told us. Our skinny arms reached around to hug this nice father.

He lifted us to his shoulders and piggy-backed us into the living room.

"Would you like me to read you a story, Ally-kitten?"

"Yes, yes!" we exclaimed, settling onto his lap and feeling comfortable and so happy.

"Which book do you want?"

"About the big sister," we told him.

"That one again? Aren't you tired of it yet?" He laughed as he reached for a green book.

"Again! Again!" we exclaimed, and I felt eager along with Alyce to hear this story that was her favorite.

It was a really nice story, too, about a little girl who was teaching her baby sister colors by blowing up a rainbow of balloons, then flying off for a magical balloon a ride in the sky. When the father finished, Alyce and I shouted out "Again!" So he closed the book, flipped back to the first page, and started over.

It was strange how while I became Alyce at this young age, a part of me knew I was still Amber, too, like a ghost of myself was hovering outside the memory. I wondered if this memory would show me how to me help the future Alyce.

I'd never met Alyce's father, but I knew that's who was reading to us. I liked how easily he laughed and his relaxed, playful manner. He seemed like the kind of loving dad who would always be there, so what had gone wrong? He sent Alyce gift cards packed with money and had set up a college trust fund for her, but he never visited. "He has a new family," Alyce had once told me in a steel tone that slammed bars across any further questions.

The book was put aside, and we curled up on the couch with "Daddy" to watch an Animal Planet show about giraffes. We asked questions about spots and long necks until we could hardly keep our eyes open.

Time passed until sounds jarred us from a deep sleep.

Mommy was home, Alyce realized excitedly. She was ready to jump and race across the room for a big welcome-home hug… until the shouting. Together, we lay perfectly still, pretending to be asleep.

Peeking out, though, we saw Mommy and Daddy. But they looked all wrong. Mommy was crying and waving her hands as she begged Daddy not to be mad at her. But

Daddy was mad, so angry that he shouted bad words and waved his fist like he wanted to hit Mommy.

"Where were you?" he shouted. "It's been over two weeks!"

"Don't know ... don't remember!" Mommy sobbed, her hands clutching her round belly.

"You can't forget something like that and you're not ... oh my God! What happened?"

"I'm not feeling well ... "

He grabbed her arms. "Why didn't you call me when you went to the hospital?"

"No hospital ... all lost and gone."

I thought she meant her memory was gone, but something darker lurked under her words and chilled me with a suspicion that the child body I visited couldn't comprehend. But Alyce knew something was wrong ... terribly wrong. Her fear shocked through us, and tears prickled down our cheeks.

"Don't talk nonsense. Tell me what happened!" Daddy insisted, shaking his wife's arms so she looked like a floppy doll. "Where have you been?"

Mommy shook her head back and forth, sobbing.

"Answer me! Where is she?"

But Mommy only cried and covered her face with her hands.

Pretend to be asleep, we told ourselves, wanting the bad dream to go away and everything to be happy again. But the yelling hurt our ears and we started to cry ...

Daddy noticed and came over to scoop us up in strong arms.

"It's all right," he crooned. Then he looked at Mommy and shouted, "What kind of mother are you? How can you just abandon your daughter!"

This only made Mommy cry more and Alyce trembled with fear, understanding enough to know why her mother looked different and what was missing. But she didn't understand why Mommy was alone.

"Where's my baby sister?" Alyce cried, tasting salty tears on our lips.

"Gone, gone!" Mommy sobbed hysterically.

"Gone!" Daddy yelled. "That's not possible—when you ran off you were ready to give birth. I reported you missing but they couldn't find you. Where were you? Where is *she?* Tell me right now or I'm calling the police!"

Mommy shook her head frantically. "Don't know… She's lost!"

"Lost?" Daddy twisted her arm.

"She wanted to sleep with angels and I found the stairway to heaven. So dark, so alone… so still in my arms. I dug a soft bed and tucked her good-night. But everything hurt and all the blood… so confusing… people and places I didn't know… and I couldn't find her. I looked and looked but she was gone. Don't tell anyone… can't ever tell!" Mommy begged in a scary voice, like she wasn't Mommy anymore.

Daddy pushed her away then covered his face with his hands. "What in God's name have you done?"

"I don't know… don't know," she cried over and over.

"But you have to!" Daddy exploded. "Where is she?"

"Lost… don't remember."

"How could you lose your own baby? Unless you…"

Daddy's voice broke and he was crying, too. "Tell me the truth … is Samantha dead?"

Then the memory ended.

My connection ended, rocketing me in another direction as if I had been snapped from a rubber band. I floated in a surreal state of energy, leaving Alyce behind as I sailed on a wave of lightness and freedom. But I was not alone—Gabe moved beside me.

Although we weren't defined by human bodies, I could see him clearly as he wanted me to see him: the authentic Gabe Deverau. His skin was rough from the wind and bronzed from the sun, and his night-black ponytail trailed down his muscled back. I had a mental flash of him standing proudly on the deck of a ship, the anchor on his blue cap seeming to bob as the ship tilted and surged forward into the vast ocean. This was how he saw himself: the passionate link of his soul to the ocean, separate from all the borrowed bodies. Only his eyes—sea-deep and mysterious—remained the same.

But it was Alyce's face that haunted me. Stealing into her thoughts felt like a betrayal of our friendship. Had she known I was there? Would she hate me for it later? I'd found out shocking things that I did need to know … but at what cost? Would I ever be able to tell her the truth, or was I now the one destined to lie about secrets?

Worry was a fish hook yanking me backwards, and I returned to Alyce's current body with a shock as soul smacked flesh. My breath caught. I felt stunned, unable to move, and only faintly aware of the electronic noise from aquariums bubbling around me.

Blinking, I stared into Gabe's face—the borrowed face that had once frightened me but now comforted me with a reassuring smile. There was no curiosity in his gaze, only approval.

"You did it," he said, with a nod of satisfaction.

But I couldn't talk, only sag against a counter stacked with bags of fish food. I had no idea how disturbing sinking into Alyce's memories would be, and worse yet was discovering that she carried this memory inside her yet had never told me. There had been hints, though, like when she got angry at the card I gave her on her eighth birthday. It had said, "You're like a sister to me." She'd ripped it up, saying that being best friends was better than sisters. She'd also said her reason for going to cemeteries was to take photographs for her Morbidity Collection. But was that really why? Or was she searching for her baby sister Samantha?

Sam.

The signature Alyce gave to her painting wasn't a random pseudonym. But why hadn't Alyce confided in me? She could have trusted me to keep her secret. While losing a baby wasn't unusual, hiding the death was illegal ... and suspicious. Why did Alyce's mother do such crazy things?

Maybe because she *was* crazy.

And I'd left her home alone.

"I need to go back," I told Gabe, jumping up, the half-eaten candy bar falling from my lap to the chair.

"Not yet!" He shook his head, the golden brown hair beneath his sailor's cap falling loosely out of its ponytail.

"Alyce's mother may need me."

"But we've only just started here—there's so much more to show you."

"I've seen enough…too much." I started for the door; my head pounding like it would burst and spill out all my emotions.

"Wait!" He moved to block me from the door, tilting his head curiously. "I don't know what happened with your friend, but obviously it was disturbing. Your energy is in distress mode—which can be dangerous to you and your friend."

"Leaving Alyce's mother alone for too long is a bigger danger. I can't believe I never guessed what Alyce was going through. I have to be the worst best friend in the world."

"You can be the best at everything if you let me teach you more powers. That was only the beginning of what you can do."

"The beginning and end," I said, overwhelmed with emotions. "I'm going to tell my grandmother to switch me back so someone experienced can help Alyce. And I'll ask her to meet you, too, Gabe. I haven't forgotten my promise."

I reached for the door but as my hand touched the knob, the floor seemed to rise and sway. My mind spun like I'd been racing on a roller coaster for days and my knees buckled.

Gabe caught me before I hit the ground, my head so dizzy that I hardly noticed the electricity from his touch.

I opened my mouth to warn him about touching me but there was no sound, only a feeble sigh.

"I was afraid this would happen," Gabe said as he led me over to a chair and gently sat me down.

"What?" I rasped out, sagging against the hard wood.

"You overstimulated your psyche."

"Huh?" I rubbed my head.

"Doing too much too quickly. The energy you tapped into is still pulsing through you, and if you don't detoxify immediately you'll risk soul burnout."

I sucked in a shaky breath and stared at him with incredulously. "Detoxify my soul? That sounds painful. Why didn't you warn me there were risks?"

"There are always risks," he said, frowning down at me. "But I can help you through this if you trust me. I may need to touch your hand so I can share some of my energy with you. Otherwise, there may be serious damage from what you've just experienced. I had no idea your connection would be so intense."

His voice, with its gentle lilt and deep caring tone, touched me with a similar tingle as the feel of his hand on mine. And I calmed down instantly, my mind and body seeming to merge together in the steady beat of Alyce's heart. I thought of her mother, miles away and sleeping safely. I'd overreacted, worrying about her when I needed to take care of this body first.

"You landed too quickly," he continued, "bringing back the same anxiety that caused your friend's crisis, and your body is reacting as if pumped full of toxins. That's why you should always separate your own emotions from those of your Host Body."

"How do I fix it?" I sucked in a deep breath, struggling for energy.

"Rise out of the physical and cleanse away the trauma."

"Leave Alyce's body again?" I asked uneasily.

"Not completely. Otherwise the trauma will attack your temporary body—like a virus infecting a computer."

"You're scaring me," I whispered, closing my eyes and focusing on his voice. For a bad guy, he wasn't so bad.

"Don't worry, I can fix everything. Take this." His strong callused fingers intertwined with my own, tingling with familiar warmth that felt friendly, not frightening. I heard the rustling paper and smelled the sweet cocoa aroma of chocolate. He pressed a square of candy against my mouth, his fingers sizzling heat as they brushed my lips.

A cool breeze of energy swept through me, and I wondered if it had more to do with Gabe than with the chocolate. He guided me like he had before, asking me to focus inwardly and gather strength. It happened quicker—the lift and pull of my soul rising, and the awareness of separating. I saw Alyce's body slumped in a chair below me. She looked so pale and lifeless, and I had to fight the urge to sink back inside her skin.

Before I could panic, I sensed Gabe's presence beside me. And then a euphoric blanket of warmth wrapped around me like a comforting hug. I again saw him in his true form: his blue cap newer-looking and his black ponytail hanging over his muscled shoulder. I even smelled the salty spray of sea. And his gray-green eyes found me, too.

Although I knew our bodies weren't flesh and blood in this surreal plane, more like holographs, when I reached out, I met his steady grasp. Shared warmth heated me like lava spilling from a mountain, and I felt strangely close to this dead guy who was supposed to be my enemy. He'd gone a long distance to find me, risked his own safety, and was sharing himself in a way that went beyond casual friendship. It was hard to remember that I'd ever feared him.

Wild excitement surged through me. I found myself leaning toward him, longing for more ... for a closeness that wasn't physically possible in a human body. But we weren't human anymore. We were two souls sharing an amazing experience, which was both freeing and terrifying.

"What's happening to me?" I asked in thoughts.

"You're detoxifying. I'm using my power to free you of negative energy." I heard his answer although his mouth didn't move, and I wondered if I was really seeing him or merely a projection he wanted me to see. It was all so confusing ... but not unpleasant. It was as if we were both whiffs of wind floating peacefully on a summer breeze.

"Am I myself or Alyce?"

"You're uniquely Amber and completely beautiful." If he'd said this in a normal voice while in a physical body, I might have been embarrassed and worried that Gabe was hitting on me, but we were beyond all that, in our purest form.

A change sprinkled around me like gentle rain. I looked down to see my own square fingers with a small scar on my thumb from the first (and only) fishing trip with my father. Long braids no longer fell over my shoulder and I reached up to touch my too-curly hair. And I was feeling wonderful—joyful, with energy that seemed endless, as if I were connected to a blissful infinity of life.

"This is incredible." I sent out with waves of gratitude to Gabe.

"It gets better," he replied in that same wordless way. A glow spun around his handsome face like silvery rings circling a planet. "You've shown me more friendship than anyone in my entire life and death. You've given me so much that I want to give you a gift in return that you'll remember forever."

"What?" I asked soundlessly.

"Fusing. It's a way to share my secrets and powers. I've never trusted anyone enough to make this offer—only you. When you learn what I can show you, you'll be able to create your own miracles."

Miracles? Like helping Alyce and healing her mother? With Gabe's knowledge and the power that came with it, I could do amazing things as a Temp Lifer. I could help everyone without making any mistakes.

"Say yes," Gabe whispered, with such passion and promise that I wanted to lean into him and discover his amazing secrets. He was so handsome, so intriguing and yet tortured, too. He could help me and I would help him.

He held out his ethereal arms, a dazzling light, shining in shades of flame, flowing from his hands. "Fuse with me, Amber."

14

"Yes!" The word fought to escape from my thoughts, the dangerous word thumping with my heartbeats like a caged bird eager to fly.

How I wanted to fly with Gabe! I couldn't imagine anything better than the euphoria already soaring through me, and I was curious to know and experience more. Desire thrilled through me. What else would I learn from Gabe? He'd already shown me so much, and to hell with the risks. The promise of power whet my appetite—like tasting only a small bite of the sweetest chocolate in the universe and longing for more.

Yet something held me back. I hesitated, racked with

uncertainty. But why? Nothing had changed on the outside…it was deep inside…a whisper from my own heart.

And just like that, I thought of Eli.

I flashed back to our first conversation, at Jessica Bradley's party, when I was feeling alone and suddenly there he was. Although we'd met briefly in school, that moment at the chocolate buffet would always be our First Meeting. In the week after that he'd shown loyalty and friendship. I loved the way his mouth tilted crookedly when he smiled, his romantic text saying his music was for me, and how he'd traveled hundreds of miles just to give me a small book. He didn't teach me secrets of the universe, but he had his own kind of power.

"No," I told Gabe, pulling away.

Gabe's eyes darkened like storm clouds. "What do you mean, *no*?"

"I-I just can't. There's Eli…my boyfriend…"

"This has nothing to do with him."

"Maybe…but it would feel wrong, and I don't want to hurt him. Besides, Alyce's mother may need me so I shouldn't stay any longer."

"But I could teach you so much more!"

"I know, and I really appreciate it. I'm just ready to leave."

Then I backed away from him, the heat fading and a chill settling over me. Was I making the right choice? Refusing knowledge that could help Alyce, her mother, and maybe others, too?

Here goes another wrong turn in my misdirectional life, I thought wryly.

Gabe had pulled away too, his energy hard to read. But I understood enough now to concentrate and tap into my energy. If focusing inward had worked to lift me out of a body, then it should work to bring me back. So I visualized happy things like my family and friends. Mostly I thought of Eli, and that seemed to work.

There was no shock of landing this time, only a mild thump.

Blinking, I looked around the semi-dark fish shop. Gabe was beside me but not moving, his expression dazed, then slowly changing. Color rushed back into his face and an electric sizzle cracked the air around him.

He seemed weakened, which made me feel guilty. Had he used up too much energy to help me?

"Are you all right?" I asked softly.

"I'm fine." He straightened his shoulders and turned away from me to pick up the discarded candy wrapper from the floor. Crumpling it into a ball, he tossed it into the trash.

He said no more as he locked up Wet Pets and led me back to his car. It was late and the road was nearly deserted, swallowing us in darkness. I tried to talk to him a few times, but he ignored me. His expression was a mask, hiding the anger I sensed. I wished he would turn on the radio or say something—or at least look at me.

"Are you angry?" I asked as he turned onto Alyce's street and parked in the shadows under a tree.

Gabe glanced out the window, then turned to me, frowning. "It's not anger."

"Then what?"

"Disappointment. We stopped too soon." He let out a weary breath. "You didn't learn how to detoxify and will need my help if you want travel by soul transit again. Unfortunately, there isn't much time for another lesson. I'll be gone soon."

"I'll be okay," I told him, touched by his concern for me. He seemed weary, too, which made me feel guilty. "Besides, you don't have to leave for a few more days."

"You'll meet with me again?" he asked eagerly.

"That's not what I meant—"

"But will you?"

I thought of all the powers he promised and how useful I could be as a Temp Lifer. My self-help books often advised being bold and unafraid in reaching for what you wanted. And what I wanted most was to help my best friend.

So I nodded. "All right."

"Excellent! We'll plan for tomorrow."

"Tomorrow?" I bit my lip. "That's so soon ... I don't know ... I'll call you."

"I'll be waiting." His eyes softened, lingering on me.

I knew this wasn't the face he'd been born into, yet his eyes remained his own, shining with the power of an undercurrent that pulled me closer. I felt a little dizzy and I found myself reluctant to step out of the car, thinking back to the incredible feeling we'd shared while out of body. It had been so freeing, honest, and ethereal. Not like going out with a human guy, but something beautifully spiritual.

As I left the car, I glanced back into his compelling sea eyes and wondered what he'd teach me at our next lesson.

I wanted to learn how to heal injured souls like Alyce and travel in soul again. I was so grateful to Gabe for teaching and sharing this with me.

And I wanted to experience it again.

Fusing together?

Maybe.

Alyce's mother slept through the night but I hardly slept at all. There was just too much to think about, and now that I knew about Alyce's lost little sister, many things started to make sense. Like how my GEM kept telling me to look for "the lost."

So the first thing I did, after making sure Alyce's mother was safe, was to pull out my GEM and fire off questions.

"Is Alyce's baby sister dead?"

Yes.

Although I suspected this answer, sorrow tightened in my chest.

"How did she die?"

Heart stopped.

"So it was a natural death?" I guessed.

Tragedy and joy are two sides of the same coin.

"What's that supposed to mean? Oh, don't bother. Just tell me where she's buried."

Underground.

"Well, duh. But where exactly?"

A cemetery.

I resisted heaving the GEM against a wall and asked which cemetery. But the GEM wouldn't give me an answer. The only thing this stupid book was giving me was a headache. I closed the book and tossed it into Monkey Bag.

Then I sorted through the facts I did know. Alyce's mother had disappeared shortly before Baby Sam was due. She'd had some kind of mental breakdown, and when she returned, no more baby. Somehow the child had (secretly?) been buried at a cemetery. Piecing together the rest of the story, I guessed that Mrs. Perfetti was disorientated, both physically and mentally ill, and becoming lost. When she found her way home, she couldn't remember what had happened that night. "Don't tell anyone!" she'd begged. And that's what happened. The secret of Sam was buried in lies. This was probably what led to Alyce's parents' divorce. While her father went off to start a new life, Alyce was left alone with her mother.

Her crazy mother, I thought, sad that I never guessed how bad things were at Alyce's home. When Mrs. Perfetti was rude to me, I'd avoided being around her.

After an hour of tossing and turning in bed, I got up and settled in at Alyce's computer, hitting the power button. I ran a search on mental illness, narrowing down the symptoms until I came up with the diagnosis of paranoia and depression. The signs had been there. If only Alyce had told me. I couldn't have cured her mother but I could have been there for Alyce.

160

Well, I was here for her now. And I'd continue the search that Alyce had started.

I'd find Sam's grave.

Energized by this idea, I dug out the papers Dustin had printed out for me with directions to the cemeteries on Alyce's list. I thought back to my visit to the Liberty Cemetery and was sure there hadn't been a grave marked "Samantha" or "Sam." So I could cross that location off the list. There was only one place left: Pioneer Cemetery in Calaveras County. That was a bit of a drive, off a country road about an hour away. I'd need to pick up Junkmobile, borrow Mrs. Perfetti's car, or get a ride from someone. Dustin would give me a ride if he was free. So I sent him a quick text and waited a few minutes, since it wasn't unusual for him to stay up half the night. But there wasn't a reply, so I guessed he was asleep.

Then I had an even better idea—Grammy!

I always hung out with Alyce on weekends anyway. Grammy could drop me off at Junkmobile, then we'd both search for Sam's grave. And when the timing felt right, I'd explain about Gabe's tragic past and convince Grammy to meet with him.

Pleased with my plan, I finally fell asleep and didn't wake up until the delicious aroma of cinnamon and pancakes set my stomach growling loudly like an alarm clock.

Not pancakes but waffles.

Thick, flakey, cinnamon-strawberry waffles.

I couldn't have been more surprised when I walked into the kitchen and found Mrs. Perfetti standing by the counter and squashing strawberries in a bowl. Makeup softened her face, and she looked elegant with her hair twisted on her head in a chignon. This was not the same ranting crazy women I'd escorted home last night.

"Good morning! Are you hungry?" Mrs. Perfetti asked cheerfully.

She didn't wait for my answer, ushering me to a chair at the table and flipping two waffles on my plate, then scooping up a huge spoon of strawberries and dumping them on the waffles. She didn't mention flipping out last night. This was a different Mrs. Perfetti, smiling as she prepared breakfast like a 1950s mom from an old TV show.

Oh. My. God! Alyce's home life was insane—literally.

How had Alyce managed to hide her problems so long without anyone—neighbors, teachers, and especially her best friend—noticing? Hiding such a big secret must have been torture. No wonder she suffered an emotional meltdown.

I was suffering, too, with Mrs. Perfetti. The way she fussed over me was creepier than her screaming "he's the devil!" I wished I had a *How to Deal with a Psycho Mom* manual. Self-help books always clarified things for me and offered solutions. But was there a solution for mental illness? When I tried to ask Mrs. Perfetti what happened last night at her office, she gave me a blank stare as if I was speaking in a foreign language. Then she switched to a "Stepford Wife" smile and offered to squeeze me some fresh orange juice.

Um … no thank you.

On the plus side, Mrs. Perfetti was so eager to please me that when I asked to borrow the car she said, "Of course, honey!" with great fervor—as if I were doing her the favor. She even offered her credit card in case I needed gas.

Then I ushered her into the living room, easing her into her favorite chair and putting on the Judge Nancy Dee episodes she'd DVRd during the week. While Mrs. Perfetti disappeared into the Judge Nancy Dee zone, I stood in front of the sink, bubbles lathering and water spilling, as my mind rushed with plans:

1. Retrieve Junkmobile.
2. Talk Grammy into meeting Gabe.
3. Look for missing grave at Pioneer cemetery.

This time when I went to a cemetery I'd know what to search for, although I had no idea if there would be an engraved headstone, a plain stone marker, or nothing at all. It was all so mysterious. How did Alyce's mother arrange a burial for a baby that died without anyone knowing? What had happened that tragic night? And what would happen to Mrs. Perfetti when her secret was revealed? I hoped it would bring closure, not more tragedy.

My plan would have worked great—except for one detail.

Grammy had plans, too.

As I was putting my list in Monkey Bag, I heard a honk from outside and peered out the window to see Grammy-As-Me at the wheel of my mother's Toyota. I looked again, just to make sure I wasn't seeing things. But that was Mom's Toyota and Grammy was at the wheel.

Then I ran outside.

My grandmother wasn't alone.

The passenger window rolled down and my heart nearly broke when my little sister Olive grinned at me and exclaimed, "Ally!" From the back seat came more excited squeals from my other two sisters.

"What's going on?" I asked my grandmother, feeling kind of dizzy looking at my physical body from the outside. Would I ever get used to this whole body-switching business? Probably not.

"We're off to an afternoon at the zoo."

"Right now?"

"Zoo, zoo, zoo!" shouted the triplet choir.

"Hop in, honey," Grammy said, grinning. "We want you to come with us."

"To the zoo? But I can't…"

"Why not? It's going to be a beautiful day—I checked the weather report to make sure. I've already folded laundry and alphabetized everything in the triplets' room. Your mother acts like raising triplets is harder than running a large country. She's too soft with them, not setting up strict rules. I'll show her that it's easy to raise triplets if you're organized. A simple trip to the zoo should be a piece of cake."

I wasn't so sure. I'd babysat a lot and just getting three toddlers to the playground without losing shoes or jackets or my mind was a challenge. But my grandmother was a competent otherworldly business-woman and capable of anything.

"What are you standing there for?" Grammy tapped her polished fingernails (apparently she didn't have a nervous biting-nails habit like me) on the steering wheel.

I shook my head. "I can't go."

"Sure, you can. Climb in the back—it'll be a tight squeeze but there's room between Melonee and Cherry. So let's go."

"But I need to pick up Junkmobile from where I left it downtown and then I have to go to Pioneer cemetery. It's an obligation." I gave her a knowing look as I leaned partly through the window. My long braid swung into the car and Olive grabbed it with the enthusiasm of a fisherman hooking a giant fish. Giggling, she petted my hair like a cat.

Grammy crinkled her brow. "What are you talking about?"

"I have to tell you alone, not in front of ... " I gestured to my sisters, and cried out when my braid jerked painfully.

"Olive," Grammy said calmly, "let go of Am ... Alyce's braid."

My little sister glanced over at Grammy, shook her head, then tickled her cheek with the end of the braid. It didn't hurt, so I just shrugged. Olive was a big animal lover and liked to pet anything that looked like fur. This could be embarrassing when someone with a beard came to visit.

"Grammy, can't you postpone the zoo or get someone else to take them?" I asked. "I need you to come with me."

"Your obsession with cemeteries is beginning to worry me."

"It's not *my* obsession. It's Alyce's search for her ... well, that's one of the things I want to tell you." I took a deep breath. "I have to find someone who's lost. And there's another thing I need to discuss with you."

"What?" She sounded impatient.

"Um … it's about a friend. It'll take some time to explain."

"Then it'll have to wait till later. Do what you have to do while I take my little darlings to the zoo. Afterwards, we'll get together and you can tell me everything."

I nodded, though privately I knew I wouldn't dare tell her *everything*——just enough to convince her to meet with Gabe.

"We're off to see lions and tigers and giraffes," Grammy said with a cheerful wave as she started my mother's Toyota.

Olive gave my braid one last tug, then reluctantly let go. "Bye, Ally!" she told me.

"Bye, Ally," Cherry echoed from the back seat.

"Bye, Sissy," Melonee added.

"Melonee!" Startled, I jerked back, banging my head on the door frame. "What did you call me?"

"Sissy bye-bye." She waved at me from her car seat.

I was dumbfounded, and I could tell Grammy was surprised, too. The triplets never did call me "Amber," finding it easier to say "Sissy."

"Melonee," I said gently. "Can't you see that I'm Alyce?"

"Sissy looks funny." Melonee giggled in her shy way, blushing and looking down at her feet, which always made it easy for me to tell her apart from her sisters. Melonee was the quiet, gentle triplet who seldom cried and loved books more than toys.

I glanced over at Grammy. "She knows!"

"Hmmm." Grammy glanced into the rearview mirror. "Interesting."

"Is that all you can say? She knows who I really am!"

"Children can be so perceptive."

"Aren't you worried? What if she tells someone?"

Grammy shrugged. "She's not even two years old. I think our secret is safe."

"You're right...still, it's freaky. How can she recognize me when I don't look or sound the same?"

"You can tell the girls apart even though they look and sound the same. I think it's much of the same with Melonee recognizing you. Still, we should be cautious. I'll drop you off at your car, but after that avoid being around the girls until after you switch back. So don't come to the house."

"But I still need to talk with you."

"Later," she promised.

Then she waited while I ran into the house to get my stuff. The drone of the TV covered my hurried steps as I whipped into my room and grabbed Monkey Bag, making sure I had a camera (I bypassed the large one with attachments and choose an easy-to-operate digital camera), a notebook, phone, wallet, and the directions Dustin had printed for me. Pioneer Cemetery was the last name on the list, so there was a good chance I'd find Sam's grave there.

I shut the bedroom door behind me and hooked the backpack over my shoulder. As I neared the living room, I saw Mrs. Perfetti dozing off while a gray-haired lady judge criticized a skinny, twenty-something guy for not cleaning up after his Great Dane in a park. I tiptoed past Mrs. Perfetti, who was sprawled across the couch, her mouth slightly open and her head resting against a pillow. She didn't look scary...only sad.

Her sadness lingered with me as I stepped out of the house.

With the triplets gibbering noisily, it was impossible to talk about anything important on the drive to Junkmobile. I enjoyed being with them, though, and wished I really was "Sissy." It was hard being away from them. But soon I'd switch back, I told myself. I'd solve Alyce's crisis and we'd both resume our real lives.

Junkmobile was where I'd left it. I unlocked the door and was slipping into the driver's seat when I heard a musical ring. Fumbling in the backpack, I pulled out the cell phone and read Dustin's name.

"Where are you?" he boomed before I could even say hi.

"Getting into Junkmobile."

"Coming to visit me?"

"You wish," I teased. "I'd rather hang out with the dead."

"We all have our fetishes." He chuckled, then added, "Seriously, I got your text and was making plans to get you a ride, but sounds like you've got that covered. You still have the directions I gave you for Pioneer Cemetery?"

"Yeah. Don't worry, I won't get lost."

"No worries here. This will work out great—it's both spontaneous and romantic. When you get to the cemetery, look for a black Civic. I wasn't sure about him at first, but he's even more antisocial than Alyce. He hates going to movies or clubs, and was cool about meeting at a cemetery."

"Oh. My. God. You don't mean..."

"He noticed Alyce around school, and liked what he saw."

"Who?" I asked, a sick knot tightening in my chest.

"Your second date, of course," Dustin said proudly. "Kyle."

15

Kyle.

The guy who might have mob connections, a criminal record, and a habit of using girlfriends as punching bags.

WHAT WAS DUSTIN THINKING?

Outraged, ready to tell Dustin exactly what he could do with this insane idea, I heard a dial tone. He'd hung up on me!

Dustin was *soooo* dead.

I tossed the phone across the seat. Dustin knew when to make his exit, that was for sure, but he didn't know anything about matchmaking. If going out with Zachary—a nice, preppy, respectable guy—had been a disaster, a date with a badass like Kyle was sure to be apocalyptic. Well, forget it. I was so not going.

But then I thought, why change my plans because of some guy? Leaning against the car's leather seat, I sorted through my conflicting thoughts. If I delayed going to the cemetery, I might switch back into my own body and lose this opportunity. I'd seen Kyle around school and despite his reputation, he didn't look dangerous. It should be safe enough to meet him in a public place in the middle of the day. Besides, what if Dustin was right and Kyle was a good match for Alyce?

Shifting the car into drive, I headed for the cemetery.

The roads became more rural, two lanes without much traffic, curving with the rolling rise and fall of spring-green hills. When I spotted the historical marker for Pioneer Cemetery I pulled off the road, parking in front of a staircase set into a steep hillside. I spotted the Civic right away.

The car was dark; no sign of Kyle. I glanced uneasily at the wrought iron cemetery gate, where only a few ghostly shapes of tombstones were visible from the street. Although the sun peaked out between smoky clouds and warmed my skin through the car window, I shivered.

There were no paved walkways at this cemetery, only a rough collage of dirt, rocks, and wild grasses. I climbed the steep steps, inhaling a sweet fragrance of spring foliage that seemed an ironic perfume for a place of death. I unlatched the gate and it swung open, creaking like old bones. I wrapped my arms around myself, wishing I'd grabbed a jacket. The gate clanged shut behind me and I stepped forward... then gasped.

A black-cloaked figure rose from a tall stone monument like the dead awakening.

My shock shifted to recognition. Not a walking corpse—only Kyle.

He wore a black coat that was so long the hem swept up dirt. He was shorter than I remembered, and draped in silver chains and spiky jewelry. He'd overdone his makeup, so that his face almost glowed white and I could barely see his dark eyes hidden under kohl eye shadow. His chin pointed sharply in a slim, V-shaped beard, and his black hair was slicked back. Was he going for a Goth or a vampire look?

"Kyle?" I stood still, reluctant to get close to him.

"Alyce," he said, nodding.

"So … um … it's cool of you to come to such a strange place to meet someone you don't even know."

"I've seen you around school," he said, with a lift of his dark brows that hinted at a deep meaning. "And your friend told me more about you—enough to pique my interest."

"You can't believe everything Dustin says," I put in quickly.

"I decide for myself. I've never done anything like this before."

"You mean coming to an old cemetery?"

"No—I go to cemeteries a lot. What I meant was I've never met anyone … a girl … like this."

"Oh … well, I never do things the usual way."

"That's cool." Kyle tilted his head as if studying me, and I noticed wicked tattoos spiraling down the side of his neck and into his coat. "So you come here often?"

I shook my head firmly. "Never before."

"Really?" he asked with a smile that showed two sharp, pointed top teeth. Had he filed them down? "I heard you've got a thing for graveyards."

"You heard wrong."

"Why were you at Red Top Cemetery last week?"

I started to deny the accusation until I realized he was probably right—Alyce had visited Red Top recently. But this just reminded me how little I knew about my best friend. She had this whole other life … without me. I pursed my lips and told him it was none of his business.

"Fair enough, but you can be up front with me. I've suspected what you're into for a long time—that's why, even though coming here was short notice, I've prepared this." He lifted a bulky paper bag from a slab of crumbling stone.

"A picnic lunch."

"Nope."

"Then what?"

"You'll find out soon enough." He gave his head a small shake. "Let's just walk around and check out our companions."

"Companions?" I looked around but we were the only ones standing in the gently sloped cemetery.

"The silent ones." Kyle gestured to the graves that were half-hidden under shadowy oak trees.

I stared down at the crumbly gravestones and monuments, most faded, cracked, and completely unreadable. Many were over a hundred years old. I scanned names and dates, searching for a small, more recent grave. But as I walked, dried weeds crackling, I was swamped with a sense of foreboding. I wondered about all the souls beneath my feet that had once breathed and danced and loved; now they were only scrawled words in stones—which was the way things usually happened.

Except for Dark Lifers.

And I thought of Gabe, imagining his name etched in stone in a distant graveyard while he defied the circle of life and death, living in stolen bodies for over a century. Although the sun couldn't shine through the web of branches overhead, my cheeks warmed at the memory of rising out of our temporary bodies together and sharing energy, power, a connection ... But thinking about Gabe felt disloyal to Eli. I loved Eli and no other guy could change that—especially a dead one with a passion for breaking rules and hearts.

So I shook Gabe out of my thoughts and focused on the graves.

The one I was looking for would be small and over a decade old. Odd that Alyce's mother might choose such a remote location to bury her baby. She'd been out of her mind, though, and not acting logically. I wasn't even sure if she'd marked the grave, and if she hadn't, then Baby Sam would be lost forever.

I must have sighed because I glanced up and saw Kyle at my side, studying my face. "Something wrong?"

"Not really ... it's just that all these graves are too old."

"Looking for a fresh grave?" he asked with a sly smile that flashed his vampire teeth. "I can help you find anything or anyone."

I gave him a startled look. Did he know about Alyce's lost sister? But he couldn't. Or could he somehow have figured it out?

Twisting the end of my braid, I acted nonchalant. "What could I possibly be looking for at a graveyard?"

"Depends on how deep you dig."

He was joking ... I hoped.

Still, I knew with a sudden certainty that no way, not in any universe, would Alyce go for this freaky dude. I didn't know what he was involved in and had no interest in finding out—only in getting out of here quickly.

Lifting my arm, I glanced down at my watch. "Wow, look at the time. I just remembered I have to ... um ... have to take my mother to an appointment. Yeah, a doctor's appointment, and you know how doctors hate to wait. So I better go."

I started to turn, but he shifted and blocked me. His dark eyes narrowed and even under his pale makeup I could see a dark flush of anger. "You're not doing this again."

"What?"

"Like you blew me off that time at lunch, when you were sitting alone on top of the garbage bin by the cafeteria and I tried to talk to you. At least you were honest and said it was because you preferred your own company to mine."

I spread my arms out, helplessly. "Really I should go ... I'm sorry."

"You weren't sorry then and you aren't now. That's part of what drew me to you, made me come here. But I won't let you rush off without some answers." There was a stubborn set to his thin, red-painted lips. "What is with the trips to cemeteries? What are you really looking for?"

"Interesting graves."

"It's more than that—for both of us." He bent down to trace his fingers across a square tombstone, his gold necklace with its dark vial swinging close to the ground.

I glanced down at a grave that lovingly remembered a mother, wife, and sister who died over seventy years ago. "I like to take photos of interesting tombstones."

"Yet you don't have a camera."

Oops. Alyce always carried her camera.

"I left it in the car but I can get it—"

"Stop already. I know what this is about and so do you."

"It's not about anything."

He shoved his hands in the pockets of his oversized black coat as he gave me a sly grin. "It was easy to figure out, what with your sneaking off to cemeteries and what I've heard around school. Who else but mysterious Alyce would want to meet here? Most girls at school only care about their clothes and popularity and dating jocks. But not you. So drop the innocent act and tell me the truth."

"I haven't lied to you," I lied.

"I know what you want from me."

"Absolutely nothing."

"Don't pull away, Alyce."

"I'm not," I said, ready to bolt for the gate and break speed records driving home if he tried to pull anything.

"I'm interested in dark magic, too." His eyes seemed to spark as if ignited. "I swear not to spill any of your secrets. Are you in a coven? I'm looking to join one, if yours has an opening. Inviting me to join can be mutually beneficial. I can dig up whatever you need for your rituals."

"Coven? Rituals?" I put my arms out like I was trying to stop an oncoming vehicle from running me over. "Are you serious?"

"I'm always serious—like you. It's cool you don't waste time with social crap."

"I'm not completely anti-social," I said defensively. "I'm vice president of the Halsey Hospitality Club."

"Only because your friend dragged you into it."

"I didn't—I mean—Amber didn't drag me. I volunteered."

"But you're not the school club type. You like nighttime and graves and the secrets of the dead—just like me." He pointed to a cluster of flat headstones tucked behind a small fence, the writing on the stones too faded to read more than a few family names like Shipp and Beans. "They checked out like a hundred years ago, so you didn't come here to see them."

"Maybe I'm into genealogy."

"And maybe I'm the tooth fairy." He chuckled, then bent over to reach into the bag I'd noticed earlier. "Although I could be." There was ominous rattle as he held out a handful of dark yellow beads.

No, not beads. Human teeth.

"Guess where I got these," he said proudly.

"I'd rather not."

"I've been digging up interesting things for a long time and if my parents ever broke the lock on my closet door, they'd get the shock of their lives." He pulled out curvy yellow strips from his bag. "Do any of your rituals call for fingernails and toenails?"

"Eww! Disgusting! You save your nail clippings?"

"Of course not—using my own for spells and rituals would be cheating. I get them from corpses. I brought these for you." He held them out proudly, as if he was a normal guy on a date offering flowers. "It's a myth that they grow after death. Living fingernails grow about a tenth of a millimeter a day and the middle and fourth finger grows fastest. Want to see what else I brought to show you?"

"No!" I jumped back from his outstretched hand.

Chuckling like I'd told a funny joke, Kyle reached into the bag again and pulled out something oblong and pale white. "Ever seen a wolf's jaw bone?"

"Those are teeth?" I asked, horrified.

"Wouldn't want them sinking into your skin, would you?" he joked.

Not funny.

"Is it real?" I asked skeptically.

"Of course. I don't deal in fakes. I can prove it." He pulled off the chain around his neck and uncorked the small vial. "Check this out—bat blood. It's rumored to have mysterious powers."

He put the vial to his lips and took a sip.

"Your turn." Red liquid glistened on his mouth as held the vial out to me. "Go ahead. Drink."

16

Sick. Sick. Sick!
This four-letter word described Kyle's demented habits, and also the way my stomach churned at the sight of bat blood dripping from his lips.

Before he could pull any more freaky things out of his bag of horrors, I spun around. Branches crackled under my feet as I bolted for the gate.

"Alyce!" I heard Kyle calling. "Wait! I didn't...!"

The gate swung shut behind me with a loud, shrill clang as I raced down the steps. I fumbled for the car keys, collapsing into the driver's seat when the door opened.

The car sparked with sweet life, and I was out of there,

burning rubber and breaking all kinds of speeding laws to get far away.

By the time the landscape changed from rolling fields to mini-malls, my breath slowed to normal. Inside, though, my thoughts were chaotic. Kyle was seriously delusional if he expected animal bones and blood to impress a girl. And all that talk about covens and rituals? *Creepy!*

Did he really believe drinking bat blood would give him powers?

I knew more about *real* powers than Kyle ever would.

This was all Dustin's fault. He'd set me up with a wacko. At a red light, I switched on the speaker phone and called him. Before Dustin could ask, I told him what I'd gone through with creepy Kyle. When I got to the part about Kyle drinking bat blood and offering it to me, for the first time in the history of our friendship Dustin was speechless. No arguments. No sarcasm. When he finally spoke, he apologized and said he'd made a mistake.

Mr. Know-Everything Dustin admitting he was wrong? That was a first, and almost worth what I'd just gone through. Almost.

My anger had faded by the time we hung up, although disappointment lingered. Despite seeing into Alyce's memories and visiting graveyards, I was no closer to finding the missing grave.

When I returned to the Perfetti house, the TV droned and Alyce's mother was still asleep, her mouth half open as she curled against a couch pillow. She looked peaceful, and younger than usual without heavy lines crossing her forehead. Too bad I couldn't just ask her what really happened.

While I heated a burrito in the microwave, I sorted through everything I'd found out and tried to calculate the time line. Alyce had been around four in our shared memory, so the baby must have died thirteen years ago—shortly before her parents had divorced. Her father never visited, which seemed harsh. But now I had an idea why he left. I couldn't blame him for bailing on Psycho Mom, but I did blame him for leaving his daughter. Could there be more to it? I wondered, as I carried the heated burrito to the table. I glanced up at a wall shelf with family photos of Alyce, her mother, and older people I guessed were grandparents. No photos of Mr. Perfetti. Had he suspected, as I was beginning to, that Alyce's mother was guilty of more than forgetting where the baby was buried?

I didn't want to believe she was responsible for her own baby's death…yet the suspicion was like a sliver stuck under my skin. If only there was a way to unlock more secrets in Alyce memories. Could Dark Lifer powers help me?

My thoughts jumped to Gabe, my pulse quickening and my skin feeling hotter than the spicy burrito burning my tongue. Why did thinking about him make me feel like this? I felt sorry for him, but couldn't call him a friend (a friendly enemy?). What we'd experienced together (near fusing?) had been so amazing. Not romantic but spiritual. He'd given me the gift of my truest self, soaring with me on a euphoric wave like surfing across the universe. Our soul journey had changed me in a profound way, and despite all logic, I wanted to go there again. And even further.

So why not call him now?

Wiping sauce from my lip with a napkin, I carried my

plate to the kitchen, my thoughts rushing with the water spilling into the sink. There were a lot of reasons to see Gabe again. I could connect with Alyce again to find out more about her visit to graveyards. I'd also ask why she'd taken the file from Green Briar, and if there were any clues to the missing grave's location, and about her mother's mental problems. But even more important, I could wash away worries by flying free of the physical plane with Gabe.

My phone was in the bedroom, a short walk down the hall that seemed miles long. I was anxious-scared-eager to see Gabe again.

Drying my hands on a towel, I wondered: could I really trust Gabe?

He had a century-long habit of lying to girls who freely offered their hearts to him. So why did he want to help me? Saying I was "different than other girls" was so cliché. Still, it sounded sincere coming from him. And I was different from his past girlfriends because I already had a boyfriend, so he couldn't break a heart that didn't belong to him. Also there was the whole Temp Lifer thing. I understood what it was like to lose your own identity while living in borrowed bodies.

Another reason for his interest in me could be my grandmother's otherworldly status. As head honcho in the TL program, she had the power to save him. I couldn't blame him for this; I even admired his resourcefulness. It seemed fair, anyway, for me to connect him with Grammy since he'd connected me with Alyce. It was the kind of strategy my book *Getting the Goal* advised for achieving success.

Only I doubted Grammy would help Gabe—not even for me. I'd been procrastinating all day about asking her. Grammy had a quick temper when she'd been alive and I was sure she still had it in her afterlife. She was not going to be happy to find out I'd been hanging out with a Dark Lifer—especially a wanted criminal.

Still, I had to call and confess everything.

Not going to be fun.

Gulp.

So after checking on Alyce's mother, who was still snoring softly on the couch, I went down the hall to the bedroom where I'd left the cell phone. I took one step inside the room—and gasped. A shadowy shape crouched on Alyce's bed! His curled tail wagged, his black eyes shone with affection, and a spinning Duty Director glowed like a holographic collar around his furry black neck.

"Cola!" I cried out, grinning.

My favorite dead dog was back.

When I was little, Cola followed me everywhere: outside to play, over to friends' houses, inline skating, and even into the bathroom if I wasn't quick enough to close the door. During meals he'd lurk under my chair, covertly gobbling down scraps of food. My mixed-everything beloved mutt was my first best friend. So I was beyond thrilled when we'd reunited a few weeks ago on the other side.

Even more astonishing then meeting my long-dead dog had been finding out that I could hear his thoughts in my head. We'd talked a lot when I was little but it was all one-sided: my jabbering away while he stared at me with adoring eyes and wagged his tail in what I imagined was a secret doggy language that only I could understand.

Now Cola was more than a loyal pet. He had an important job as a Comforter, where he could change into the shape of any animal to ease a dying person's final moments. Once I'd watched him change into a Siamese cat, which had seemed like a miracle. The old man he'd "comforted" recognized him as a beloved pet, which made his passing from this world to the next peaceful. To me, it had all seemed amazing and miraculous. I couldn't be prouder of Cola.

So my first reaction to finding him on Alyce's bed was to wrap my arms around his fuzzy body in a big hug. He lapped my face and in my mind I heard him say how good it was to see me again.

"It's great to see you, too," I told him.

Then I noticed that his Duty Director (a computerized collar energized by a higher power) whirled with images in a speedy blur. It was like trying to look at a rainbow while riding in a Ferris wheel. And I wondered why he was here.

He stopped wagging his tail, and reached out a paw as if holding my hand. In my mind I heard him say, *Amber, I've come with an urgent message.*

"Is something wrong?" My heart skipped.

There is a problem, he admitted.

"Is Grammy all right?"

She's fine—but this problem affects her, too.

My gaze lifted to the dark ceiling with all the painted stars on infinite black, and I felt as if the darkness stretched down to swallow me whole. "It must be something huge for you to come all the way here from the other side."

He lapped at me with his wet doggy tongue and I patted him on the spot between his ears where he loved to be scratched. *I came to warn you. I wanted you to hear this from a friend, not a random Temp Lifer. You're vulnerable because of your recent contact with a Dark Lifer.*

Recent! Did that mean he knew about last night?

Don't be afraid, he assured me, clearly misreading my anxiety. *The DD Team is working on the situation so it should be resolved soon. You've done a remarkable job as a new Temp Lifer—following the GEM rules and reporting the Dark Lifer when you encountered him on his boat.*

Oh...the boat! Relief swept through me. Cola was talking about what happened when I'd been in a different body, on spring break in Venice Beach. He had no idea about my more recent Dark Lifer encounter—and I wasn't about to tell him.

"What's going on?" I asked my dog.

Nothing yet, but we're on high alert, Cola mind-spoke to me. *Although Dark Lifers can be dangerous, it's rare for them to harm a human. Acts of violence drain their energy, making it easier for the DD Team to apprehend them.*

"So a Dark Lifer can't really hurt me?"

They can if they touch you with focused energy. But there's only been one occurrence ever, and that was partly the Temp Lifer's fault for breaking rules.

I glanced over at Monkey Bag lying on the floor, imagining my GEM book inside and those nine rules—I'd broken at least three. "What happened to that Temp Lifer?"

Not important. Cola's dark eyes clouded over. *Still, don't go anywhere alone and immediately report anyone you suspect could be a Dark Lifer.*

I didn't *suspect* Gabe—I *knew* what he was. So, technically, I wasn't lying to Cola when I nodded. Still, I couldn't quite meet his gaze and glanced down at my hands.

"Anyway, I doubt I'll meet another Dark Lifer," I said evasively.

I'm more concerned with the one you already met. Gabriel Deverau isn't an ordinary Dark Lifer. He's the most wanted DDT criminal. He's been a fugitive for generations, but he can't hide forever.

"It's been almost a week since I saw him on the boat."

Yet his essence still remains on you. Cola tensed like a hunting dog on alert, his fur bristling as he sniffed me. *This is very odd. The smell should have faded by now, but you still stink with foul darkness.*

I sniffed but didn't smell anything except Cola's doggy breath. Not pleasant, either. And he had the nerve to say I smelled bad?

"I can't help how I smell," I said defensively. "Besides, Gabe didn't seem dangerous. I actually felt sorry for him. Maybe Dark Lifers aren't all that bad."

How can you say that after what you've been through? Or have you forgotten your first encounter with a Dark Lifer?

"No, I'll never forget." I frowned. "But I got away and nothing terrible happened."

Only because the Dark Disposal Team captured him before he could steal your energy. If he'd touched you long enough, your essence would have spilled out like blood from a deep cut.

You could have lost your mind and soul, which is worse than death.

"He *was* horrible," I admitted. "But it's not fair to say that *all* Dark Lifers are evil. Maybe some are just misunderstood."

Don't waste sympathy on the soulless ones who abuse humans. His sharp teeth flashed in a growl that sent shivers through me. *Gabe Deverau is soulless and dangerous. But the DDT is closing in on him and soon he'll no longer be a threat in any world.*

"So all Dark Lifers deserve punishment? Haven't any of them ever been reformed?"

Never. He shook his head, ears floppy like an ordinary dog, but the cold chill in his gaze froze all hope. If my own dog felt this way about Dark Lifers, how could I hope to convince my grandmother to forgive Gabe?

Cola was sniffing again, his Duty Director sparked with red lights like flares in the night flashing danger. *Your dark odor worries me. Why is it so strong?*

"I need to use a different brand of soap?"

Do not make jokes. This is far more serious than you realize.

Oh, I realize it's serious, I thought anxiously. But I couldn't let on or the DD Team would capture Gabe. He'd made mistakes, but I knew he wasn't really bad. There was always hope for change. And I was determined to give that hope to Gabe.

Amber, listen to me. Cola's mind-voice was both stern and gentle. *My fur is bristling in a warning of trouble. I don't want anything bad to happen to you. Our roles have changed*

*since my Earth life, but I'm still your faithful and loyal friend.
I'd give my soul to protect you.*

"Thanks," I said softly, so touched by his words that I forgave him for saying I smelled bad. "But I'm fine, Cola. And I'm getting close to a breakthrough with my assignment. I'm sure I can solve Alyce's problem." I didn't add that a Dark Lifer was crucial to my plan.

Solving problems isn't a Temp Lifer's job.

"Yeah, I know. Grammy has told me the same thing. But Alyce is my best friend and helping her will only take a few more days."

Days you won't have, my dog said gravely.

"What do you mean?" I clutched at the soft quilted bed comforter.

Cola straightened, haunches tense and fur bristling, looking fierce like a warrior dog readying for battle. *Amber, the Dark Lifer you encountered on the boat—Gabriel Deverau—has been psychically located in this area.*

"Psychically?"

Those with intuitive skills living on Earth contact the other side when they sense the presence of a Dark Lifer. We've had several psychic reports of Dark Lifer activity in this area. If the DDT hasn't located him within forty-eight hours, all Temp Lifers in the area will be pulled from their mission.

"But that's not fair! I need more time."

Then hope that Gabe Deverau is captured. Soon.

17

I'd been lying on my back and staring up at the ceiling forever, or maybe ten minutes, since Cola left in a rather spectacular lightning flash.

Trying not to stress over Cola's message, I told myself that being pulled from my mission wouldn't be all that bad. It would be great to be me again, to play with my sisters and do mundane chores around the house. I actually missed hearing Mom sing off-key to country music while she jogged on her treadmill, and Dad's corny dinner-table lectures. I wouldn't even mind the stink of cleaning Snowy's litter box.

But my TL job wasn't finished. I was *not* a quitter.

And what about Gabe?

I needed to warn him and fulfill my promise of a meeting with Grammy. No more putting this off—I had to see my grandmother.

So I dug into Monkey Bag for the phone. I flipped it open, glancing at a wall clock and figuring Grammy should be back from the zoo by now. Only before I could hit her number, the phone burst with song. When I saw the caller ID, I couldn't answer fast enough.

"Eli!" I cried, flopping back on Alyce's bed and leaning against a pillow. It was amazing how just seeing his name on the phone perked my spirits up.

"Yeah, it's me," he rasped, wearily.

"You don't sound like yourself. Are you sick?"

"I'm losing my voice."

"You sound good to me. It's been, like, days! I've really missed you."

"Me too."

"So when can I see you?"

"That's why I'm calling. There's … um … something … " He paused in this really awkward, uncomfortable way, like he was about to knock me over with bad news.

"What is it?" I gripped the bed's comforter.

"Uh … I don't know how to tell you."

"Just say it."

"Okay … only it's hard. I hate letting you down, but I thought you should hear it from me first."

Oh. My. God. He was breaking up with me.

I went rigid, holding the phone like it was a grenade that could blow up my entire world. I should have expected this; Eli was on TV and had all those girls screaming his name and waving posters. Then there was his gorgeous competitor Mila who'd clung to him like she was applying for the role of Siamese twin—or new girlfriend.

How could I compete with glamorous and talented Mila? They'd travel on concert tours together, sharing cozy meals and adjoining hotel rooms. It would be torture reading tabloids that buzzed about their showmance. Photos of them together, smiling, dancing, kissing, would be all over the news. I'd never turn on the TV again and join a nunnery.

"Amber, are you there?" Eli asked through the phone.

I didn't want to be, not if it meant losing him.

"Yeah ... I'm here."

"You're so quiet. I thought the connection died."

Something worse was dying, I thought miserably. Then I closed my eyes, the way people did when facing a firing squad. Ready, aim ...

"Go ahead ... tell me."

"It's over," Eli said with a sigh.

My heart plunged off a cliff, shattering.

"Oh," was all I could say.

"I'm really sorry, Amber—I know how much it meant to you—but I'm out of the *Voice Choice* contest. I've been eliminated."

"The contest ... this is about *the contest*?"

"What else?" he asked, clueless. "The judges came to a unanimous decision—I'm out. Everyone will know once it airs. I've been dreading telling you, but there it is."

"Wow! That's great!"

"Didn't you hear what I said?"

"Yeah." I tried to work up some sorrow or at least sympathy. And I really did feel bad for him...at least, the parts of me that weren't jumping up with joy. *Wicked selfish girl,* I chastised myself. Good thing we were talking on the phone and not in person because I couldn't stop smiling.

"Your boyfriend is a loser," Eli said.

"Pul-leeese, you're not a loser. Must you always be so overly dramatic?" I teased, paying him back for once accusing me of the same thing.

"But you wanted me to be a star—then you could be my manager and we'd both go Hollywood together."

"All I want is for you to come home. I'll make it to Hollywood on my own someday. For now, I'm where I want to be—or at least I will be soon. My assignment may end in two days, then I'll return to my own body."

"Now that's good news. I miss your body...not that way...well, maybe a little that way...but not like...you know what I mean," he said, stumbling over his words in that adorable klutzy way I loved.

"I know," I said, smiling.

"Are you sure you don't hate me for losing?"

"Over a dumb contest? Never happen."

"I didn't even make the final three—number four and out the door. And Mila didn't waste her time telling reporters that there wasn't any showmance between us. Everyone says she'll take top prize."

"Wrong," I told him in a flirty tone. "She doesn't have you."

Sappy? Yes, but true, and it led to Eli saying some sappy stuff, too, that would just look dumb written down, but it meant a lot to me. And I sensed Eli's confidence returning, too, which made me feel good. I asked him to tell me more about the competition and he had me laughing out loud with the crazy stuff the fans did to get noticed.

"They'd wait outside the hotel every day, screaming our names and throwing gifts like flowers and stuffed animals while they screamed for autographs. One little boy, about five years old, asked me to sign his sneaker."

"Did you?" I asked.

"Sure." Eli laughed. "That was safer than where some girls wanted me to sign. And before you even ask, no, I didn't sign any of those places. I can't believe how insane fame is. I'll be glad to get home and forget all about Rocky, and just be boring Eli again."

"Boring? You? No way."

"I'd make a great accountant. I'm not cut out for this whole fame thing, being fussed over like a celebrity. It's not just strangers, either. Can you believe my brother actually asked me to send him a signed photo for his girlfriend?"

"You can't mean arrogant, stuck-up Chad. Do you have a brother I don't know about?"

"Only Chad. Since I made it on TV, he's suddenly noticed I exist and actually seems proud of Little Bro."

"About time he appreciated you." Then I realized what else Eli had said. "Chad wanted your autograph for his girlfriend? But Leah is so not the fan-girl type."

"Not Leah. Chad has a new girlfriend."

"He broke up with Leah?" I'd spent some time in Leah's perfect body, living her not-so-perfect life, and I remembered how much she loved Chad.

"Actually I think Leah broke up with him, but Chad didn't say. He never does, he just finds a new girl. When I started to sign my real name, Chad said 'no, write Rocky.' I guess that's an improvement over him calling me Dufus or Geekwad—but Rocky isn't who I am. I got my fifteen minutes of fame but it was like living someone else's life."

"I know how that feels. Exactly."

"I give you kudos for doing it not once—but three times. You're amazing."

"Insane is more like it," I said with an ironic chuckle. "At least I didn't switch into someone famous like this other Temp Lifer I met once, who couldn't go anywhere without being mobbed. You can have fame…" I paused, then added wickedly, "Rocky."

"Don't call me that! And I'm not famous. No one ever remembers the singers who get kicked off. I'm just relieved it's all over now and I can go back to my home and school. This is the first spring vacation that I can't wait to end."

"But it was pretty awesome," I admitted. "And to me you'll always be Eli."

After that our conversation turned silly and sweet and all about us again. Talking to him made Dark Lifers and lost graves seem unimportant. We were all that mattered, sharing thoughts and feelings and hopes for when we were together again.

Tomorrow night, he'd return to his real life.

And soon I'd be joining him.

As Amber.

I didn't accomplish much the rest of the day, although I did finally hear from my grandmother. Sounding frantic enough to pull out all her (my!) hair, she complained about my sisters' lack of zoo etiquette.

"I gave them strict rules," she complained. "I told them we were playing a game of 'Follow the Leader' and that I was the Leader. They promised to do everything I said. But when I tried to organize them in alphabetical order, they wouldn't hold each other's hands. When I offered to buy them healthy snacks, they screamed that they wanted cotton candy and sodas. One would use the restroom, then minutes later another one had to go. And they whined about being too tired to walk. I explained the importance of behaving like proper young ladies, only they completely ignored me!"

"They're babies—not young ladies," I reminded her. "You can't expect them to be perfect."

"Oh they were perfect all right—perfect little monsters! Olive climbed into the flamingo enclosure and chased the flamingos to grab their feathers!"

"Pink is her favorite color," I said, trying not to laugh.

"But that wasn't even the worst! When I took the girls to the restroom for the third or tenth time, they unraveled rolls of toilet paper and ran around me until I was covered like a mummy." Grammy's voice broke. "My own grand-babies TPd me."

This time I did laugh. "They've done it to me, too."

"But I was sure I could handle them better than your

mother. Now I'm not sure of anything—except your sisters have been banned from the zoo."

"Mom does okay," I said. "She gets support from her Mothers of Multiples group. She doesn't believe in being too strict or get stressed when the girls mess up because she believes they'll learn more from making mistakes then from doing everything exactly right. Mom says being organized is great in theory but a little disorder strengthens character."

I was repeating what Mom had told me when I was going through a rough time adjusting to not being the only child anymore. For a while, I'd had this love-hate thing with my sisters. So much had changed, too quickly—moving from a lake condo to the suburbs, sharing my parents, and money suddenly being tight. I'd blamed the triplets for ruining my life. But I got over that when I realized that no one can ruin my life without my permission (advice from *The Blame Game Myth*). Now I was all about loving and missing those little TPing monsters.

Grammy had grown silent on the other end of the phone. When she spoke again it was in a subdued voice. "I owe your mother an apology."

"You do?" I asked, surprised.

"I never told you, but I was completely against your mother having any more children. You and I were always so close, and I was more worried about your feelings than my own daughter's. When she asked for a loan for the fertility treatments, I refused. I said awful things about her mothering skills and warned her that if she went ahead with her crazy plan, not to look for any help from me... and she never did." Grammy's voice broke. "When I saw those beautiful baby girls, I wanted to tell Theresa how proud I was of her and that I was sorry. But I kept putting it off—then I died."

"Mom still loves you. She couldn't stop crying at your funeral."

"I know—I was there. I tried to reach her through dreams and signs but she didn't notice. And now that I'm with her, if I told her the truth, I'd break Temp Lifer rules."

"And seriously freak Mom out," I added wryly.

"Theresa was always easily shocked."

"Finding out your daughter is actually your dead mother would be shocking."

"I know." Her sigh carried through the phone, soft and wistful. "Being with my Terry again has been a wonderful gift, and I can't complain."

"Still, it's got to be hard, too, when you can't say what's on your mind." I meant this in more ways than one as I tried to work up the courage to tell Grammy about Gabe. But with her confession about Mom and the whole TPing thing, this wasn't the right time to mention my secret meetings with a Dark Lifer. I'd call her back tonight.

The rest of the day was quiet, mostly because Mrs. Perfetti had as much life as a zombie. She alternated between sleeping and watching TV, taking time out only to share a pizza with me. Her depression worried me, but at least she wasn't ranting about the devil or hiding under furniture.

Exhausted from my previous late night with Gabe, I fell asleep early. I dreamed that a giant woodpecker was tapping on my brain. *Tap, tap, tap.* The sound wouldn't go away and grew louder.

When I jerked up in bed, I was relieved that it had only been a dream and that giant woodpeckers didn't exist.

Then I heard it: *tap, tap, tap.*

I looked at the window and saw a shadowy figure right outside it.

With a start, I jumped back, ready to run and call 911. But when the shadow waved an arm in a "come here" gesture, I recognized the broad shoulders, wavy hair, and cap.

Gabe!

My emotions surged forward like a wild thrill ride that I couldn't wait to take. I hurried over to the window and slid open the glass. Gabe was straddling a thick branch of the tree I'd climbed so many times.

"What are you doing here?" I spoke softly, although there wasn't anyone close enough to overhear and I doubted any neighbors could see Gabe. He blended in with the shadows, as if the darkness was welcoming one of their own.

"I had to see you," he whispered through the grainy screen.

"But you shouldn't have risked coming here. It's not safe!"

"Not safe for whom?"

Good question, I thought uneasily, at the same time impressed with his grammar. I never could get the hang of who and whom.

I told him to climb down and wait for me. Then I grabbed a jacket and slipped quietly out of the bedroom, ignoring the voice inside me warning that this wasn't a good idea. Earlier today I'd spoke of love and the future with Eli. Now here I was sneaking out to meet another guy. I loved Eli—that was something I was absolutely sure of—yet I couldn't resist seeing Gabe again any more than I could resist licking the spoon when I mixed cookie dough. My roller-coaster emotions whirled up and down, spinning out of control and flying off the rails.

I couldn't wait to see Gabe again.

When I peeked into the living room, Mrs. Perfetti was still sleeping, which worried me a little since it didn't seem normal to sleep so much. Still, I was glad, since it would be easier to sneak out without her knowing. The DVD had ended and the TV screen showed a blank blue screen, humming slightly. I stepped softly through the door in the mud room and into the backyard.

It took a minute for my eyes to adjust to the dim light.

And there was Gabe, sitting on the edge of a brick planter, smiling up at me in a way that flip-flopped my stomach. His eyes, shadowed underneath the brim of his cap, were impossible to read. But his lips curved with secrets and promises. And I smelled a heady salty scent of fathomless seas.

There was something forbidden, dangerous, and irresistible about being here, a few feet from a dead guy who could easily slip into bodies and minds. When he tipped his cap, staring deep into my face, I seemed to dive into the fathomless sea-green of his eyes. We stood, neither moving forward, staring at each other for a long moment.

Not sure what I was feeling, only that I had no right to feel anything for Gabe, I shook off this weird mood and went straight to business.

"Gabe, before you ask, no, I haven't set up a meeting with

my grandmother yet. But I will, either tonight or tomorrow morning. Time is running out fast, and you're in danger."

"I am?" He didn't sound alarmed, only curious.

"The DDT knows you're in the area."

"You're breaking rules by telling me this," he said, gazing deeper into my face.

"I expect to be struck with lightning any moment," I joked.

"They won't harm *you*."

"But you could lose everything. It's dangerous for you to even be here with me."

"The risk is worth it to see you. You're wrong about why I came here—not because I want to meet with your grandmother. It's to share my power with you. We have unfinished business."

He didn't say it, but I knew he meant fusing.

And I wanted to—help me, God—I wanted to.

"I can't." I shook my head, backing away from him.

He followed, his brief touch shooting fireworks through me.

"Please, Amber."

When he said my name, with that faint English lilt to his voice, I lost all reasonable thinking ability and melted like chocolate over a bonfire. He'd risked his soul to come here for me. He was so gallant, not like any one I'd ever met before ... or would meet again.

So I nodded and whispered, "One last time."

18

"Is there someplace private we can go?" he asked, sweeping his gaze around the dimly lit backyard with its scattered patio furniture and grass that needed mowing. There was a doghouse, too, although the Perfettis hadn't had a dog in years. Except for a wisp of wind that rustled the leaves and shadows, the yard was as still as death.

I glanced over at the bright lights shining from neighboring windows. "The garage, I guess. No one ever goes in there since it's easier to park the cars in the driveway."

I led him into the detached garage, pushing open a door that squeaked from lack of use. Reaching out, I felt for the light switch and flipped on a fluorescent tube light fixed into the open rafters. Dust swirled as I took a step inside, and I sneezed.

"Bless you," Gabe said, coming up behind me.

"A blessing from a Dark Lifer?" I teased.

"Being a fugitive doesn't mean a lack of manners."

I shoved aside a pile of old newspapers and some boxes to make a path through the cluttered junk, then turned to Gabe curiously. "I can't figure you out."

"If this were a movie, I'd be the villain."

"I'm not so sure. You're polite, poetic, and you've offered to help me even though I reported you to the DD Team."

"Ah, so the truth comes out at last. You're the villain." He folded his arms across his chest, giving me a wry smile. "Life isn't black and white; people aren't all light or dark. It's the gray inside all of us that makes things interesting."

"You're definitely interesting."

"I hope to be much more than that…" There was a deliberate pause, something dangerous smoldering in his sea eyes. Then he added, "To you."

Lost for words, I broke away from his gaze, tripping over a garden hose coiled like a snake. Stumbling but catching myself before I fell, I moved deeper into the garage, assuring myself that I was doing the right thing. This was all about helping Alyce and had nothing to do with any attraction for Gabe.

With its dust, dried grass, and oil smells, the garage was not a great setting for a spiritual ceremony. I glanced with some embarrassment at scattered tools, a broken lawn-mower, and old bikes stacked up against the wall. A pink bike with a banana seat reminded me of Alyce, when we were little and used to ride bikes all over the neighborhood. Everything had seemed so simple then, and I had no idea that beneath Alyce's smiles lurked a tragic secret. It was still hard to believe she'd been searching for the grave of a sister she'd never told me about.

Of course, there had been clues—moments when she seemed sad and cried for no reason. She'd say her mother was mad at her for stupid stuff like not finishing homework or cleaning her room. But now I suspected her tears had been for more serious reasons. Why hadn't I guessed she was suffering? How could I be so blind? I thought I knew everything about her... but I'd been wrong.

Now I had a chance to make it up to her, to find the missing grave and give closure to this family secret. Gabe had the key to accessing powers and learning more than was humanly possible.

He gestured to a ripped brown-leather couch that had been pushed up against a wall. "Let's sit there."

I nodded as if under a spell, unable to refuse him anything.

"So how do we start?" I asked, heart thumping. "Can you, um, connect with your powers when you're not near sea water?"

"When in doubt, improvise." He pulled out a small paper bag from his pocket. "I brought something that should help both of us focus."

When he said "both of us," like we were one entity instead of two, I leaned closer to him as if pulled by a magnetic force. Everything about him radiated charismatic power: the confident lift of his chin, the narrowed intensity in his expression, and the lilting cadence of his words. Although his body may have been borrowed, Gabe's true personality dominated its flesh and features. I longed to be even closer to him—which frightened yet thrilled me. What was going on with me? My body, thoughts, and desires were strange and traitorous.

"What's inside?" I looked down at the ordinary paper bag, hoping to hide how my cheeks flamed as I anticipated what we were about to do together.

"You've heard of gateway drugs? What I have isn't a drug, but its ordinary sweetness can open our gateway to alternate planes of consciousness."

"I don't get it." I furrowed my brow.

"But you will," he said with a mysterious smile. "You'll get more than you can even imagine."

"I have a pretty good imagination."

"You'll need it."

"Are you trying to scare me?"

"Prepare you," he corrected. "As Einstein said, *Logic will get you from A to B. Imagination will take you everywhere.* And I will take you to everywhere else. Are you ready?"

I took a deep breath, then nodded.

"Concentrate and keep focusing, no matter how strange things may seem. What you experienced last time was only a taste of power. Now I'll show you the real thing—merging soul energies. Fusing."

That ordinary-yet-eerie word hinted at a closeness more profound than anything I'd ever experienced. I wasn't afraid in a young-girl-with-older-guy way, because I knew this wasn't physical. I didn't understand how our souls could merge. I wanted to learn, though, especially if I could gain abilities that would help with my Temp Life job.

"Close your eyes and hold out your hands," he told me in a commanding way I couldn't refuse even if I'd wanted to ... which I didn't.

I cupped my hands together, closing my eyes. A memory flashed in my mind of another girl holding out her hands for Gabe and his heartless betrayal of her love, but I pushed it aside because that was the old Gabe, not this upgraded version.

There was a whispery rustle of paper, then something small and smooth fell into my palms. Opening my eyes, I stared down at a colorful rainbow of wax-wrapped candies.

"Saltwater taffy," I said, moving my fingers so the wrapped bundles rolled like tossed dice against my skin.

"Combining your hunger for chocolate with mine for the ocean."

"But there's no saltwater in taffy. It's an urban myth."

"Right." He beamed at me like a teacher giving kudos to a top student.

"I read about it somewhere," I said, smiling. "I think the candy was created on the Atlantic Beach Boardwalk like a hundred years ago."

"Longer—in the 1880s. Some people credit it to Joseph Fralinger, who was known as the Saltwater Taffy King."

"Did you know him?"

"Sure, I know all famous dead guys." Gabe chuckled. "Not really. That was even before my time."

"If there's no saltwater in taffy, how will it work for you?"

"I'm skilled enough to connect without any stimuli. Still, there is salt and water in the candy mixture, and I associate this candy with the ocean even if it's not made with sea water. I brought the candy to help you focus, choosing chocolate varieties like rocky road, caramel, and chocolate chip cookie dough."

"Mmmm ... cookie dough." My mouth watered.

"Go ahead," he urged. "Unwrap a candy and put it on your tongue, tasting and enjoying it as it slowly melts."

"Can't I chew?" I asked.

"Hold off until you can't resist, building on the sweet taste until you reach a happy, peaceful state of mind. Allow the candy to seep into all of your senses: see the chocolate in your mind, hear your throat swallowing, feel and smell melting sweetness and savor the taste. Combined together, the five senses create a sixth and more energized sense that lifts you to a higher plane."

I nodded, listening to the crinkle of the waxy paper as it fell from my fingers to the floor, and then bringing the soft smooth taffy to my lips.

As I sank into all my senses, I was still aware of Gabe. He was pulling seven small, spiraled candles from his jacket pocket, arranging them in a circle on an upturned barrel. Almost reverently, he lit each candle, whispering foreign words. Then he pulled two cushions off the couch and tossed them to the concrete floor, near the barrel. He gestured for me to sit down on one while he knelt on the other, his arm so close to mine that our elbows brushed.

I was on fire, probably more from his touch than the heat wafting from the candles. I could heard my own heart, thumping like it was competing in a race. I wondered what I'd find at the finish line.

Gabe swirled his hands in circles over the candles, stirring up the smoke so it seemed to merge and blend into a gray cloud.

"Do you feel the energy, Amber?"

"I feel ... everything."

His eyes shone approval. "It's beginning. Now things will move fast and you must promise to follow my instructions. It's already starting, more intense than last time."

"What's happening?" I said through a dizzy fog.

"Fusing," he whispered and an electric charge shot through me.

"Fusing," I repeated, awed by the wondrous exhilaration of Gabe's nearness. This wasn't lust or love and had nothing to do with my feelings for Eli. Gabe was guiding me on a non-physical soul journey; I was guilt-free.

Unable to resist any longer, I chewed and swallowed, closing my eyes. The taffy melted like sugared wine, intoxicating and hot, as it spilled down my throat. I started to reach for another candy, but Gabe was already unwrapping one and offering it to me. When his fingers touched my lips, I tasted warm, delicious bliss. Beyond thinking or questioning, I soared somewhere that seemed both familiar and terrifying.

"Amber," he intoned my name with the soft intensity. "Take my hand and repeat everything I say."

Some part of me resisted, because the mere touch of

his hands could destroy me, yet this wasn't about destroying—this was about learning powers. So when his fingers found my own, I held on.

I wasn't sure what I was feeling or even who I was anymore. I seemed to be disconnecting from flesh, rising away from the body I knew to be Alyce.

My eyes were still shut but I saw Gabe against a backdrop of dazzling stars, as if he stood poised against the edge of a world with infinite galaxies. And there I was beside him, looking like myself although draped in luminescence. We held hands, suspended together in soul. I didn't understand, and was struck with acute fear that he'd let me go and I'd fall into a black void of nothingness.

"Don't hold back, Amber."

"I'm not…I'm just confused. How will this help Alyce?"

"Don't think of her. There is only now. Only us."

"I don't understand." The stars darkened and my fingers slipped, but he grabbed and held tight.

"You will soon," he said.

And I wanted to, as I was swept along a current of absolute joy, rejoicing in the freedom of being in spirit. Energy was building like powerful clouds, lifting us away from mundane things. Gabe no longer wore his borrowed body so I saw him in true form, with his dark ponytail and sun-kissed skin and those compelling, gray-green eyes. His hat slouched over his brow, drawing attention to the sharp curves of his cheeks and soft, full promise of his lips.

His lips curled up at the corners, as if he was thinking of deep secrets. His soul body moved slowly, lightning strands of energy connecting us in a way that seemed more intimate and personal than human touch.

An ocean scent swirled around me as Gabe pursed his lips in invitation. "So close now," he intoned in a sultry voice. "Come seal our union. All it takes is a kiss."

"I can't!" I jerked away. "I have a boyfriend."

"We are no longer bound by human rules. Here, we make our own rules."

"Still, no kissing ... Eli wouldn't like it."

"Eli is unimportant."

"Not to me, and I can't lie to him."

His sea eyes darkened and for a moment I was afraid he was angry. But then he smiled. "I understand. If not with a kiss, entwine both of your hands with mine."

"Is that safe? Won't it drain me of energy? I mean, since you're a Dark Lifer."

"I promise—it's completely safe."

"But how will this teach me powers to help Alyce?"

"You'll have infinite power, Amber. Trust me."

But his words, rather than offering reassurance, shot me with fear. "Trust me." I'd heard him say that before—once on a cliff to another girl, and then to me on a boat. Instead of trusting, I pulled my hands back.

"Never be afraid of me, Amber," he assured with a nod of his head that seemed to shower me with a cool wave of calmness. And I did feel calmer, sinking into that sweet dizziness again. His spirit form rose and shone so dazzlingly bright that he reminded me of an angel. His hands were the most amazing of all—exploding with luminescent rays as if he held the sun in his palms.

And I wanted to share that sun, to let it fill me, too. It would be so easy to do as he asked, to take his hands and fuse our energies. More intimate than anything physical I could imagine on Earth, as if we were truly one spiritual being.

His eyes were completely of the sea, waves of blue and gray spilling into me. "Clasp my hands," Gabe told me. "I swear it won't hurt and afterwards you'll share my powers and more. No loneliness, sadness, or grief. All past sorrows will be washed away and I'll be your protector, teacher, and soul mate."

"Soul mate?" A tremor rocked me.

"We're destined for each other."

"To help each other, you mean," I corrected.

His tone sharpened. "Amber, do you understand what I'm offering?"

"Not exactly," I murmured, uneasy but unwilling to break away from his radiant gaze. "Tell me."

"When I saw you on the boat—not your Host Body, but the real Amber—I knew you were the soul mate I'd been hoping to find; a girl I could finally trust."

"I turned you in to the DD Team," I reminded him.

"That showed bravery and resourcefulness, as well as compassion because you gave me time to escape."

"That's not how it really—" I started to explain, but he wasn't listening.

"I was intrigued that an Earthbounder would choose to be a Temp Lifer," he went on with intensity. "I knew you were the soul mate I longed for, so I followed you. Even in another's body, your beauty shined through, and I was willing to wait until you were ready. But waiting is over. Soon your earthly ties will be gone. There will be no going back, only forward as my companion."

"Companion! You mean to stay with you … like this?" I gestured to his glowing essence, which was more like a holograph than solid body. "Forget it. I want my real life with my family and friends. If anyone's my soul mate, it's Eli."

Gabe frowned. "He can't offer you what I can. I meant it when I said I wanted to change. I'm weary of lying and loneliness. Fuse with me and we'll see the world, travel endless lives in borrowed bodies, together forever."

Forever? Um … no thanks.

And what would happen to Alyce if I suddenly left her body? Would she automatically zap back or would she be lost in soul limbo?

"No!" I wanted to run, but didn't know where to turn or how to escape. Trapped in a spirit limbo, I wasn't flesh and blood, only energized soul. Gabe had all the power and knowledge. Instead of teaching me, he tricked me—as he had tricked countless other girls—and I'd been stupid enough to believe him.

"You can't stop what we've started," he told me, as if he were a wise adult and I were a foolish child. "Take my hands and I'll guide you into this new journey."

"NO! I can stop it and I will."

"Amber!" His tone snapped with warning. "You don't know what you're doing!"

But I did know, as if by some inner instinct, and I visualized the happy feelings of my first meeting with Eli over the chocolate buffet. This memory buoyed me and I felt something shift away from Gabe. I thought of another happy moment—dressing up as a vampire with Dustin so Alyce could snap a photo. We'd used raspberry jam for blood, and soon were completely covered in the sticky jam.

I jerked away from Gabe so sharply that the shock of separation ripped like tearing through fabric. I pulled all my energy away from this surreal place and threw myself back into Alyce's body. I landed with a thud that sucked out all my air. Then I was breathing, on my own.

Blinking, I started when I saw Gabe—or at least the body he'd borrowed—slumped over on the couch. He didn't move; his tanned skin was as pale as a corpse. Was he still in that limbo plane? What would happen to him if he couldn't come back to his borrowed body? Or, more urgent—what would happen to *me* if he did come back?

Got to go—and fast!

I jumped to my feet, poised to run, but I had barely lifted my foot when something hard and steel-like clamped around my ankle. Looking down, I saw Gabe's hand.

"Leaving so soon?" he said, in a chilly tone of controlled fury.

"Let go! You can't force me to become like you."

"I won't have to. You'll come willingly."

"Never!"

"Oh yes, you will. You have forty-eight hours." He paused, his smile wicked. "Or the next body I possess will belong to your beau Eli. A fall from a high building or in front of a speeding train. I can switch to another body quickly, but your beau won't escape. Earthbounders are so easy to kill."

19

Gabe didn't stop me from leaving the garage.

There was no need for him to go after me physically, not when his threat bound me tighter than duct tape. He knew I'd do anything to save Eli.

Before I left, Gabe told me to not to bother setting up a meeting with my grandmother. He'd never planned to meet her, he admitted proudly—he'd only used that pretense to gain my trust. And heaven help me, it had worked. Not only had I fallen for his lies, but there had been something more in my feelings for Gabe.

"Stupid, stupid," I repeated as the garage door slammed behind me and I returned to the house.

I was angrier with myself than with Gabe. I'd been

warned over and over not to trust a Dark Lifer. Yet it turned out I was no smarter than Sharayah and the other girls who'd fallen for his poetic, old-world charm. He'd told me what I'd wanted to hear and I'd believed him.

Now I had to figure a way out of this mess.

The GEM!

I could use it to alert the DD Team. Gabe couldn't have gotten far yet, which should make it easy for the DDT to capture him. But could I trust the DDT? If they hadn't caught Gabe in over a century, how could I expect them to get him now? And if Gabe found out I reported him, he wouldn't take his anger out on me—he'd go after Eli.

Lying on Alyce's bed, staring at nothing, I tried to think logically. I didn't turn on a light because Gabe might still be lurking outside, waiting for me. Although why should he bother? In less than two days he would take a new body (and if he wasn't caught by then, my mission would be cancelled anyway). If I didn't go with him willingly, Gabe would possess and destroy Eli's body.

That wasn't a choice.

It was a death sentence.

And only I could offer a reprieve.

I slept uneasily that night, waking up only when Mrs. Perfetti came into my room to ask if I was asleep. That had to be one of the dumbest questions ever. She sounded kind of spacey, and I had a feeling I should get up to make sure she was all right. Instead I brushed her off. "Yeah," I murmured. "I'm asleep."

She apologized, then shut the door.

After that I couldn't go back to sleep. Awake, tormented, thinking of everything that had happened and searching for a solution. There had to be some way out. But if I reported Gabe, he'd go after Eli. And if I did what Gabe asked, I'd lose more than my life.

I'd lose my soul.

What would it be like to be a Dark Lifer? Living a month at a time in stolen bodies, always hiding and afraid of being captured by the DD Team. I'd never go to college, become an entertainment agent, get married, have kids, or grow old. I'd live forever but never really live at all. And my own grandmother would add my name to the *Wanted, Dead and Alive* list of other-side enemies.

I smashed my fist against my pillow and sat up in bed. Gabe could *not* win! I wouldn't let him. But I'd need help.

Glancing at my bedside clock, I saw that the illuminated dial read 5:13 A.M.

Sure it was early, but Grammy would understand.

It took three rings before she answered.

"Amber?" Grammy greeted sleepily.

"Yeah, it's me." My voice cracked and I had to swallow fast so I didn't cry.

"Is everything all right?"

"Uh ... sure. It's just that I can't sleep."

"Is this about the Dark Lifer?"

I gasped. "You know about him?"

"I may be away from my desk, so to speak, but I'm still

the overseer of Temp Lifers. I sent Cola to warn you, but I didn't mean to scare you."

"*You* didn't." It was Gabe who scared me.

"Cola warned all the Temp Lifers in the area as a precaution, but it's unlikely you'll encounter a Dark Lifer. The warning was routine and nothing to worry about."

"I'm not worried … well, not much. I just couldn't sleep."

"Bad dream?" she guessed.

"It was more than a dream … "

Here's where I tell her the truth, I thought. She'll be upset and contact the DDT, which will result in my being pulled off my mission. I'll be safe. But would Eli? I'd seen only some of Gabe's powers and suspected he was far more dangerous than anyone realized. Could I trust the DDT and my grandmother with Eli's life?

"I had a horrible nightmare," I told Grammy. "Sorry I woke you so early."

"I'm always here for you. Make some hot tea or cocoa and you'll feel better."

I wish it were that easy, I thought with a sigh. "It's good to hear your—well, my—voice. Can we just talk a while?"

"Sure, hon. Want to tell me about your nightmare?"

I wanted to tell her far more. "I guess so … it was about Dark Lifers."

"The DDT will take care of them. You have nothing to worry about."

"I know. But I wondered if any of them are dangerous."

"Nah," she said dismissively. "Most are just lost souls afraid of change."

"But the one that Cola warned me about—the same Dark Lifer I met on the boat—isn't lost or afraid."

Grammy sighed. "Gabe Deverau is an unusual case."

"He bragged about having unusual powers. Is that true?"

"Never believe a Dark Lifer."

"But he … " I shifted the phone to my other ear, hiding the catch in my voice. "He seemed capable of anything."

"Don't worry, honey." I imagined her sitting in my room, swiveling at my desk chair or perched on the edge of my bed. "Dark Lifers can slip into bodies but that doesn't make them powerful; in fact, switching bodies weakens them. Also, they can't jump into a body without placing both hands on the person's skin—which isn't easy."

"Do they knock their victims out, or drug them?"

"Nothing so dramatic. It's not in a Dark Lifer's best interest to damage a body they want to possess. They simply wait till their target is asleep."

"I may never sleep again," I said wryly.

"Sleep with no worries," Grammy assured me. "It's impossible for a Dark Lifer to possess a body occupied by a Temp Lifer."

"Really?" This was news to me.

"The TL process is thorough. When you're switched, there are powerful protections placed on the Host Soul's body."

"If I'm protected, why are you and Cola so worried and planning to pull me off the job?"

"I didn't say an experienced Dark Lifer *couldn't* hurt

your body—he could do great damage if he gets close enough to grab you with both hands. He could drain your energy so you can't speak, think, or even breathe. This has only happened once—with tragic results."

A tremor quaked through me. Tragic—that meant death. To both Temporary and Host Soul.

Grammy must have noticed my shocked silence. "I didn't mean to scare you," she said quickly. "Only to advise caution. Gabe Deverau has a long history of Earthbounder abuse. I can't even tell you how many young girls have needed Temp Lifer replacements after he damaged their spirits. I want to believe there's good in even the darkest soul, but I've seen no evidence of compassion or decency in Gabe Deverau. The sooner he's captured, the better for everyone. But he always seems to know when the DDT is coming for him and is gone before they get there."

"Then how can you stop him?"

"Leave that to the DDT," she assured me. "Put him out of your mind, because the one thing we do know about Gabe Deverau is that he's smart—too smart to come near you again."

"You'd think so." I frowned, glancing out the dark window. "But how can you protect the people he steals bodies from? Let's say a Dark Lifer jumped in front of a moving train, but then jumped out of the body before impact. What would happen?"

"The Host Soul would die," she admitted. "But nothing like that has ever happened."

"Not yet," I worried.

"It would take an enormous amount of energy for any

Dark Lifer to leap from a falling body without damaging his own energy. Then he'd have only ten minutes to find another body, all the while eluding the DD Team which would have spotted his beacon light the moment he left the body. The Dark Lifer would be captured immediately. But if you're worried, I can arrange for you to switch back right away."

"But then you'll switch back too, and I thought you wanted to fix things with Mom."

"I tried already and it didn't work out. Maybe we should both go back where we belong. What do you say?"

I considered this, tempted to just run home, but I quickly discounted the idea because wherever I ran, Gabe would follow. He would recognize me no matter whose body I wore. And I didn't want him near my family. So I assured Grammy that I wanted to finish my assignment.

It was still early, and my bed looked so inviting that I curled up under the covers, missing the warm furry comfort of my cat Snowy, but suddenly so tired I couldn't keep my eyes open.

When I woke up, I felt an eerie sense of quiet in the house. And when I got dressed, I couldn't find Mrs. Perfetti anywhere—even her car was gone. Alarm changed to understanding when I found a note on the fridge saying she'd gone to church like she did every Sunday. Alyce stopped going a few years ago, although I'd never known the reason why. I'd just been glad because it meant Alyce could spend more time with me.

Only now it wasn't Alyce I was thinking of … and when

I heard a musical tone coming from my phone, I couldn't check the text message fast enough.

Driving.
Home 2nite.
C u soon.
Eli.

I wanted so badly to call him back … to hear his voice and tell him how much I missed him and longed to see him … but I didn't. Because I had to think this through, figure out how much I could tell him. Considering that Eli didn't even know that Gabe had found me and we'd been meeting in secret, the whole wanting-to-kill-my-beau thing would be hard to believe. And Eli might consider it a betrayal, too.

Still, he deserved to be warned—even if he'd hate me and our relationship would be over before we'd shared a real first kiss. So, steeling my heart against breakage, I picked up the phone. Only I'd delayed too long. My call went straight to voicemail.

Anxious and frustrated, I couldn't do anything now except wait for him to call back. So I kept busy doing random stuff like cleaning the room and flipping through Alyce's photo books, feeling sad whenever I saw pictures of us together. There was an entire album of the theme baskets she'd created for the Halsey Hospitality Club, and underneath each basket was the name of the new student who received this "Hello Halsey" gift. She never personally handed out the baskets—that was my job, because she couldn't stand gushy emotional scenes—but I could feel her pride over her artistic work in each photo. And I felt something inside me soften, letting me know it wasn't only about the art. She cared about helping people more than she'd ever admit.

Sighing, I put the albums away and searched the room again, checking drawers, shelves, and even under furniture for any clues, but finding nothing new. There was so much I didn't know and little time left to find answers. At least I'd be able to get into Alyce's locker tomorrow at school.

School.

A familiar yet foreign word, from a language I'd spoken in a past life. Thinking about walking the halls, going to classes, and facing people with my borrowed face freaked me out. Talking, walking, looking like Alyce ... who always wore lots of black, which was so not me. I shared a few classes with Alyce and knew her schedule, so I wouldn't get lost. Still, I'd be my own best friend and my grandmother would be me.

I should have taken Grammy up on her offer to switch back early.

Sorting through Alyce's closet—seeing so many familiar shirts, jackets, boots, and skirts—made me feel like she was here with me. I could quit now and she'd return. Only what would she return to? A depressed mother, a grave that was still lost, and a best friend who might be a Dark Lifer.

I now had less than forty-eight hours to find a way out of this crisis.

Or tomorrow would be my last day.

Alive.

Mrs. Perfetti returned from church acting almost normal. I was getting used to her mood swings, and noticed the way her smile didn't quite reach her eyes. She didn't say much, as if socializing had drained her. She asked me to make her some tea, then wearily sank down on the couch. She expected me to fuss over her, rather than the other way around like most mothers. So while she watched TV, I made linner—Alyce's word for a late lunch/early dinner.

Rather than place a cooking SOS call to Dustin, I made the only thing I could think of: stuffed French toast. Cream cheese and blackberry jam slapped between two slices of battered bread, grilled, then served up with whipped cream on top. High in calories but even higher in delicious-factor, and for a while I was able to forget my problems.

Eli called while I was washing dishes.

"I'm back!" he exclaimed in happy exhaustion.

And it was so good to hear his voice—soft, sweet, buttery warm. I thought of his smiling face, his tender blue eyes, his soft lips...until I remembered Gabe's threat and snapped back to harsh reality.

"Eli, I need to see you right away," I said before I lost my nerve.

"I've needed to see you all week. Should I come there or will you come here?"

I glanced over at Mrs. Perfetti, who was back to lying on the couch and staring zombie-like at the TV. I didn't think Alyce would want me to leave her alone. "Come here," I finally told him, then added, "Hurry."

"Can't wait to see me, huh?" he asked, teasingly.

"More than that—there's something I have to tell you."

"So tell me now."

"I-I want to…and I will when you get here. It's just better in person."

"What about Alyce's mother? Will she let me in the house?"

"She's the least of my worries. Just get here."

"Sure. I'm really beat after driving seven hours and am practically falling asleep on my feet." He yawned. "I got some things to do before I can see you."

"Soon?" I persisted.

"Within an hour," he promised.

I hung up, feeling better for the first time all day.

I finished filling the dishwasher then turned it on, all the while checking the clock, counting the minutes and preparing how to dump my horrible news on Eli. How could I explain about meeting with Gabe despite knowing Dark Lifers were bad news? I couldn't—not without admitting how Gabe had made me feel and how much I'd enjoyed our secret rendezvous. Thinking back now, I ached with shame as if I'd cheated on Eli.

And in a way, I had.

Eli was going to be so pissed.

Maybe hurt, too.

While I waited, I rehearsed what I was going to say, hoping he'd understand.

But an hour passed, then another. Mrs. Perfetti turned off the TV and went to bed. I waited by the window, hand poised on the curtain to check the streets, but no sign of Eli. When I tried his phone, it went straight to voicemail. After checking the phone book, I dialed his house. His brother Chad answered and I almost dropped the phone, flashing back to kissing him when I'd been in a different body. But that was two body switches ago and he didn't even know Alyce.

"Is Eli there?" I asked cautiously.

"He's sleeping," Chad said.

"Sleeping! But he promised to come right over."

"Eli's a big star now—lots of girls have been calling him."

"They have?" I had the absurd impulse to smash the phone.

"Well, sure. Didn't you hear he made it to fourth on the *Voice Choice* contest?"

"I heard," I said dryly.

"Eli hasn't had time to go through his messages or gifts—can you believe girls send him gifts? I've won some impressive golf tournaments but girls never gave me the rock star treatment." He laughed in that charming yet egotistical way I'd once crushed on. "Anyway, Eli was so beat from driving all day, he fell asleep. I can wake him if it's important."

I was feeling less than important, more like abandoned, but I wasn't about to admit this to Chad. "That's okay," I said. "It can wait."

"Should I give him a message?"

"Um...not really. I'll see him at school."

Then I hung up, disappointed. Not much later I went to bed.

At first it was hard to sleep, so many things running through my head, but I eventually slept soundly with no horrible dreams. And when I awoke, the sun streaking golden warmth through the window, disappointment (and admittedly, some jealously) seemed far away. Energized with hope, I felt like I could conquer any problem today. Soon I'd be with Grammy, Dustin, and Eli, and we'd come up with some way to defeat Gabe and find the missing grave for Alyce.

As I slipped into black jeans and a lacy black vest over a dark purple crepe shirt that went nicely with Alyce's velvet ankle boots, I was thinking all about Eli. So it was like my thoughts had materialized into reality when I glanced out the window and saw him coming up the walkway.

I heard the knock and suddenly I was nervous, thinking about kissing him, wondering if it would be okay even though I was in Alyce's body. Would she mind? Would she know if I didn't tell her?

Another knock, and I hurried to the door.

I grasped the knob, twisting.

And there he was.

"Eli!" I cried softly.

"Not quite." Smiling in a strange way, he shook his head. "Guess again."

There was husky lilt in his voice and a confident lift of his chin as he stared hard into my eyes.

And I smelled the salty scent of the sea.

20

"Noooo!" I choked out, reaching for the door to slam it.

But he grabbed my hand and, with a swift yank, pulled me outside with him, the door shutting behind us. And there I was, staring into the face that I'd been longing to see again.

Only this wasn't Eli.

"Gabe!" I covered my mouth. "Ohmygod! What have you done to Eli?"

"Nothing yet." His smile made me ill. "It all depends on you."

"Get out of him right now!" Tears streamed down my

face. Seeing Eli's body possessed by such a despicable soul was more than I could take.

"Why would I want to do that? This is a comfortable body—younger than what I usually choose, but it'll do nicely ... at least for a short while."

"Don't you dare hurt him!"

"I hope it doesn't come to that. He's rather an interesting fellow, with all those puzzles on his bedroom ceiling. He was very accommodating when I came for him. He was sleeping so soundly, he never even felt my hands on his skin."

"You're ... you're a monster!"

"No," he said, his shoulders dropping. "I'm lonely. If there were another way to make you come with me, I would do it. I don't want to hurt you."

"You're not hurting me! You're hurting Eli!" I turned on him furiously. "Get away from him or I'll report you to the DDT."

"You wouldn't do that. I always know when the DDT is coming, and if that happens, I'd have to leave—and that could end tragically for this body."

I knotted my hands into fists, wanting to smash his face—only that dear face didn't belong to Gabe. How ironic that I'd waited so long to be with Eli and now that he stood before me, it wasn't even him. And there was only one way I could save him.

Reality slammed into me, sucking away the air and all the fight in me. I pulled away from him, clinging tight to a porch rail. There was no one I could turn to—it was just me against a powerful Dark Lifer.

"Please, leave Eli alone," I whispered.

"That depends on you."

"But I can't...don't make me!"

"It's your choice. You should act normally until you decide, though, or the consequences could be devastating."

"Normally?" I blinked. "Like going to school?"

"Ah, school." He touched his chin with his finger. "I learned about that while enjoying a fascinating breakfast of frosted pastries—Pop Tarts, the brother called them. The father was most thoughtful, too, offering me the use of a vehicle."

I could hardly bear to look into his face and hear him speak in Eli's voice with that chilling detachment. "At least give me this day at school with my friends and no weirdness," I said finally. "If you do that for me and promise not to harm Eli, then I'll...I'll do what you ask."

"I solemnly promise." He held up two fingers like a Boy Scout.

Dreams, hope, life faded from my voice. "You win."

"I always do."

Rank odor of diesel from yellow buses, the shouts and laughter of kids, and the crush of hundreds of students heading down narrow halls to lockers and classrooms—today was like any other first day back to school after a week of spring vacation, for everyone except me. It was hard not to think about what I'd agreed to do … and how this first day back could also be my last day.

One of my self-help books, *It's Not an Addiction, It's a Goal*, talked about the fine line between obsession and goals, how creative people—like writers and actors—could be obsessive in their ambitions. This book advised to take control of emotions by creating lists of "major" and "minor" goals, then crossing out everything you had no control over and focusing on what you had the ability to achieve on your own. Alyce was the creative type, not me, but I did do my fair share of obsession when it came to my goals. Becoming an entertainment agent had always been my major goal, followed by graduating with honors, getting accepted into a top college, sharing a dorm room with Alyce, and getting an internship at a top talent agency. On the minor goals list were things like falling in love, marriage, and kids.

Only now I knew that falling in love was the most major goal of all. And as I walked through the halls, weaving through a blur of faces who meant little to me, I could only think of the one face I longed to see—with its sweet smile and clear, honest eyes shining at me.

Oh, Eli, what have I done to you? I thought as I held onto Monkey Bag. *This is all my fault, but I swear, on every self-help book I own, that I'll fix this and bring you back … no matter what happens to me.*

When I heard my name called, I almost didn't stop because the first thing on my "To Do" list was getting Alyce's purple notebook. But then it registered that the name being called was "Amber" and not "Alyce." I stopped abruptly and spun around.

"Don't call me that!" I warned Dustin, putting my finger to my lips and looking around anxiously. Still, it was so good to see him, to be with a friend who knew me, that I softened my criticism by reaching out to hold his hand. The human contact was warm and real—something I would miss.

"Oops…I meant, Alyce." He didn't carry a backpack, only a small electronic lifeline resembling an iPhone, which he'd nicknamed "Headquarters .02." It contained all his textbooks, homework notes, and the Internet, any of which could be activated with a simple voice command.

"It's okay. I don't think anyone noticed."

"Still, I should have known better. Won't happen again."

"You're right…it…it may never happen again." A tear slipped down my cheek and I wiped it away, but not fast enough.

"Hey, what's wrong?" He furrowed his brow, studying me. "Is this about those stupid dates? I'm so sorry about that—Zachary and Kyle were jerks and I should have never put you through that."

"It's not about…about them." I couldn't meet his gaze and glanced down at Alyce's velvet black boots, noticing a smudge of grass on the right toe but not bothering to wipe it away.

"Has something else happened?"

Lying would be the easiest hard thing to do.

"Yes," I admitted, nodding. "But it's my problem and no one else can solve it."

"No one?" He snorted. "Since when did you become

Goddess and rule the world? Come off it, Amber. Tell me what's wrong or I'll start singing to you at the top of my lungs so everyone will stare at us like we're crazy."

And he would have. He'd done it once...no, twice...before. He didn't give a crap what anyone thought of him. I was going to miss him so much.

Dustin was opening his mouth, ready to belt out a Broadway tune or something equally humiliating. So I reached out and put my hand over his mouth. Then I led him down the hall to Alyce's locker, which was in a remote corner away from the rush and bustle of other students.

"It's Eli—he's in terrible trouble because of me..." My voice caught and, to my own surprise, I told Dustin the truth. Well, the least humiliating parts. I admitted to meeting with Gabe, believing that he wanted to change but turning him down when he asked me to be his "forever" companion. But I didn't mention "fusing" or the way Gabe made me feel when we lifted out of our bodies.

"So Eli is now this Dark Lifer dude Gabe?" Dustin asked with wide, dark eyes.

"Yeah," I answered, shivering.

"And where is Eli?"

"I-I don't know." Worry sliced like a knife through my heart.

"He's not..." Dustin's breath caught.

"No...not yet. He's just lost, somewhere in soul limbo, waiting to come back to his body. But he might not be able to...not if Gabe hurts him, and he will if I don't go with him willingly."

"But you can't go with him! That's suicide—literally!"

"What choice do I have? He threatened to kill Eli." I bit my trembling lip, shoving away my fears so I could do the right thing. "I won't let that happen."

"You mean … you'd just give up and die?"

I nodded.

"That's the stupidest thing I've ever heard you say and I've known you for a long time. I repeat—you do not rule the world. Use that smart head of yours and get some help from someone with the right contacts."

"Who?"

"Your grandmother." His expression brightened and he pointed beyond me. "And here she comes now."

Grabbing his arm, I leaned close to hiss in his ear, "Don't you tell her anything!"

"But she can help you."

"No, she'll switch me back before I finish my mission and I won't be able to help Alyce. Then Gabe will get revenge by killing Eli!"

"You don't know that for sure."

"Trust me on this," I said, wincing at my own words. "He will."

"There you are!" Grammy said, coming over with relief on her face. Well, my face, although she'd done something with blue eye shadow and pink lipstick that made me cringe. My hair, usually a mop of curls, hung straight, which actually looked cool. But the clothes Grammy chose for me were like something a four-year-old would wear to a birthday party.

I was hurting too much inside to care, though, and had

to struggle just to speak in a normal voice. "Hi...Amber," I said carefully. "What are you doing here?"

"Following my Host Body's schedule—no matter how painful. What's with the two-ton backpack?" She groaned as she shifted the weight of my canvas backpack on her shoulders. "There are like a dozen books in here. You'll be stooped over like a senior citizen before you're thirty. Aren't you worried about having back problems?"

"No—I have worse problems. Like my grandmother going to school in my body. Why didn't you fake being sick and stay home?"

"And miss experiencing high school again? This is like a second chance. I probably shouldn't admit this, but I wasn't a good student like you. I was too busy flirting with cute guys, cutting classes to sneak smokes, and staying out late drag racing. I was the oldest of seven kids so my parents didn't catch what was going on until I was suspended."

"Suspended?" My hand flew to my mouth. "Why?"

"For getting caught in the teacher's lounge—with a cute teaching assistant. Not one of my proudest moments. I'm much wiser now and—" She stopped abruptly, tilting her head to look closely at me. "But why are your eyes so red? Amb...Alyce, have you been crying?"

"I...I...um..." Speechless, I shot Dustin a "Help me!" glance.

"Allergies." Dustin patted my arm sympathetically. "She's a weepy, snotty mess."

I sniffled dramatically. "Alyce is allergic to pollen, trees, and grass."

"And she's too thin," Grammy added with a disapproving

head shake. "Make sure you eat healthy so she'll be in better shape when she returns."

"Is the switch still on for tonight?" I asked uneasily.

"Unless the Dark Lifer is found before midnight. You've done a good job, honey, but you can't expect to solve everything. Being a Temp Lifer isn't about solving problems, it's about standing in so your Host—"

"—Soul can solve their own problems," I finished.

Only I didn't believe it and ached with guilt, knowing I was letting Alyce down. So that Grammy couldn't read my expression, I turned to Alyce's locker and spun the combination I knew by heart: 13-46-03. It was easy for me to remember number combinations, but Alyce (not math-gifted) had to use memory tricks. "Thirteen is my favorite number since most people think it's unlucky," she'd told me. "Mom will be 46 when I'm 20 and I have three freckles on my right thumb."

I looked down at her thumb, my eyes filling and blurring the tiny freckles. But everything else was crystal clear to me. I would do what whatever it took to protect the people I loved.

With new determination, I told Grammy there was one last thing I had to do for Alyce. Then I searched the locker, checking folders, books, and papers until I saw purple.

I'd found Alyce's top secret, private purple notebook.

Pages full of drawings and Alyce's handwriting. I flipped through them, while Grammy and Dustin watched me curiously. There was too much to explain, so I gave Dustin a look that translated to "I need some time alone." He gave me a "gotcha" nod, then offered to take Grammy to my first class since I was headed the other direction to Alyce's homeroom. I could tell Grammy was suspicious, but she also seemed a little nervous (first-day-of-school jitters?) and left with Dustin.

The warning bell rang, so I skimmed faster, searching for the words "grave," "Green Briar," or "Sam." And in the middle of the notebook, I found them all—along with a strange drawing of a large, steep staircase leading up to a beautiful angel. Something about the drawing tickled my memory, as if I'd seen this angel before, but that wasn't likely since Alyce didn't share her private notebook, even with me.

I understood why, too, as I read her heartfelt agony over her mother's depression; Mrs. Perfetti would cry for days and wouldn't get out of bed.

Mom makes me crazy and scared. I don't know what to do to help her. She won't see a doctor and she wouldn't even eat if I didn't cook for her. She keeps crying about needing to find a lost grave. Alyce's tiny, slanted letters combined calligraphy and printing. She'd joked that it was her signature style, one that would be easily recognizable in the artistic world someday.

But the Alyce writing here was more concerned for her mother than any dreams of a career. *I wish I could tell someone ... especially Amber. Only she'd feel sorry for me, which I'd hate ... and her life is so perfect anyway that she wouldn't understand. I wish we could trade mothers ... I wish I wasn't me ...*

On the next page her letters were calmer, looping with elegant swirls as she listed the same cemeteries I'd found on the list in her backpack. Next to the one that said Green Briar, she'd written, *"Mom freaked out last night, screaming for her baby. It was scary, but I learned more and convinced Mom to draw a picture of where Sam was "sleeping." Mom drew a tall iron fence and an angel with giant wings and a marble tombstone engraved with a green bush symbol above the name Angelica. Not far away lies baby Sam, the only marking a wooden plaque inscribed SAM. The bush logo could mean the headstone came from Green Briar."*

That was on the last page ... and I knew what had happened next. Alyce had stolen the Green Briar file, but I'd jumped into her body with no clue how to use it. Now I did.

Digging into Monkey Bag, I pulled out the Green Briar file and searched for the name "Angelica." And there is was, near the bottom of the page. Angelica Hightower, who died in the 1960s at the age of ninety-eight. A woman named Jane Hightower had purchased the headstone for the grand sum of $325 (which was a lot back then from what Grammy used to tell me). But there was no mention of where Angelica had been buried.

I regretted sending Dustin away, now that I could really use his online link via Headquarters .02. I'd try to catch him between classes.

Then I hurried off to my class, thinking how ironic it was that on what could be my last day of school ever, I was in Alyce's body. When I walked down the halls, I had to remind myself to keep my head low and not act too friendly. Alyce ignored people while I enjoyed smiling and waving, even to kids who couldn't remember my name.

So I was startled when I heard someone shout out, "Alyce!"

Turning, I saw a vision of silky black hair, cinnamon skin, and a beautiful smile. "Jessica Bradley?" I murmured, shaking my head.

. "Hey, Alyce." She sounded rushed. "Could you give Amber a message?"

"Oh … sure."

"Great!" Jessica always sounded like a cheerleader even though she was more involved in student government and community service. "Tell her that there's a meeting of the Basket Club at lunch today."

"Don't you mean the Halsey Hospitality Club?" I said sarcastically.

"Oh, sure. Whatever."

"And Amber's the president, so shouldn't she be the one arranging meetings?"

"She's been through so much lately, I'm happy to help her out." Jessica beamed her beauteous smile. "We have so many new members since her accident, and I have this wonderful idea to announce. I know Amber will love it! So FYI her about the meeting, and you should come, too."

Before I could say something sarcastic about Alyce being Vice President of HHC and the one who made all the gift baskets, the final bell rang and Jessica dashed off. I was running late, too, and I hated to be tardy. It was kind of funny, really, how although my life might soon be over, I was afraid of being late to class.

I turned a corner and spotted Alyce's homeroom up ahead. Breaking into a run, I arrived at the door and bent over to catch my breath. But when I straightened and reached for the knob, someone else grabbed it first.

"Allow me to open your door," said a familiar voice, with eloquent politeness.

And I turned to face Eli.

21

Of course he wasn't Eli—which broke my heart all over again. Despite wanting to break down and beg for my boyfriend back, I knew that wouldn't work on Gabe. So I channeled my grief into rage.

"What are you doing here?" I demanded.

"Same as you. Going to school."

"You don't belong here."

"I have my class schedule." He pointed to a zippered pouch in the blue backpack I recognized as Eli's. "But I'm not sure where my first class is—can you help me find it?"

He was playing with me, like a spider spinning a sticky web around a trapped fly. And I hated him more than ever.

"Can't you let me enjoy this one last day before destroying my life?"

He only smiled. "Don't forget—we have a meeting later."

"I haven't forgotten anything."

"Good. Although I regret upsetting you, I have survived this long by following strict rules. Promises are binding—those I make and those that are made to me. Despite what you may think of me, I have never killed anyone and would sincerely regret having to do so. Enjoy your day at school and say your good-byes. Afterwards, you're mine."

Hearing those words from Eli's lips was torture. I coped by imagining the DD Team lassoing their silver ropes around Gabe and hauling him away so he'd never steal another body—especially someone who meant so much to me.

"When will it happen?" I asked numbly.

"At sunset. We'll finish what we started last time. Change shouldn't be feared but embraced."

His poetic talk, which had once impressed me, now made me want to throw up in my mouth. "I hate change," I argued.

"You'll feel differently when you experience the unlimited power I can show you. I'm doing this for you." He reached for my hand but I drew back. "On the boat, when you saw through my disguise, I knew we were meant to be together. For the first time in over a century, I felt honest feelings."

"Honest?" I scoffed. "You survive by lying and stealing."

"But I follow a code of ethics. I never steal money or

possessions from my Host Souls. I never borrow the same body twice. And if a body I'm about to borrow successfully resists me, I respect that and go on to someone new. When I give my word to someone, I never break it. You have my word that I will make you happy."

"Happy? Not when I have to leave everyone I love."

"I'll be your friend, family, and lover," he said seductively.

But I was in no mood to be seduced. I'd rather kick him where it hurt and watch him double over in agony. I hated him! I hated his twisted "ethics." Yet anger wouldn't solve anything, so I tried to reason with him.

"I'm sorry you're lonely," I said softly. "But you don't have to live like a fugitive anymore. Grammy can help you find a place to belong."

"I don't belong anywhere—except with you."

"Please … don't make me go."

"I'm not forcing you to do anything."

"But if I don't come to you, you'll kill my boyfriend."

"Tragedies happen." As he spread his arms in a shrugging gesture, his hands glimmered gray underneath his sprayed-on tan. "Now I need to find Room 46. And tonight, I'll find you."

Not a promise—a threat. Shaking all over, I fled into the classroom, stumbling over a backpack left in an aisle and landing in the lap of a skinny kid with a bad case of pimples. The class roared with laughter, but I hardly noticed … I was dying inside.

All my emotions numbed after that, and I only went through the motions. To anyone watching, I was typical, antisocial Alyce, keeping to myself and not saying much.

I'd always admired her independence and thought she was smart for doing her own thing. But mostly she was just alone—except for our friendship.

Alyce did surprisingly well in math today, but disappointed her biology teacher. I asked myself over and over why I was bothering being at school when I could enjoy my last hours of freedom with my parents and little sisters. Not that I was giving up. No way! I would meet with Gabe, but I wouldn't leave my life willingly. I had several hours to come up with a plan. I'd managed to talk briefly with Dustin after homeroom, and I hoped he'd have some ideas when we met for lunch.

We usually hung out in the computer lab, and since Grammy wouldn't know how to find us, I met her as she left my fourth-period class. I called "Amber!" She hesitated, then turned toward me, the look of relief spreading across her face almost comical. Obviously I wasn't the only one having a bad day, so I gently took her hand and led her into the computer lab.

"I thought I was wild when I was a teen, but compared to the spitting, swearing, and talking-back to teachers going on here, I was a saint." She sank down on a hard plastic chair beside me.

"Saints are overrated," I teased, glad not to dwell on my problems. "I'd rather hear more about your drag racing."

"Not even going to go there. I am still your grandmother."

"How long did you smoke? And just how many guys did you date?"

"Now you're just being rude." She gave me a disapproving look, then opened the sack lunch I knew Mom had made. Mom took pride in the stay-at-home motherhood thing and put together great lunches, with thick sandwiches, chips, fruit, and homemade cookies for dessert.

"So are you having a tough time at school?" I asked Grammy as I bit into a hoagie sandwich I'd gotten from a vending machine.

"Everything is so high-tech now," she said, gesturing around the room to some kids challenging a teacher to an online role-playing battle. Not far away a few girls sat together, not talking, just holding cell phone and texting.

"It's just what it is." I shrugged.

"Definitely not what I expected." She sipped her mango-peach juice, then added, "Your mother isn't what I expected, either. I've seen a whole new side to my daughter, and although I don't always approve of her methods, Theresa is an amazing mother."

"I could have told you that."

"And you did—only I wasn't listening. I wish it wasn't too late to tell her."

I hated the finality in her tone. It touched a nerve and anger surged through me. It was never too late for anything important. I wanted to believe in justice and dreams and happy-ever-afters. As long as you kept trying, there was always hope.

Maybe I couldn't win with Gabe, but I could help Grammy with Mom. A thought struck me, and for the first time that day, I smiled.

When I told Grammy what I had in mind, she gave me a big hug and said it was a great idea. As thanks, she offered me one of Mom's homemade cookies, and as I took a bite, my heart melted like warmed chocolate. I already missed Mom, Dad, my little sisters, my cat...

If only I could stay.

The door to the computer lab burst open and for a nervous moment I expected to be dragged away by Gabe. But it was just Jessica Bradley, looking exotically gorgeous in an oriental-print dress and silky red jacket, but also angry, with pinched lips and her hands on her hips.

Oops. I'd forgotten her "Basket Club" meeting. I braced myself for attitude about missing the meeting. Only she walked past me, and gave it all to Grammy-As-Me.

Grammy sputtered in confusion, glancing over at me for help, but I just shrugged when Jessica insisted that "Amber" come back with her to the cafeteria. I tried to argue, but Dustin cut in and urged them to go. "Alyce and I have a project to finish," he added, with a meaningful look for me. I got the hint and played along.

Once Jessica and Grammy were gone, Dustin scooted his chair over. "I checked out that address and number you gave me for Angelica, but the house she lived in was torn down when they put in Gossamer Estates."

"Jessica's neighborhood." I'd been to Jessica's mansion home a few times and was awed by the beautiful garden and luxurious decor. It was the kind of home I dreamed of living in when I had my big career... if that ever happened.

"So I tried finding Angelica's relatives... and I'm waiting to hear from a grandson. He could call anytime. He should know which cemetery his grandmother is in, which will tell us where Alyce's lost sister is buried."

"Then Alyce and her mother can accept their loss and move on—and I can, too."

"You are *not* going anywhere." Dustin wagged his finger at me. "No self-sacrifice allowed. If you won't ask your grandmother for help, then I'll take this dark dude down."

Imagining Dustin—who had techno-geek pasty skin and zero muscle-tone—taking Gabe on, I almost laughed. But I actually came closer to crying. He was so sweet...and after tonight I may never see him again.

"Gabe was here—at school," I admitted in a low voice, glancing around the computer room anxiously, as if expecting Gabe to materialize from a computer monitor. "I didn't want to freak you out before, but he was waiting for me by Alyce's homeroom."

"Damn!" Dustin balled his hand into a fist. "We've got to find a way to beat him."

"You can't beat someone who plays with Earthbounders in a game where he's made all the rules," I said miserably. "Sure, I can report him to the DDT, but they're not powerful enough to catch him and Eli could end up dead."

"We'll figure out something. I know! I'll go with you tonight and hide nearby. We can drug him and lock him up until he has to change bodies again."

"He won't have to change again for a month. But he could steal your body any time just for kicks. He can't take Alyce's body from me, but if he touches me with both hands he can drain my energy until I forget to breathe. There's no way to stop him."

"You sound like you're giving up."

"I don't want to...but I'm scared." Saying these words

made it seem more real, as if a toxic breeze had swept into the computer lab and was slowly poisoning me.

"We have fifteen more minutes before lunch ends," Dustin said, glancing at the large clock on the wall. "Tell me everything you know about Dark Lifers. The more information we have, the better the chance of finding a solution. We'll come up with a plan and take down that Dark Loser."

I wanted to believe him and clung to the small rope of hope he was offering. So I did what he asked, telling him everything I knew about Dark Lifers.

A few minutes before the warning bell, his cell phone rang. He snatched it fast, glancing at the text message and then swearing.

"Bad news?" I asked, biting my lower lip.

"Worse. No news at all." Dustin shook his head. "Angelica's grandson lost touch with that side of his family after a nasty divorce. He doesn't know where his grandmother is buried—only that it's somewhere in California."

"That tells us a whole lot of nothing. How can we hope to find a grave in a few hours when Alyce has been searching for months with no luck? She hasn't left us much more than a drawing of an angel with huge wings."

As I said the word "angel," a picture sprang into my mind of a crumbling stone angel, and I felt the sting of nettles. Excitedly, I pulled out the purple notebook, flipping to the page with the drawing. The stairs, the unusually large angel wings, and the location ... it all added up.

I knew where the lost baby was buried.

A few weeks ago, I'd been driving to a party given by the glamorous Jessica Bradley and I'd taken a wrong turn—a turn that marked the beginning of the weird string of events that led me into three different bodies. But at the time, all I'd cared about was getting to that party, positive it would raise my status at school and lead to influential new friends. When I'd gotten lost on a dead-end road at a cemetery, it had seemed like the end of my world. Then bad went to worse and I landed on my butt inside the locked cemetery gates in a prickly bush of nettles. When I picked myself up, itching and miserable, I'd climbed up a granite stairway to a crumbling but still-beautiful statue of an angel.

The angel in Alyce's drawing.

This explained why the drawing looked so familiar, and why Alyce hadn't been able to find the grave. Angelica's headstone may have been purchased at Green Briar, but her final resting place was in a different cemetery. In the 1990s, when developers bought the land for Gossamer Estates, they'd closed down the old Gossamer Cemetery—which I never would have found if I hadn't taken that wrong turn. Dustin had told me that the most recent graves had been moved but the older ones were considered historical and the fate of the cemetery was still tied up in courts. This was the final resting place where a grieving, mentally ill mother had buried her stillborn baby almost thirteen years ago.

I knew this was true, but I still needed to see it for myself.

But in a few hours the sun would set and Gabe would find me. He'd take me so far out of this body that I'd never be able to return. What would happen to Alyce? Her switch back wasn't scheduled until midnight. Would her body survive until she could reclaim it? Or would the heart in her empty body stop beating? I could only think of one way to make sure she was safe.

So after the final period, I met Grammy as she was leaving the classroom. She came out last, with tangled hair and a dazed expression. "We had to use computers." She threw her arms out in frustration. "I couldn't find the button to turn it on or figure out how to use that mouse thing. Everyone was looking at me ... laughing like I was an idiot."

"You're not," I assured her. "You're just old ... I mean, well, you know."

"I suppose you think it's funny." She glared at me. "You and Dustin weren't any help when Jessica dragged me off at lunch. Do you have any idea what I went through? Suddenly all these girls surrounded me, saying we were having a meeting and I was in charge. My head hurt so much trying to remember names and figure out what was going on. Something about a party and making baskets for charity. Being dead is a big job—but high school is impossible. How do you survive?"

"I just muddle through like everyone else," I said with a deep sigh. Then I switched to what I hoped sounded like an upbeat tone. "But you won't have to deal with computers or meetings or school again. I'm ready."

"Ready for what?" she asked, puzzled.

"To switch bodies. Let's do it now."

Unfortunately, switching back wasn't that easy.

Grammy explained that she'd need to made arrangements with the other side to prepare Alyce for the return. "If the Dark Lifer isn't apprehended, other souls are switching tonight, too. It's wiser to wait till midnight when it's already scheduled to happen. What difference will a few hours make?"

"A lot," I said as we walked to the school parking lot.

Grammy narrowed her gaze. "Is there something you're not telling me?"

I hesitated, thinking of everything that was at stake. "Nothing important."

"So we'll stick with the original plan—the switch will happen at midnight."

I knew there was no point arguing, not unless I was willing to tell her the truth, which I couldn't because she'd prevent me from meeting with Gabe—which was as good as signing Eli's death warrant.

Grammy had been driven to school by Dad, so I offered to take her home. Starting the car, merging with other cars, I went through the motions of normalcy as if on auto-pilot. I had to make idle conversation, too, and act like my world wasn't ending in a few hours. I could tell by the way Grammy kept studying me that she was suspicious.

When I dropped her off, I longingly looked at my ordinary home in a quiet suburb that had always seemed boring and too crowded for a family of six, but now shone with a beauty that made my heart feel close to bursting. I memorized everything: the lawn that was never quite green enough, with its spotty patches of weeds; the bricked planter spilling over with blooming hydrangeas; Mom's car in the driveway (Dad was still at work); and a porch cluttered with tricycles, a plastic princess castle, and naked dolls.

"Want to come in?" Grammy asked.

Did I ever! But if I went inside, I'd never come out.

When I shook my head, Grammy gave me one of those probing looks, then stepped out of the car. "Wait here a minute while I get something for you."

I was so choked up I could only manage to nod. A few minutes later, she came back out.

"Here," my grandmother said, as she held out her hand and pressed something small and soft into my palm.

I looked down and saw the rainbow cloth bracelet she'd woven for me before her death—the "lucky" bracelet she told me I could use to contact her whenever I needed help. With all the body-switching I'd lost track of it, but I was glad to slip it on.

Then I waved good-bye with a soft rainbow swirl around my wrist.

And I drove away from my grandmother, my family, and my life.

I had one more thing to do before sunset—grave searching at Gossamer Cemetery. Dustin insisted on going with me, so my next stop was his house. I was secretly glad to have his company; besides, I needed his help to get through the locked gates. He worked part-time as a locksmith and had this slightly weird but impressive collection of keys—most hanging from the ceiling at Headquarters (his bedroom).

Dustin was waiting for me with the same key that had once before unlocked the Gossamer gates. I offered to drive but Dustin argued, pointing out my "directionally challenged" problem. He was right—I usually turned wrong when it was right, or was that left? We compromised: I would drive but he would navigate.

Once we were on our way, he pulled out a stack of print-outs.

"I've been analyzing our Dark Lifer facts," he said, flipping through the papers. "And I have a theory about why the DD Team has never caught Gabe."

"Why?"

"It's important to understand his abilities and past history. From everything you've told me, we know more about him than the DDT. That's why they underestimate him, assuming he's like other Dark Lifers. But one big difference is that he doesn't need to steal energy from Temp Lifers like average Dark Lifers."

"True," I said, nodding and slowing for a red light.

"And he doesn't panic or cower in fear of being caught."

"He's not afraid of anyone."

"And why should he be? He obviously has financial means or he couldn't rent a pricey boat. He probably has secret bank accounts all over the world. But money is only a convenience for him. Can you guess his deepest goal?"

I thought for a moment, remembering how casually he spoke of material things but his passion when he spoke of his past. "Power," I said. "He was dragged to the gallows for a murder he didn't commit, which had to make him feel completely powerless. So now he's all about being powerful."

"Yes—in this world and others," Dustin continued, reading from a paper. "He can astral travel without losing his connection to his borrowed body. And he was able to show you how to do this, too. Right?"

"He took me out of body to Alyce, in some other-side plane where she was resting. I couldn't have gone there on my own," I said carefully, not mentioning the second time we'd left our borrowed bodies, when I'd been swept up in overwhelming emotions.

"He also can find you, even when you're in a different body."

I nodded. "He said he can see my soul, like the way psychics see auras."

"And the other side actually uses psychics to locate Dark Lifers." Dustin made a notation on his paper, then scratched it out and wrote something else. "That's my theory about Gabe, too. He's psychic."

I was so shocked I started to drift into the next lane, but stopped myself and steadied the wheel. I saw the turnoff for Gossamer Cemetery ahead and slowed down.

"Not psychic about everything," Dustin said quickly. "Only when it comes to energy being directed at him. Thoughts can produce energy, and that's what alerts him. When he first found you at Alyce's house, had you been thinking about him?"

I flashed back to that first strange night in Alyce's body, when I'd seen a shadow out her window. Yes, I'd thought of Gabe. Was it cause and effect? Had I thought of him first, or had his being nearby made me think of him? Either way, Dustin's theory made sense—and it scared me even worse. It wasn't like I could just stop thinking about him. Was he aware of my thoughts now, listening?

"You're not making me feel better," I said, slowing down as the road dead-ended.

"There's still two hours before sunset."

"One hour and forty-seven minutes." I groaned, then killed the car engine and opened the door.

Even though I was in Alyce's body, not my own, I started itching when Dustin used his key to unlock the cemetery gate and I stepped on the hallowed ground. Large chunks of broken concrete from what was once a paved path poked up like sharp warnings not to enter. Wild bushes and dying trees blocked our way, too, so we had to climb over or around to proceed. When I saw familiar prickly weeds, I moved away, careful not to touch the nettles.

It didn't take long to find the crumbled stone staircase and the angel. I didn't see Angelica's grave, though, and wondered if it had been moved to a newer cemetery. Still, the angel was a solid clue, and that's where we started looking for Alyce's missing sister. There were many uneven patches of ground where wild grass had grown over what was once someone's resting place. We had to really look, but then Dustin called out, "Come here!" I ran over and saw a cross-shaped wooden marker with faded letters scratched in the wood: *SAM*.

And as I stared at the name, thinking about Alyce, I felt an odd sense of connection. I could see Alyce's face in my mind—smiling as she gestured to me with a thumbs-up. There was an enormous relief, too, as if her worries were sailing away from her and she was lighter now. Ready to come back.

"Let's go," Dustin said, twirling a key ring around his hand.

My gaze swept around at the cemetery and I thought about Dark Lifers. Dustin had tried so hard to study their abilities, searching for a weakness in Gabe. But there was no weakness. He was stronger than anyone on the other side, in soul and psyche. And as long as he chose to live off humans, no one could stop him. His only limitations were the time restrictions on body switching.

As a Dark Lifer, I wouldn't actually die…but living in

a new body every month, stealing into strangers to survive, would be a nightmare. How could I invade innocent lives? I'd rather die—or turn myself in to the DD Team and leave Earth forever.

And I thought about time: how little I had left and how my future would consist of constantly changing into stolen bodies, staying in each one no longer than one month—a full moon cycle. A rhyme I'd learned to help remember the days in each month sing-songed in my head:

> Thirty days hath September, April, June, and November; all the rest have thirty-one, except in leap year, coming once in four, which gives February one day more.

This now seemed like a life-in-death sentence.

But wait—there was one other time restraint on Dark Lifers, in addition to the restrictions of the moon cycle. If their temporary body got injured, they only had a short time to switch to a new body.

As I thought about this, an idea formed—too risky, dangerous, and horrible to consider. Still, I kept thinking about it, calculating that the odds of it succeeding were less than ten percent. Terrible odds...yet what did I have to lose?

"Come on, Amber," Dustin tugged my hand. "We found the grave. We're done here."

"No," I told him. "We're not done yet."

Then I told him my plan.

23

The sun was sinking fast—my fears were rising faster.
So many things had to work perfectly, and even then
there were no guarantees.

We'd driven back to Dustin's house and gathered some
things for my plan. To the contents of Monkey Bag, I had
added a flashlight, a first aid kit, a key, and a knife.

Not a large knife, no longer than six inches, but sharp
enough to ... well, I didn't want to think about that part of
my plan. I just hoped that when the time came, I'd find the
courage.

My biggest obstacle turned out to be Dustin.

"You can't come back with me," I told him firmly.

"I'm not letting you wait in a cemetery without help," he said stubbornly.

"If you're there, Gabe can use you like he used Eli." I put my hands gently on his arms and stared into his face, pleading. "It's the only way this can possibly work."

"But you'll be alone without anyone to protect you."

"I'll protect me," I said, much more bravely than I really felt.

Then I drove back to the cemetery, finding it again without making any wrong turns. I switched off Junk-mobile's engine and stepped out of the car.

Time ticked by like a heart counting down to its final beat. I had no doubt Gabe would come for me. As he'd boasted, he never broke his promises.

Carrying the flashlight in my hands, I slipped the knife in my skirt pocket and left the remaining items in Monkey Bag. Then I entered the cemetery, leaving the gate open for Gabe.

To ease the waiting stress, I pulled out Alyce's purple notebook and a pen, flipping to a new page:

Alyce—I don't know where or who I'll be when you read this. I just want you to know, in case you don't remember, that your lost grave is in the old Gossamer Cemetery. Also, I know that you've been hiding your mother's problems, but hiding a problem won't make it go away. You need to let other people know so she can get medical treatment. Maybe start with her coworker, Edna—she seems like a good friend to your mom. I'm sorry I wasn't a good enough friend for you, and even sorrier that I won't be around to make it up to you. Dustin will always be your friend but you should find other friends, too. Be happy, Alyce. I'll miss you ... your BFF, Amber.

"A good-bye letter. How touching."

I slammed the notebook and jumped to my feet to face Gabe. His tone dripped with smugness; he had no doubts of his supremacy. But then why shouldn't he feel victorious? Here I was, waiting for him, defeated.

It was still unnerving to look at Eli and see Gabe's mannerisms and the glimmer of the sea in his eyes. He'd changed his clothes, too. No longer in Eli's comfy jeans and T-shirt, he now wore flannel over a button-down navy blue shirt and snug black slacks. His cap with the anchor tilted to the side.

Dusk had fallen like a cool, dark blanket. I switched on my flashlight, shining the light on the ground in front of me. "So you're here," I said with no emotion.

"I told you I would be. I expected to find you with your family, not out in the middle of nowhere."

"I didn't want you near my family."

"But a cemetery? Is there some black humor in your choice for our meeting?"

"Everything isn't about you," I said stiffly. "I was helping a friend find something lost a long time ago."

"And you found it here?" he arched a brow. A faint gray glow shone from his palms, giving him a silvery glow.

"I found it. And I waited for you."

"Thank you, my dear," he spoke in a more formal tone that usual.

"I have come to you willingly." I bowed my head,

spreading out my arms in surrender. "I've fulfilled my promise."

"I shall, too. I promise not to harm your precious Eli."

"So what now?" I asked, noting the bag in his hand. "Will you light candles again?"

"Candles do set a nice romantic tone," he told me with a meaningful look. "And fusing, although not at all physical, is the ultimate romantic bonding of souls. If we hadn't stopped so soon before, you would have enjoyed an emotional high far beyond any human experience."

Heat surged through me as his words created images in my mind. I realized I was leaning toward him, and pulled back abruptly.

"Candles would help," I said with forced calm. "Then I won't need to use my flashlight."

"I brought saltwater taffy, too." He smiled. "Sweets for my sweet Amber."

I cringed at his possessive tone, but didn't show it. I stood quietly for a moment, watching him kneel down on the ground and remove candles and candy from his bag. While he was preoccupied, I backed away. I had taken about five or six steps and was close enough to reach for the gate when his head jerked up, toward me.

"Where are you going?"

"Just moving to stay warm," I lied.

"Come closer to the flames. If that's not warm enough, I'll give you my jacket."

"No, I'm fine. I'm just a little nervous and feel like moving."

"Amber, don't stall. The candles will burn out."

"Only two candles? But you used a lot more last time. I don't think I'll be able to concentrate with so little flame."

"You *are* stalling, but I'll play along—for now. Walk if you want, but don't go far." His tone was that of an amused parent humoring a child. "This will only take a few minutes."

Again, I backed away, aiming my flashlight low so he couldn't see exactly where I was going. Large chunks of broken concrete and fallen trees were useful camouflage, as I made my way to the wrought iron gate and grasped a rusty bar, shivering at the shock of cold metal. I turned off the flashlight to hide what I was doing, then slowly eased the gate into a closed position so that we were both shut inside. Now all I had to do was grab the lock and—

"Come back, Amber," Gabe called. "No more games."

"But isn't this all a game?" I spoke loudly, feeling with my fingers for the lock. "You chose me, pursued me, and now I'm here with you."

"I can't even see you. Isn't your flashlight working?"

"Battery died, I guess. But I can see fine—my eyes adjust quickly."

"So hurry back now. I'm ready to start."

My fingers closed around the curve of the lock, then pushed down until I heard the most wonderful click. "I'm ready too," I said with grim resolve.

As I walked back to him, I paused to look at the crumbling staircase leading to the angel statue. I spotted a piece of the broken angel wing and paused, dropping the gate key under the bone-white wing. Then I hurried toward glowing candles and Gabe.

"Sit beside me," he urged.

I hesitated, then did what he said.

"Take a piece of taffy. You know what to do."

"Okay ... sure."

"Here." He held out his hand.

Sick to my stomach, I picked the candy up, careful not to touch his gray-glowing skin. I couldn't bring myself to unwrap the candy.

"Go ahead, eat it," he urged.

"Gabe, you can stop this now ... we don't have to do this ... you know it's wrong."

"Wrong to want to spend eternity with an intelligent, compassionate, beautiful soul?" Compliments, like charisma and charm, were easy for him, but hard for me to hear because I wanted, *needed,* to hate him.

"Eternity in stolen bodies is no life at all," I said bitterly. "It's wrong to force me."

"You came here willingly."

"Yes ... I did. Remember that." I swallowed hard. "It's not too late—you can change your mind."

"No." The flames from the candles illuminated the determined set of his jaw.

But I was determined, too, and closed my eyes to gather courage.

Think of home and family and Eli, I told myself. *Shut out everything else except this moment and what needs to be done.*

Something shifted inside me—a lifting, like wings flying toward a shining light. A girl with long black hair and gentle hands was reaching out to me. Alyce. Somehow, a part of her had come to help me—nodding, encouraging, and offering support. Calmness, soft like summer rain and sweet like spring flowers, fell over me.

Jumping to my feet, I reached into my pocket.

And swiftly drew out the knife.

Gabe stood, scowling. "What in the blazes are you doing?"

The blade glinted scarlet from the flaming candles.

"This is not funny," Gabe snapped. "Give me the knife."

I shook my head, my gaze fixed on his hands, ready to act if he moved toward me.

"Amber, I'm tired of your games. You promised to come to me."

"And I did. I'm here and you're here, but I won't go any further. No fusing or anything else. I'd rather die than live forever in stolen bodies."

"Is that what you're planning to do?" he asked incredulously. "Kill yourself?"

My heart thudded and my fingers tightened on the knife.

"You can't be serious." The expression on his face was so like Eli's when he was confused and vulnerable that I panicked, afraid I couldn't go through with this. But I reminded myself that he only looked like Eli because he'd stolen Eli's body and would easily destroy it—if I didn't stop him.

"Amber, don't be stupid. Put that down."

He lunged for me, but I moved back, knife lifted.

"You want to go with me—admit it and stop pretending otherwise," he added irritably. "You're not foolish enough to kill yourself, not when you can have an exciting life with me forever. And what can your Earthbounder beau offer you? A boring, short, dull life. You'll forget him quickly and realize you made the better choice. He doesn't deserve you." Gabe gestured to his stolen body with his gray-glowing hands. "But I do."

That's when I lashed out with the knife.

And slashed Gabe.

Twice.

24

"My hands!" Gabe shrieked as blood from the slashes in his ripped palms streamed down. "What have you done?"

"What I had to," I said, the knife trembling in my fingers. The cuts weren't more than scratches, but to a Dark Lifer, any cut to the hands was dangerous. I clutched the knife tightly, afraid he'd attack if I let go of my weapon. Even with his blood energy draining away, I knew he could overpower me if he got close enough.

But he didn't seem interested in me, staring with horror at the dripping blood.

Pressing his hands together, as if that would hold his

soul intact, he looked around frantically. "I have to get out of here!"

"Ten minutes," I said.

"Damn it! Don't you think I know that? This isn't the first time I've been injured. That time on the cliff was a close call, but I found another body within ten minutes. I know what to do. I'm not weak and scared like other Dark Lifers."

"Nine minutes," I said, with a glance down at the illuminated wrist watch I'd borrowed from Dustin.

"You planned this!" He started toward me with the fury of a charging bull, but stopped when I waved the knife. "Now I'll have to find another body or I'm done."

"Yes," I said, sickened by my own violence.

"After all these years... so many lives." Holding his palms together, he shook his head. "I can't believe you did this."

"I had to."

"No, you didn't. You could have trusted me and we could have been happy forever."

"Your definition of happy. Not mine."

"I have to give you credit. No one else has ever stood up to me. And I can't take your body because you're a Temp Lifer."

"Eight minutes," I murmured, keeping my distance.

"But I could touch you and drain your energy, leave you close to dead."

"That would waste valuable time—and you wouldn't have much energy left to take another body."

"True. And I don't want to hurt you—despite everything."

"Approaching seven minutes."

"That is plenty of time to take a new body."

"You think so?"

"I know so." He stared hard at me. "There are homes close by—I'll find someone. And then I'll come back for you."

I moved aside—far out of his way—as he bolted for the gate. I knew what would happen next and I steeled my heart against pity. I also reached down for the rainbow cloth bracelet on my wrist and quickly did the "good luck" ritual of turning it right and left, then kissing the cloth and whispering the lucky chant. I needed all the luck I could get.

"It's locked!" Gabe exploded.

He rushed around the fence, rattling iron bars and swearing with crazed fury.

I glanced down at my watch.

Five minutes.

With a shout of rage, Gabe stormed back toward me, reaching with his bloody hands but sharply pulling back as I waved the knife. "Amber, give it to me now!"

"What?" I asked innocently.

"The key!"

"I don't know what you're talking about."

"You do too! Give me the key *now*!" he demanded, but suddenly he wasn't so fierce; his voice was weakening. Before my eyes, his energy was fading.

I steeled my emotions, shutting off sympathy. "What key?"

"The key to the damned gate!"

"The gate was open when I got here," I lied.

"I don't believe you! The gate was open and now it's locked. It didn't just lock itself. You did it!"

"Why would I trap myself in here with you?"

"Give me the key!" he bellowed.

"I can't give what I don't have."

He cradled his hands, shaking uncontrollably. I could see flickers of silvery mist blending with the blood, as if his soul was slowly seeping out.

"I'm starting to glow...I have to go now! They'll find me."

I knew he meant the Dark Disposal Team. That had been part of my plan, so I didn't say anything, only gave another grim nod. This was the only way to save Eli and myself. With Gabe captured, unable to use his psychic sense and flee before the DDT arrived, for once and for all he'd be stopped.

He knew it, too, and regarded me with a look that was terrifying and tender at the same time, as if he both respected and hated me. He was desperate now, and angry, a caged beast with no way out.

Only two minutes left. I still gripped the knife, although there was little reason to, since he was rapidly losing strength. Gabe sagged down to his knees, moaning and clasping his bleeding hands, almost as if praying.

There was a flash, and a group of figures in formal business suits, wielding silver lassos, materialized. I'd never seen so many DD Team members before, as if they'd called in everyone on the other side to bring down their most-wanted fugitive.

I could hardly bear to watch as the silver whips snapped toward the spectral glow that was seeping from Eli's body. As his glow spiraled upward, like a flame rising from a fire, the DD Team's whips lashed out and curled around it. Energy crackled, and light exploded like bursting stars. Then the shape of the glow shifted, spreading and growing, until I could see a handsome young man with a dark pony-tail, seaman's clothes, and ocean-green eyes.

"Amber," I heard him whisper one last time. "I won't forget...you."

The whips curled tighter, spinning Gabe's ghostly essence. His glow faded, like a dimmer switch slowly turning off. And as Gabe disappeared in the throws of silver ropes and business suits, I felt something strange and familiar happening to me. My world tilted and shifted into sensations I recognized.

The switch.

Grammy had managed to pull harp strings and speed up the process like I'd asked. But I wasn't ready to go yet! Eli's body was still here, bleeding in a cemetery without anyone to help him. Gabe would be gone and Eli would be alone. Alyce would take my place, but she wouldn't know what to do. But there was no time. I was swept by a whirl-wind and pulled into a roar of swirling colors and move-ment.

Flying forward, spinning...then impact.

When I opened my eyes, I was swimming in darkness, blinking. My vision gradually adjusted and I could make out furniture and familiar objects like stuffed animals on a shelf, a bulletin board tacked on a wall, and a furry white cat curled on a bed pillow.

My bedroom, my cat, my body.

Thank heaven—and Grammy.

I was home.

I had no memory of falling asleep but I must have, because I was awoken by a rough tongue licking my face. Instinctively I reached out to push Snowy away until memory crashed back and I wrapped my arms around my cat.

"Snowy!" I cried, loving how her soft fur tickled my skin. "You're the most beautiful, wonderful, best cat in the world. It's so good to hold you again."

She replied by wriggling out of my arms and scampering out of my room.

"Still the same old attitude," I said, smiling.

Then I leaned back against my pillows and waited for my thoughts and feelings to catch up with each other. Being back in my own body felt like being reborn, although it wasn't anything new. I had this crazy urge to sing or dance, like there was something to celebrate. Yet I was sick inside with dread, too, remembering the terrible things had brought me to this moment.

Still, for a moment, I reveled in being back home and danced across my sunlit room to the mirror. "I'm me, I'm me, I'm me!" I sang, as if inventing a brilliant new song.

Gazing in the mirror was like magic. There I was: too-curly brown hair, freckles sprinkling my pale skin, and dark eyes just like my father's. I was wearing a nightgown that was too long and old fashioned to have been my own choice. And when I looked around my room, which was completely reorganized so that everything was color coordinated and neat, I recognized Grammy's work.

While I knew Grammy had gone back to the other side and I guessed that Alyce was herself again, I didn't know what had happened to Eli.

Ohmygod! What if he was still in the cemetery?

Quickly, I looked around for a phone and found one on the dresser.

I called Eli's cell and waited, listening to ring after ring after ring and then finally reaching voicemail.

My anxiety mounting, I hung up and called someone who might have answers.

Dustin picked up before it rang twice.

"Amber?" he asked at the sound of my voice.

"Yes—I'm home. But I don't know what happened after I left last night."

"I do," he said a little too smugly.

"Have you heard from Eli?" I asked. "He was bleeding and then my switch happened and I couldn't help him."

"Relax," Dustin said. "He's fine."

"Are you sure?" My knees went all rubbery and I collapsed on my bed.

"Positive. Did you really think I'd stay completely away last night? I was outside the fence ready to jump in if your plan failed. Wow! I couldn't believe it when you actually sliced Eli … I mean, Gabe. Way to go, Amber."

"I'm not proud of what I did."

"Well, I am. You're my new hero."

"I don't feel heroic—mostly sad. Gabe wasn't all that bad. In his own egotistical way, he thought he was helping me."

"He tried to kill you!"

"I don't think he would have hurt me, not as badly as I hurt him. It was so hard to do what I did . . . then watch him bleed."

"I nearly rushed in to make sure he didn't attack you," Dustin added.

"Thank God you didn't! Gabe would have jumped into you body and things would have even been worse."

"Which is why I stayed hidden. I'm not stupid," he added dryly. "Those people in suits with the whips—wow! I've never seen anything like that. And the way Gabe just floated out of Eli's body was freaking weird! Those silver whips spun around him and then everyone was gone."

"What about Eli?"

"Oh, he was there and so were you. But you were both just lying there, not moving. So I used a spare key—you didn't think I gave you the only copy, did you?—and went to help him. I found the first-aid kit you'd left and bandaged his hands. The bleeding stopped—the cuts weren't deep. But he didn't wake up."

"What about Alyce?"

"She woke up and seemed confused at first, but then she said she had to go home to her mother. She had her own car, of course, so she didn't need a ride. I couldn't stay around to explain things but I showed her the grave. You know the one I mean."

"Yes, I do," I said solemnly. "But what about Eli?"

"Since he wouldn't wake up, I took him to his house and gave his family a story about his being mugged. His parents, brother, and sister were really upset."

"His sister?" I asked. "Sharayah was there, too?"

"Yeah. It was weird seeing her, considering you were wearing her body just a week ago."

"I'm glad she's back with her family, but how is Eli doing?"

"Last I heard, he was still sleeping."

"I tried his phone and he didn't answer."

"Give him time."

"I will. Suddenly I have a whole future ahead with lots of time." I was overwhelmed with conflicting emotions.

"Not that much time—I have to get to school. And you should, too."

School? The word startled me, but in a nice "life must go on" kind of way. And well, why not? My family had no idea what I'd been through. They'd expect me to follow my usual routine. So I told Dustin I'd see him at school, then hung up.

My stomach growled—a familiar sound that reminded me again of how good it felt to be me. I got dressed quickly, then hurried to the kitchen where I saw a picture-perfect family: mine.

My little sisters complained when I squeezed them too tightly.

"Hurting me!" Cherry whined.

Olive squirmed away and ran to Mom, who was pouring cereal into bowls.

Only Melonee didn't complain, and hugged me back with gusto. "Sissy home," she said, then offered me half of a buttered slice of toast.

Dad was in the living room, sipping coffee while he watched the news. When I went in to give him a hug, he looked up at me curiously.

"I just heard on the news about a boy from your school," he said, clicking the remote to a different channel. "He was mugged last night. Eli Rockham—"

"Rockingham," I corrected, a chill shivering up my skin.

"Yeah." Dad nodded. "I thought the name sounded familiar."

"It's on the news?"

"It's a big story, I guess, because he was in some contest. Is he a friend of yours?"

"Something like that." Much more than a friend, I thought, blushing. "What exactly did you hear?"

"They think he was attacked by an obsessed fan."

"But is he okay?" I held my breath.

"Yeah. They said he was resting at home—no mention of a hospital."

I breathed out in relief.

Still, I wished he'd call so I'd know how he was doing.

Would he be awake by now? I wondered.

Looking down at my wrist, I saw my own watch, not the digital one I'd borrowed from Dustin. My lucky bracelet was gone, too—but I knew exactly where to find it.

Alyce... how was *she* doing?

Would she remember anything from the last few days? Did she know what happened last night and that I'd been the one to find her sister's grave?

As if just thinking of her held magic, I heard a honk outside. Rushing to the window, I saw Junkmobile pulling up in front of my house.

Without bothering to find a jacket, I raced out of my room.

To see my best friend.

25

I climbed into the passenger's seat, shutting the door behind me before slowly turning toward Alyce.

We didn't say anything, both studying each other like strangers meeting for the first time. And it was strange for me—seeing the body I'd recently inhabited from the outside. She had her hair pulled back into one long black braid, wisps of curls escaping around her forehead. Purple-black gloss simmered on her lips and kohl shadowed her dark eyes. She wore black leather and black suede in a Native-American-meets-vampire style. Totally original Alyce, and I smiled.

"I wasn't sure I'd find you here," she said, with obvious relief.

"Why not? This is where I live."

"But you had me really worried," she added.

"I did?" I asked, surprised.

"What did you expect after leaving that letter in my purple notebook? I didn't find it until this morning, and I drove over here right away—I was so relieved when you walked out front door." She shifted in the seat, her knee jingling the keys in the ignition. "My memory is fuzzy, but I know enough to say thanks."

"Well ... you're welcome. After everything ... I just hope you're okay."

"Okay?" She gave a brittle laugh. "Have you met my mother? Of course you have—so you know that nothing will be easy with her. But now that I know where the grave is, I'm going to make her face reality. It might get complicated, since what she did was illegal, but we'll work through it."

"And I'll help you," I added. "I'm sorry I wasn't there for you before."

"I'm the one who shut you out."

"Still, I should have known."

"I was the idiot who thought that if no one knew what Mom was really like, I could pretend everything was fine—that my family was great like yours. I got so jealous sometimes, watching your mom take care of you instead of the other way around. And it was hard seeing you with your little sisters, knowing that I had almost had one of my own."

"I'm sorry." Tears sprang to my eyes. "I wish I'd known."

"Me too. But that was my fault, not yours. I see that

now." She twisted the end of her braid. "With all the body-switching and other-side weirdness, you know what I find the most hard to believe?"

"What?"

"I spent months looking for that stupid grave, and you found it in just a few days. How did you do it?"

"Dustin helped. He even helped me set you up on dates."

"Dates?" She looked horrified.

"Zachary wasn't bad, but Kyle was a nightmare."

"You went out on dates as *me*?"

"Only two. There would have been three but Dustin goofed and Taylor turned out to be a girl."

Her glossy lips fell open. "I don't remember anything about it."

"I'll fill you in." Then I grinned and told her every-thing—starting with Kyle and his bat blood.

I was still talking when there was a knock on Junk-mobile's window. Dad gestured to his watch and mouthed, "School."

Alyce told me she wasn't going to school, that she was going to be busy for a few days taking care of her mother. But she offered to drop me off. On the way, she filled me in on her experiences.

Waking up at the cemetery and finding Dustin ban-daging Eli's bleeding hands shocked her. But even more shocking was to see the grave marked "*SAM.*" She stayed in the cemetery awhile, staring at the small plaque, before going home to have a serious talk with her mother.

"Thank you," Alyce said, with such sincerity that I

nearly cried as I stepped out of her car at school. Fighting tears, I nodded and smiled to show that I understood.

Then I heard the warning bell ring and hurried to my locker.

As I was grabbing my books, I heard a musical beep from my cell phone and read a text from Eli.

> I m ok.
> Being watched.
> Will talk l8r.
> L Eli

I stared at the message, reading deep meanings into every letter, especially that *L* in front of "Eli." Did it mean what I thought it meant? Or was it just a typo? And why was he being watched?

I found out why when I met up with Dustin later for lunch in the computer room. Dustin said everyone was talking about Eli's attack. The status of having a stalker had renewed the media's interest in him, and reporters were swarming his house. With his family under siege, he wasn't allowed to answer the phone or go to school.

While I was glad to know why Eli had been a no-show since the switch, I was still tense with anxiety ... and eager to see him.

The door opened, and I glanced past the computers to see Jessica Bradley sweep into the room. She pulled up a chair between Dustin and me and launched into an excited description of her ideas for a fundraising party on Saturday. She had bought hundreds of baskets and fun items to fill them.

"Party?" I repeated, completely clueless, although I vaguely remembered Grammy mentioning a party when she'd been me. But she was back at her other-side job now, so I couldn't call her—not by phone or even GEM. I'd searched my purse and backpack before coming to school and the GEM was gone. This was proof that my career as a Temp Lifer was over.

Somehow I managed to fake things with Jessica and she left me with a glittery-pink party invitation—similar to the first party invitation I'd received from her a few weeks ago. And since this party was for the Halsey Hospitality Club, I wasn't just a guest—I was on the planning committee.

And so was Alyce. But when I told her later, she refused to go, slipping into her old habits. She couldn't use the excuse about her mother needing her, though, since her mother had entered a treatment facility and Edna was staying at her house with her. So after some begging and threatening, Alyce gave me this exasperated look. "All right, all right. I'll go, but only because you're my BFF."

I smiled. Yeah, best friends forever.

Saturday morning, I was ready to go, my hands full of folders with plans and basket-creating ideas.

While I waited for Alyce to pick me up in Junkmobile, I heard a strange sound coming from the kitchen. A gasp, or maybe a sob. When I went to investigate, I saw the walk-in pantry door open and Mom standing there with a shocked expression, holding something in her hand.

Finally, Mom had found it.

I'd suggested to Grammy that she leave a letter for Mom to "accidentally" find—so that Mom would know Grammy loved her and the triplets. It had been Grammy's idea to buy a gift. While I'd been facing the dangerous Dark Lifer and stabbing my boyfriend, Grammy had been shopping for a special gift. She'd wrapped the box and hidden it in the kitchen pantry. When Mom found it, she'd assume it had been there for over a year, rather than for less than a week.

Now Mom was kneeling on the floor, ripped wrapping paper all around her, as she cradled a photograph album with the words "Grandma's Darlings" on the cover. Tears fell down her face as she read the note from Grammy inside the flap of the book. A simple message of love for triple granddaughters. But it was enough, and I could tell by Mom's face that all the bitterness was forgotten.

Junkmobile honked from outside, and I grabbed my bag.

A short time later, we walked up the elegant steps of Jessica's home and were welcomed by the maid. I had taken care with my appearance, wearing embroidered jeans and a shirt that shimmered a silvery color like rain. My too-curly hair was pulled back with a sparkly scarf. I'd used only a touch of makeup: foundation to tame my freckles and a hint of shimmery peach lip gloss.

When I walked into the back garden, recognizing familiar faces from school, I received smiles and waves. Everyone knew my name, and a lot of kids had ideas for making spectacular baskets. Alyce hung back a little, but when

I explained she was the creative brains behind the baskets, soon she was talking and warming up. She seemed to really hit it off with this one girl with short dark hair and a similar taste for black leather and draped skirts. Her name was Taylor—the same Taylor that Dustin almost set up as Alyce's date. I couldn't help smiling at the irony.

Then I heard my name called…in a voice that almost stopped my heart.

And I turned away from Alyce and Taylor to find Eli.

I was so mixed up with happiness and uncertainty that I could hardly speak. This was the first time I'd faced Eli in my real body since we'd first met—in this very same garden. We'd never…well…anything.

"Great party." Eli's eyes shone in a way that made me all soft inside.

"Yeah…greater, now."

"I know what you mean. But I checked, and there's no chocolate buffet."

"You can't have everything."

"Who says you can't?" he asked, teasing.

"Someone famous and dead, I'm sure." Using the "D" word kind of made things awkward, and we stood there for a moment. We'd been through so much—it was like starting off a relationship at the fiftieth anniversary, only now we were back to the beginning.

"So…" I said with a glance around at other people, who were laughing and talking with total ease. "How did you manage to get here without being stalked by paparazzi?"

"That's not a problem anymore—they found better

news. A popular singer—can't remember her name—quit the business to join the marines. So I'm off the media radar."

"And onto mine," I said, stepping closer.

"I've been waiting a long time ... to be with you."

"Me too."

"We still haven't kissed."

"Really?" I said in a flirty tone, tilting my face up toward his.

He reached into his pocket and held out a silver-wrapped triangle.

"A candy kiss!" I said, laughing. "That's not exactly what I had in mind, although I never refuse chocolate."

When my fingers touched his as I took the candy, I felt a shock of electricity that had nothing to do with the other side—it was all about living on Earth. He must have felt something, too, because he stumbled backwards, bumping into someone carrying a cup of punch. The cup flew and dumped sticky red punch on Eli's shoes.

Eli looked so embarrassed, which was kind of sweet and made me love him even more. While he went to wash up, I plopped the chocolate kiss in my mouth and imagined how much sweeter the real thing would be.

I was staring in the direction that Eli had gone when I became aware of a smell ... a salty breeze, a whiff of the ocean. I sensed someone behind me, but when I whirled around, no one was there.

Just my imagination, I decided with a shrug.

Someone tapped my shoulder and I turned with a start.

"Eli!" I cried out with delight.

"Expecting someone else?" he teased.

"No one," I said firmly. "Only you."

"I like the sound of that."

"You know what I'd like even more?" I asked with a flirty smile.

"Chocolate?"

"Guess again." Then I reached up to hook my arms around his neck, pulling him close and lifting my lips.

Finally, we shared our first kiss.

The End.

About the Author

Linda Joy Singleton lives in northern California. She has two grown children and a wonderfully supportive husband who loves to travel with her in search of unusual stories.

She is the author of more than thirty books, including *Dead Girl Walking* and *Dead Girl Dancing*, the Strange Encounters series, and The Seer series (all from Llewellyn/ Flux). She is also the author of the Regeneration, My Sister the Ghost, and Cheer Squad series. Visit her online at www. LindaJoySingleton.com.

Don't miss the first two books in the Dead Girl series,
Dead Girl Walking
and
Dead Girl Dancing